D0397505

ALSO BY JEN MALONE

Map to the Stars

Wanderlost

Changes in Latitudes

WITHDRAWN

THE ARRIVAL OF SOMEDAY

JEN MALONE

HARPERTEEN

An Imprint of HarperCollinsPublishers

HarperTeen is an imprint of HarperCollins Publishers.

Names: Malone, Jen, author.
Title: The arrival of someday / Jen Malone.
Description: First edition. | New York, NY : HarperTeen: an imprint of
    HarperCollins Publishers, [2019] | Summary: After the liver disease she
    was born with flares up unexpectedly, roller derby star Amelia, eighteen,
    must come to terms with the brevity of life while hoping for an organ
    transplant.
Identifiers: LCCN 2018034258 | ISBN 9780062795380 (hardback)
Subjects: | CYAC: Sick—Fiction. | Medical care—Fiction. | Transplantation
    of organs, tissues, etc.—Fiction. | Best friends—Fiction. | Friendship—
    Fiction. | Family life—Fiction. | Roller derby—Fiction.
Classification: LCC PZ7.M29642 Arr 2019 | DDC [Fic]—dc23 LC record
available at https://lccn.loc.gov/2018034258

Typography by Torborg Davern
19 20 21 22 23   PC/LSCH   10 9 8 7 6 5 4 3 2 1
❖
First Edition

To Laura, who lives on

Our deepest fear is not that we're inadequate.
Our deepest fear is that we're powerful beyond measure.
It is our light, not our darkness, that most frightens us.
We ask ourselves,
"Who am I to be brilliant, gorgeous, talented and fabulous."
Actually, who are you not *to be?*

—MARIANNE WILLIAMSON, ACTIVIST

BEFORE

1

"CAREFUL, GIRLS—WE DON'T CALL OUR JAMMER INVINCIBLE for nothing." My best friend, Sibby, gestures at me, smirking as she catches my eye above the pack of women skating into place for the starting whistle. "She's so badass, she gets her cavities filled *without* novocaine."

I flutter my eyelashes and nudge my soft plastic mouthguard out just enough to point playfully at rows of molars boasting metal, before sucking it back into place. No one has to know three-quarters of those "fillings" are actually tooth wax from a zombie costume kit, painted silver and applied in the locker room less than an hour ago.

Sibby's Australian accent is pronounced when she continues, "You'd be wise to steer clear."

Roller derby can be as much about showmanship as it is sport, even on the track, and Sibby and I are *all* about dramatic flair, both here and whenever we're rallying behind any of our causes. We have a whole routine rehearsed for our pre-jam lineups. Unfortunately, the opposing team isn't showing any signs of being rattled by our trash talk; no one responds beyond an eye roll.

I give Sibby a tiny, one-shouldered shrug and grin. *There's more than one way to skin a cat.* Then I turn my smile on the crowd in the bleachers and sweep both hands into the air repeatedly, urging their cheers. They respond in full force, their energy traveling across the modest arena and into my chest, giving me a familiar jump.

Snippets of our skate-out song—American Authors' "I'm Born to Run"—blasts through the arena and I sing along in my head to the familiar refrain:

I wanna see Paris, I wanna see Tokyo
I wanna be careless, even if I break my bones

Maybe not so much on the broken bones, but a definite yes to the rest.

A short whistle blows, and all ten of us jump into action as the music cuts off abruptly.

As jammer, my job is to zoom through the pack of blockers, using whatever methods and force ethically and legally necessary (and some that ride the dizzy edge between the two), because once clear of them, I can skate free and rack up points.

Sibby and my other teammates are on defense, both preventing the other team's jammer from getting out in front of them and simultaneously clearing a path for me to do it instead.

It's no sport for the meek, but luckily, I'm far from that. I live for these bouts. *All glamour to the jammer*, as Coach says.

I tuck my head low, relying on the colored tape we have wrapped around the toes of our skates to let me know which belong to those with friendly hands that will push me ahead, versus those who might lock on to my wrists to halt my progress. My breathing is even, despite the excitement pumping through me.

As I straighten, there's a weird twinge in my gut that disappears before I can fully process it. I stumble for a half second, but then right myself and let the game suck me back in.

Sibby's war cry sounds just beside me as she knocks the opposing team's jammer out of bounds. Cheers erupt in the stands and a deep voice announces over the loudspeaker, "The Wizard of Aussie executes a smooth move on Rainbow Migraine, who can now rejoin play only if she enters the track behind the same skater who sent her off course."

Sibby drops back, slowing her roll—literally—to achieve the derby version of a cockblock, and I grin around my mouthpiece as I surge forward.

My focus snaps to the last two skaters I need to clear. The crowd chants my derby name: "Rolldemort! Rolldemort!"

This.

This right here is where I feel most alive. It's not the fans cheering for me or the potential for glory. It's the instant where all of that external stuff goes fuzzy and what's straight in front of me sharpens like a camera in portrait mode. I see the elusive path through the blockers as clearly as if it's a lighted airport landing strip and my breathing deepens, low in my diaphragm. Endorphins fire, and I hit the roller derby equivalent of a runner's high as I pop up on my toe stops and jump left to evade my first opponent, before pivoting and tucking low to fake out the next.

And then I'm through, staring ahead at a wide-open track laid out like a red carpet for me alone. I increase speed and cross one skate over the other as I lean into a graceful turn, then another. In less than fifteen seconds, I've rounded the last curve and hit the straightaway, where the pack has re-formed tightly to block my approach.

In the mess of helmets ahead, I spot Sibby's and I shift to re-enter the pack by her side. I've only been skating with this team since I moved up from junior derby after turning eighteen last fall, but I already adore all my teammates. Still, there's no one I trust with my life more than my best friend. She'll block out of straight love as much as out of competitive spirit, and she's got both in alarming quantities.

Sure enough, she grabs on to my wrist with one hand and propels me forward, past the blocker on her left, while her right arm is straight out to stop another opponent. (My girl is a beast.)

I wish I could find a way to bottle this feeling. Eyes forward, I weave and duck around women, clipping one's elbow hard in the process. I offer no apologies. Lacing up your skates and stepping onto the track is permission granted, for all of us.

I rack up three easy points, but the last one looks like it will be much harder. The other team's pivot, the one blocker who is eligible to become a jammer during play, is skating backward fast and has her attention fully locked on me. Except she trips over someone's skate—I can't tell if it's one of my team's or not—and goes down!

I zoom by!

The audience screams their heads off, gearing up for my next lap, where I can add even more points to the board. I'm mentally mapping the distance to the next turn when the pain in my stomach returns. This time it's so sharp I can barely keep from doubling over. *What the hell?*

Before I can think through my decision, I pat my hands on my hips twice to signal the ref that I'm calling the jam off, which is my right as jammer, but not something I'd ordinarily ever do when there are easy points to be scored. Four rapid whistle blows from her alert the rest of the players.

The crowd quiets and I sense their confusion. I'm feeling it too—though mine is tied to the cramp and whether or not I could have imagined it, because it's completely gone now. *How is that possible?*

Arms drop to sides, skaters snowplow and tomahawk to stops, music pumps again, and the announcer updates the score for the audience: "Beantown Ballers pick up four points, which increases their lead over How Ya Like Them Apples to an impressive fifty-seven to forty-four. And we're just getting started, folks!"

I'm the last to reach the circle my teammates have formed on the track, and I catch the silent questions they're asking each other with their eyebrows and baffled shrugs. But there'll be time for explanations once we get to the sidelines. For now, we bunch up and put our hands in the center of our circle, ending the period the way we always do, with the jammer—meaning me—yelling, "What's the boss of us?"

"Courage!" my teammates scream in reply, waggling fingers.

"What's never the boss of us?" I shout.

"Fear!" they answer.

We wave our hands above our heads before settling into triumphant power poses the crowd adores. They reward us with catcalls, and we preen and bow, then break apart and move toward the sidelines to await the start of the next period.

I keep my hands on my hips and glide slowly, savoring the rush of being on the track.

Sibby appears at my side. "How ya going? Not keen to add too many points to our lead that jam?" she teases, but with a hint of concern underneath her words.

I sigh. "It was super weird. I had this intense cramp, but it's completely gone now, like it never happened." I massage my abdomen absently and shake off a tiny prickle of fear. "Anyway, bizarre."

Sibby's mouth pinches down. "Are you sure you're okay? Should you sit out the next jam?"

Coach jerks her chin our way, summoning me.

"I'm fine now," I tell Sibby, pulling the cloth cover from my helmet and acknowledging Coach with a nod. One of the girls from the opposing team is right on our heels, close enough to have eavesdropped.

She taps my shoulder, and in a perfect Regina George mocksweet voice says, "Not to worry, Rookie, it takes a few years to get used to menstrual cramps. Once you pass puberty, you'll be fine.

Don't be too bothered about letting your team down in the meantime."

You've *got* to be joking. Sure, derby is full of trash talk in the name of fun, but it's also all about girl power to the millionth degree, which is one of the reasons I love it so hard. This chick is hitting low.

"Speaking of our nether regions," Sibby shoots back, "why don't you channel your energy into trying to grow a pair. I saw your rubbish attempt at a block."

"Whatever," the girl tosses over her shoulder as she turns to skate toward her own team. "Go throw another shrimp on the *bahhhhbie*."

I kick into gear, passing her easily, then executing a T-stop in front of her. Smiling serenely, I pop one hand on my hip and slap the other over my mouth in exaggerated surprise before saying, "Wow. Just . . . wow! That's so, so *clever*! I've never heard *anyone* say that to an Australian before! Where did you come up with it?"

The girl is sandwiched between us now, though we aren't crowding her, and my eyes twinkle as I catch Sibby's. I skate toward her but stop just beyond the other girl's shoulder and call back cheerfully, "Maybe once *you* manage to pass *infancy*, you'll pick your head up, look outside your bubble at the big world around you, and realize how ignorant you sound. Wanna know the fallacy in your oh-so-witty cliché? They don't even *have* 'shrimp' in Australia. They call them *prawns*. So, yeah."

Sibby licks her finger and puts it in the air, making a sizzle noise and touching it to mine. "Solid burn, babe," she says, in her best American Teen accent, which always makes me laugh.

We watch the girl skate away in clear disgust and Sibby cocks her head. "Wow, she was a bit aggro." She taps her thumb on her lip, pretending to contemplate, then adds, "Reckon I should ask her out?"

"This is why I love you so much, you know that, right?" I ask, bumping her toe stop with mine.

"Because I'm adorable? Because I use Aussie words like 'reckon'? Because I'm clearly descended from the witches they couldn't burn?" she responds, tapping back playfully.

"Let's go with D: all of the above."

"*Ta, dah-ling.* Or *maybe* it's because I encouraged you to apply for the mural grant and you have me to thank for winning it?" We resume our path toward Coach, in no rush now that she's deep in conversation with Hannah, our team captain.

"Um, excuse me, I don't remember any arm twisting involved!"

I'm always in a good mood on derby days, but today's is especially great because of the email I got on the drive up here, letting me know my design had been chosen to decorate the entire exterior wall of a new restaurant opening near Harvard Square. It's a pretty big deal. I've been doing chalkboard art since I was eleven and my hand lettering skills are seriously legit (I don't believe in humblebrags—if you got it, own it), but so far I've mostly only done chalk menus for the store-owning friends of my parents. I've never attempted anything on this scale. Or anything this permanent; I'll be switching mediums to work in paint.

"Hey, the mural's not stressing you out, is it?" Sibby asks. "You have a bit to get used to the idea before you start, yeah?"

"Are you kidding?" I answer. "I can't *wait* for it to warm up enough for me to get out there with my cans of paint! The rest of this winter is gonna be endless."

Part of me wishes we could zoom past the next month and just have it be spring already. The other part of me knows I'm supposed to savor the remaining days of high school before everyone scatters into our different futures. Plus, there's plenty to keep me busy in the meantime, between the lead-up to derby playoffs and the road trip to DC Sibby and I are planning so we can take part in a march for gun control legislation.

Coach is still in conference with Hannah, and she puts up a finger as we approach, so we pivot and rejoin our team on the sidelines.

"You okay, Rolldemort?" a couple girls ask, while others offer congratulations on the points I scored. Desiree, aka Char-Broiled, points at my knee. "Hey, stellar bruise, Rookie. Wall of Fame–worthy."

Bruises are badges of honor in roller derby. I spin to show off another impressive one on the back of my shin. "You should only see the two I found last night on my torso. Must have happened at practice."

Only we would get this excited over painful injuries. But I definitely don't tell them I'm a little alarmed at how serious those two on my sides look, especially given that I can't remember any impact that would have caused them.

"Imagine the ones we'll get once we're on the all-stars!" Sibby whispers for my ears only. I nod hard, tucking away my nagging concerns.

Come fall, Sibby and I will be on different teams. I've already been accepted early admission to Amherst, in western Massachusetts, so I'll transfer onto the regional team there. I have every faith Sibby will get off the wait list at her top choice, Tufts, which would keep her on our current team and make us occasional opponents. Not cool. So we hatched a plan—if we can both get onto the all-stars, a separate unit composed of the best players in our league, we'll be reunited again for those bouts. The trick is edging out all these older players who've been at it way longer, but I'll put my money on the unstoppable force of Lia + Sibby any day.

"Ah, the eternal, unwavering optimism of youth," Desiree teases. Clearly, Sibby needs to work on her whisper volume. Desiree makes her voice shaky to mimic an elderly woman. "I remember having that once upon a time . . . vaguely."

Desiree is the ripe old age of twenty-four, so neither of us takes her remotely seriously. She drops the put-on voice and gestures to the stands. "Speaking of all-stars, did you catch your cheering section?" She waggles her eyebrows meaningfully as she takes a swig from her water bottle, then skates off while we survey the bleachers.

I suck in a breath when I spot at least half the all-star team. They're scheduled to play here tonight, but I hadn't considered they might arrive so early. This means they were on hand to witness us in action!

A few are looking our way, so I exaggerate air kisses before spinning my backside to them and cheekily (pun intended) flapping up the top of my miniskirt to reveal tight bicycle shorts below.

Sibby gasps. "What are you doing?"

I glance back at the stands; one girl has two fingers in her mouth, whistling at me. See? All good. "One: Outlandish behavior is synonymous with roller derby," I remind Sib. "Two: Since when are *you* a shrinking violet? Do I really need to pull up pics of the outfit you wore to the pride parade last year?"

Her smirk tells me my point hits home, and confirmation comes when she glances up again at the all-stars across the arena and drops them a deep curtsy. Catcalls follow from their section, and I can't contain the smile that stretches across my face.

I'm about to gloat to Sibby some more, but instead my breath is stolen when the pain returns, full force.

I grab my side and cough, choking on something liquid and metallic-tasting that rockets up my throat without warning. Sibby's eyes widen in alarm and mine must match. I reach for her arm to steady myself but instead sway into her as my lips fall open and I projectile vomit blood all over her uniform and the track.

Oh god!

Oh god, oh god, oh god! What's happening?

It's candy-apple red, nothing like the deeper purplish blood from a cut. Someone screams—I think it might be Sibby, though I can't lift my head to check because I'm doubled over now, clutching my abdomen as blood continues to shoot from my mouth. It's like someone turned on a spigot somewhere inside me.

Where is it coming from?

My hands grasp my knees, fighting to grip them with clammy palms. Sweat drips from my forehead too, and stings my eyes. The arena is full so there should be all kinds of noises, but other than the scream, I can't hear any of them.

The blood keeps coming.

How can there be so much? What does it mean?

It sprays from my mouth like water splatters from a hose when someone holds a finger over the nozzle. The scent clobbers my nostrils. It's nothing I've ever smelled before—sharp, coppery, dank, and otherworldly. It can't have been more than a minute, but there's already enough to puddle.

My wheels slip and my feet go out from under me, but someone catches me from behind, their hands sliding under my armpits. I'm lowered toward the ground, my legs sinking with relief. I'm dizzy and wild; my heartbeat is a rabbit being chased.

Please, please make it stop. Please *let me be okay.*

Another skater appears in my peripheral vision, wearing the opposing team's uniform. "Don't! You need to keep her upright so she doesn't aspirate."

I'm hauled to standing again. No. I want to lie down. I'm so weak.

"I hear the ambulance!" a girl says.

"Can anyone please tell me what's happening to her!" Sibby's accent makes her voice distinct—otherwise I may not have recognized it through the tears clogging her words.

I fight the terror clawing at my throat as I wait for someone to answer her . . . but no one does.

DURING

2

"I'M FIRING CHRISTOPHER," MY DAD SAYS.

"You're not firing Christopher," my mother replies.

I drift awake to my parents' voices, but I'm still in that dreamy in-between state so I keep my eyelids closed and let the morning chatter wash over me.

I can usually hear their kitchen conversations pretty clearly through the heating vent in my bedroom, but this is way crisper than usual, almost like they're in the room with me.

"If he hadn't called in sick, I would have been there," Dad says. "I should have been there."

Huh. This is juicy stuff. My father took over the neighborhood hardware store my grandfather started and I would bet my winning mural commission no one's been fired in the seventy-two-year history of the place.

Been there for *what*, though?

"None of this is Christopher's fault and it isn't yours either," Mom says.

Something beeps over my left shoulder. *What the*— The alarm on my phone is a guitar strum and I don't have anything else that would beep in my room. My mattress sinks low and I startle, my eyes flying open.

Not my bedroom.

Not remotely.

The ceiling above me has the same dropped panels as my school, and a silver stand holds an IV bag that dangles over my right shoulder.

"Lia! I'm so sorry, baby!" my mother says. She's positioned next to my torso and holding a thin plastic tubing that she drops in order to grab my hand. Behind her is a long curtain acting as a partition. "I was trying to see where your IV line was pinched, so I could stop that blasted machine from going off. I didn't mean to wake you."

Her eyes drink me in like I'm some kind of mirage.

"Hey, Sunshine," my dad chimes in, and I turn my head to find him in a chair on my other side, his expression soft with sympathy. He takes my free hand. "How ya feeling?"

How am I feeling?

I don't know. *How* should *I be feeling?*

I'm feeling . . . disoriented. But it only takes another second for scenes to line up behind my eyes, flipping from one to the next as though I'm scrolling through them on my phone. The arena. The EMTs. The ambulance. The ER.

I remember the anesthesiologist leaning over to tell me I'd be put in a "twilight sleep" so I could have an operation and her waking me up immediately afterward, telling me I'd done beautifully.

I remember the blood.

Blood.

More blood.

I squeeze my eyes shut to banish the memory of it, but the smell is back in my nostrils. *What if it never leaves?*

The machine continues to emit a beep every few seconds and my mother strokes the back of my hand with her fingers. "It's okay, sweetness. You're safe. Everything's gonna be fine."

I peel my lids open again with effort. There are faint mascara tracks on Mom's cheeks, and her normal "lawyers work on Saturdays" blouse and dress pants combo is all wrinkled. Dad, with his shaggy hair and habit of forgetting to shave, is the one who usually corners the market on the rumpled aesthetic. I love the guy, but most of the time he looks like a walking unmade bed. My mother, on the other hand, sleeps in her pearls.

I swallow over the worst sore throat I've ever had and try to wet my lips. "What—what happened?" I manage.

Mom's gaze goes directly to my father and I catch the flare of unease in it. "You had a—" she begins, but is interrupted by a nurse poking his head around the curtain.

"Aha! I *thought* that beeping was coming from in here." His eyes fall on me and light up. "Well hey there, sleepyhead. I'm Anthony.

Do you remember me rolling you here to recovery?" When I reply with a tentative nod, he smiles. "Good."

Anthony steps to the machine behind me and does something that makes the noise cease.

"That's better. Do you feel up to trying some ice chips, Amelia? The doctor should be in to check on you—"

"Right about now," a voice from the other side of the curtained partition calls, and my eyes widen as a familiar face rounds the corner.

"Hi, Amelia," she greets me. "You had quite the eventful afternoon." She turns to the nurse and asks, "Has she been up long?"

Anthony looks to my mother, who answers, "Just a couple minutes."

Why is Dr. Wah here?

The doctor steps closer and presses a button on the side of my bed to raise me to a halfway-seated position, then drops into the chair Dad vacated. She scoots it next to my shoulder and rests a hand on the rail beside me.

"The sedative should be almost out of your system by now, but you lost a lot of blood, so I expect you might feel woozy for a little while longer. Does anything hurt?"

I swallow thickly and croak, "My throat."

"That's to be expected. The pain when you swallow should also recede in a couple of hours. I'm sure you have a lot of questions. Have your parents brought you up to speed?"

"We were just about to," Mom answers.

Dr. Wah nods, keeping her eyes on me. "I know it probably felt quite chaotic when you first arrived, so you may not have processed all of what was going on. Would you like me to walk you through what happened when you reached the ER?"

"Okay," I rasp, but my brain is stuck on the same question: *Why is Dr. Wah here?*

I'm still so unfocused, I'm having a hard time maintaining eye contact. Both of my parents jumped from their seats when Dr. Wah arrived, and now Dad stands awkwardly in the corner and Mom perches on the very edge of my mattress, next to my toes. Anthony's disappeared, and I can make out his deep voice teasing a patient on the other side of the curtain.

"You had an upper GI bleed that was caused by ruptured esophageal varices," Dr. Wah says, her voice soft and steady. "I'm sure it was incredibly scary to see that much blood coming out of you."

My nostrils flare at the memory, but I can't bring myself to do more than nod. She gestures at a bandage on my arm. "We gave you fluids and blood to make up for what you lost, and some medicine to decrease the flow to your intestines."

I fight to process her words through the fuzz that is my brain at the moment, but she's already continuing. "Then we did a procedure called a band ligation, where we use small rings of elastic—basically like baby rubber bands—to tie off the bleeding portion of the vein. We'll have to scope you to check them periodically going forward, but the hope is they'll keep this from happening again."

Of all the words she throws at me, only the last line really penetrates, and when it does, I exhale.

Okay then. I don't know exactly what scoping is, and it doesn't sound like a picnic, but at least they fixed the problem. *Thank god.*

A thought intrudes. "Does this mean—I can still do roller derby, can't I?"

Dr. Wah laughs. "Maybe we can revisit the question in a couple of weeks, but I think you should be able to return to it before too long."

Phew. Her laughing. Her saying I can go back to derby. They all send a reassuring message to my gradually clearing brain, and my shoulders soften as the tension leaves them. It's going to be fine. *I'm going to be fine.*

"This is a lot to take in at once. Do you have questions for me on anything I've told you so far?" Dr. Wah asks.

I shake my head gingerly. "Not really. I just don't understand how a hit I don't even remember taking could cause so much damage."

"A hit?" The doctor's eyes narrow and my shoulders stiffen again in response to the lines that appear in her forehead. She glances at my mother, who squeezes my foot, and my father's sigh travels the length of the room.

Dread forms hard and cold in my belly.

"Lia," Mom whispers before regaining her voice to tell me, "this— this didn't happen because of any rough contact at your bout."

I blink slowly, and Mom continues, "It happened because of your biliary atresia."

Wait, what?

But as soon as she says it, the inconsistencies begin to click into place. Why Dr. Wah, a hepatologist, is here. Why the EMTs nodded when Coach handed them my emergency contact form. Why I can't remember any traumatic blocks happening during the jams.

The fact that my brain took this long to connect the dots is partly a result of the sedative, but it also speaks to how little the liver disease I was born with has affected my life. Most of the time I can go months without even thinking about it, and when I do it's usually only because the faded scar on my stomach happens to catch the light in my bathroom in a way that makes me notice it, or because someone offers me something alcoholic at a party, or because it's time for my annual checkup at Dr. Wah's regular office, where they take some blood, pat me on the back, and cheerfully say, "See you next year!"

It's a minor inconvenience, if even that.

BA is a pretty rare disease that basically means my bile ducts didn't work properly when I was born. I had to have an operation when I was six weeks old to fix the flow from my liver (where the bile was backing up) into my intestine. The procedure they did was only a temporary fix, but for some people temporary can mean a month and for others it can be well into adulthood. I'm one of the lucky ones. Bile ducts of a rock star, that's me.

Fingertips creep up my spine as a realization begins to seep in. *Is this my luck running out?*

"We ran some bloodwork to check for excess bilirubin and enzymes that could indicate liver damage," Dr. Wah says. "I'd like to get some imaging to give me a clearer picture, but I'm sorry, Amelia, the preliminary tests all point to decompensated cirrhosis."

I stare at her. I vaguely know these terms, but my brain still isn't functioning properly. I wish she'd just speak English.

As if I've said the words aloud, she clarifies. "It means your liver has a good deal of scar tissue that's hardened and is keeping things from functioning properly."

My mother coughs to cover a tiny yelp and my eyes slide to her.

"Sorry," she whispers.

From Dr. Wah's comment earlier, I know she's filled them in on all of this already, although I guess it's not any easier to hear a second time. Dad's hands fold over Mom's shoulders.

I tear my gaze from them and return it to my doctor. "But how come I didn't notice? Why haven't I had any symptoms?"

Aside from turning a derby track into the set of a slasher film, that is.

I flutter my hands. "I mean . . . other than what happened today."

"Upper GI bleeds like yours commonly hit without warning. Any other indicators could have been mild or even nonexistent. Have you noticed yourself getting fatigued more easily?"

I shake my head. I was *just* skating my ass off and feeling strong as ever.

"Any yellow tinge to your skin or the whites of your eyeballs, to indicate jaundice? Have you been really itchy?"

Again I shake my head.

"Bruising?"

I picture the two unexplained splotches of purple on my torso, the ones I'd been so proud of I'd referred to them as battle wounds. Dr. Wah notices my eyes widen and nods. "You can probably expect to see more of those. You've been among a small percentage of my patients who've managed to stay symptom-free all this time—but this was always how we expected your BA to progress at some point."

At some point, maybe, but not now! *I'm powerful and fit and firing on all cylinders. I'm about to graduate and take on the world,* I want to scream at her.

She takes my hand, and the compassion on her face sends foreboding prickling under my skin. "You knew that, right?" she asks.

Wrong. I mean, yes, right. Sort of. I just—

My mother answers for me. "We talked to her about all this as soon as she was old enough, but she didn't want to dwell on it and we figured it was okay to just . . . stick to the basics until the time came." She sounds somewhere between apologetic and defensive. "We make sure she takes care of herself and stays up to date on all her immunizations, and we've lectured her about what alcohol or drugs could do to her liver, but we were treating it like, well . . . you know how some people who might be carriers of the breast cancer gene or the Alzheimer's one get tested right away and others choose not to find out because they would feel like they were a ticking time bomb?"

My father, his hands still encasing my mother's shoulders, interjects before Dr. Wah can answer. "Amelia, she—she's full of energy and passion, and she's just got this 'in the moment' personality, and we didn't want to squash that. We never wanted her to feel like she had a shadow chasing her."

Dr. Wah's understanding smile is enough to keep him from continuing. "It sounds like exactly how I would have recommended handling it."

But the flash of warmth in my chest at hearing my father's description of me chills to icy tendrils when I finally grasp what this conversation is circling.

"You—you're saying I need a liver transplant, aren't you?" I whisper.

Mom rubs my leg and Dr. Wah presses her lips together briefly before answering, "I am."

For the space of several heartbeats, my world shrinks to a pinprick of light on the ceiling as the words bounce against the edges of my brain. I feel them rather than hear them. They are hot and pulsing and prickly.

Dr. Wah lassos me back by saying, "I know this is a lot to take in, Amelia. Especially when you're still recovering from the shock of the GI bleed and coming off the anesthesia. If you want, I can leave you to process this, and we can discuss further steps at your next appointment, which I'd like to have happen in a couple days' time, okay?"

I'm shaking my head before she even finishes. I may not be completely coherent, but information is power and I need to cling to any control I can get right now. I'm not as naive as Mom and Dad might be making me out to be here. Of *course* I paid attention when they sat me down in third grade and told me I would likely need a new liver at some point in my life. And I haven't been burying my head in the sand since then either—I check in on organ transplant advances every so often. Just a couple months ago I read an article online about two women in Silicon Valley who are working on a way to create organs using a 3D printer.

Reading things like that, though, it was easy to let myself believe that by the time my existing liver became an issue, a transplant might be some outpatient procedure I could schedule on my way home from saving the environment or solving world hunger or whatever it is I might be doing with my time ten or twenty years from now. So why waste mental energy on worrying in the present, when it could be a completely different landscape by the time I actually *needed* to confront things, right?

"When?" I ask. "I mean . . . how urgently?" I would rather have the blood back in my mouth than taste these words on my tongue, but I need to know the answer.

Dr. Wah sighs. "I can't tell you that. It depends on how the scarring progresses from here and how your liver function holds up. For some people it can take a year for the transplant need to be critical."

"And longer for others?" my dad asks, hope giving inflection to the word *longer*.

Dr. Wah's eyes stay trained on me, though. "For others, a bit less."

My breath evaporates, leaving my lungs an empty cavern. I rip my gaze from hers and settle it on the ceiling, willing the echo of her words to fade in my ears. They're all I can hear, though—if my parents have their own reaction, I don't even register it. If Dr. Wah says anything next, I don't hear her. I'm underwater, kicking for the surface.

Breathe, I order myself.

Again, I instruct.

Okay, focus, Amelia. This is an obstacle, and what do you do with obstacles? You slay them, that's what.

I inhale deeply once more as I curl my fingernails into my palms and let the pain of their digging chase off my panic. I exhale. "So how do I buy myself enough time to reach the top of the transplant list?"

Dr. Wah tilts her head and grins at me. "Grit like that will help." Then her smile fades and she speaks more seriously. "But really it's less about the amount of time you've spent waiting and more about how urgent your need for a liver becomes. Someone could present for the first time today and move immediately to the top of the list, if they're sick enough."

"Are you saying we actually *want* Amelia to get sicker, so she can get a liver faster?" my mother asks.

Dr. Wah shakes her head. "Not necessarily, no. It's a bit of a catch-22; the sicker you are, the closer you move to the top, but there's also a point of no return where your body becomes too weak to receive a new organ, and that's a tightrope I'd rather we didn't have to walk."

"Would—would you be able to—to give us any odds right now? If you had to guess Amelia's chances?" Dad asks, avoiding my eyes.

Even more than the gut punch the question itself delivers, it kills me to hear my father's voice crack. He's usually such a giant goof— he's never met a cheesy line or an awful pun he could resist. I'm convinced he is the actual man responsible for the expression "Dad jokes."

Lately he's been on a corny "Have you ever wondered?" kick. *Have you ever wondered why sheep don't shrink when it rains? Have you ever wondered who named grapefruits when we already* had *grapes and* they're *a fruit? Have you ever wondered why Tarzan doesn't have a beard?*

But, *Have you ever wondered what my daughter's odds of survival are?* Not words I expected to hear leave my father's mouth. I bite my lip, waiting for the reply, but also desperately not wanting to hear it.

Dr. Wah sighs again. "I understand why you're asking the question, but I'll give you the same answer I give everyone. If I wanted to be an oddsmaker, I'd have skipped medical school and bought a horse track. I'm not trying to be glib; it's just that there are too many unknown variables to take into consideration. I wouldn't even be able to offer an educated guess, other than to say that I'm always optimistic, and I think you should be too—let's leave it at that for now, okay?"

A rush of love for my doctor and her finesse courses through me. Her response was exactly what I needed.

My parents nod and Dr. Wah offers a tight smile. "Look, I know it's frustrating to have your fate in the hands of a computer algorithm. But the list is set up in a way that prevents anyone from 'gaming' it—there's no priority given to the rich or to celebrities and no prejudices based on religion or occupation or political affiliation. The only factors taken into account are biological and geographical. Who needs the recovered organ the most, who's the best physical match for it, and who can be on an operating table in time to receive the transplant. You can make yourself dizzy trying to guess when the call will come, but please don't do that. Honestly? Here's the advice I give all my patients. You ready?"

She's staring straight at me as she asks, and I nod.

"You're going to recover from the GI bleed very quickly. In fact, you'll be released shortly and once your sore throat wears off, you should feel just like your regular self, possibly for some time to come. So you go about your life as normally as possible and you do what you need to do to stay strong, mentally. There's a lot we don't understand about the mind-body connection, but I've seen enough to believe in the healing power of a positive attitude."

I grasp at the lifeline she offers. The worst thing I can imagine being is powerless, and her words are lightness and hope. Resume normal life? Stay strong? I can follow that action plan. Coach's favorite call and response—the one I'm in charge of leading at the end of every jam—plays in my head:

What's the boss of us?

Courage!

What's never the boss of us?

Fear!

The perfect mantra for this. The words are metal rods burrowing into my spine, straightening it, shoving up against the spaces where panic had invaded and serving notice. I can hack this waiting game thing.

No. I won't just hack it . . . . I'll find a way to own it.

My lungs fill with air again.

"Now, beyond the mental game, let's cover some other considerations to keep you healthy." Dr. Wah's words snap me back to the recovery room. "Your mom mentioned you being up to date on all your immunizations, but we're going to confirm that. Your liver plays an important function in fighting off infections, so if it's not running at full capacity, neither is your immune system. I'm talking double the hand washing, got it?"

"Got it," I tell her.

"We'll buy stock in Purell," Dad says.

"I also want you to start taking an antacid daily. Tums. Rolaids. Any kind is fine."

I'm tempted to answer, "I have a serious disease and you're prescribing *Tums*?" but instead I simply say, "Okay, that's easy."

"Other than that, if you start having the other symptoms I described—itching, fatigue, yellowing—or any pain, I want you to check with me before taking any over-the-counter drugs because your liver is going to have a hard time processing them. In fact, check with me on anything you want. I'm going to be seeing you for bloodwork every couple of weeks, but if you need me between appointments, you call my office. Someone tells you about a homeopathic treatment they're heard of and you're curious about it, you call me to discuss whether it's something we should explore. You have *any* questions, you call. Sound good?"

What would sound better is going back to yesterday, when none of this was remotely on my radar.

"Sounds good."

"Okay then," she says, standing. "I'm going to take care of things on my end to get you placed on the transplant waiting list. We'll cover all this in more detail in future appointments, but as far as basics go, you're going to want to keep your phone close to your body and your body in easy driving distance to the hospital. Recovered livers are only viable for eight to twelve hours, so time is always of the essence."

So much for the march in DC with Sibby at the end of the month. I know that should be minor in light of everything else, but the pinch of disappointment is real.

Dr. Wah puts her hand on my knee. "You're strong, Amelia. I have a good feeling about your ability to handle this. You have me to lean on anytime you need it. And your parents too, of course."

She turns to acknowledge them and both share closed-lipped smiles with her, but I notice the tightness in the corners of my dad's eyes, and my mother seems to be having a hard time swallowing. I have to look away to tamp down the tickle behind my eyelids.

Fear is not the boss of me; courage is.

I will *not* let this disease ruin my life.

Dr. Wah's shoes click out of hearing range and a heavy silence descends.

There is both everything to say . . . and nothing to add.

After a few seconds Dad clears his throat and pulls his cell from his pocket, pointing it to the hallway. "I, um—I should fill Alex in while we wait for them to discharge you."

My older brother is a sophomore at college in Maryland. We're close, but not super tight or anything, and I wonder how much he's been looped in already and how he's reacting.

Mom's sigh is soft. "Tell him I'll call him later too."

Dad slips from the room and my mother reaches under my bed to haul her purse into her lap. "Speaking of calling, I have your phone in here. Sibby's been texting every five seconds, so you might want to let her know you're up. When Dad and I got to the ER she was simultaneously manning a phone tree to update your teammates and badgering the woman at the registration desk for information on you. I had to promise her we'd call as soon as you were awake to keep her from staging a mutiny."

I smile at the image, then flash back on how panicked Sibby was at the arena, having to watch me spray blood everywhere.

Mom jams her hand inside her purse, feeling around. "Do you want some privacy to talk to her?" she asks. "I could find Dad out there and we could grab a coffee from the cafeteria or something."

My mother's giant bag is the one place she surrenders to disorder and chaos, and the sight of her rummaging through it in search of some elusive item it's eaten is such a normal sight, while everything else about this scene is so surreal. I can't make myself reconcile the two.

"Why can I *never find anything in here*!" Mom glares death rays at the purse before she dumps it upside down and begins shaking items loose onto the blanket covering me.

"Mom!" I yelp, when crumbs from a half-eaten PowerBar scatter onto the floor.

She huffs but lets the bag fall from her fingers. "Sorry." She lowers her chin and shakes her head. "I'm sorry," she repeats, sounding defeated.

"It's fine. It's in there somewhere and in the meantime, I can call Sibby from yours—this is nothing worth getting worked up about."

She half snorts, half chokes, her eyes still on the floor. We both know her being upset has nothing to with my phone, but neither of us is willing to go there. Despite all my resolve to stay strong following Dr. Wah's pep talk, I have to fight the urge to turn on my side and draw my knees tight to my chest.

Mom exhales slowly and her expression turns rueful. "Bet you didn't picture your day ending here when you woke up this morning."

Truer words have never been spoken.

Not my day, or my year . . . or even my decade, if I'm being honest.

I've always known my BA could catch up with me . . . someday. I just never expected *someday* could be *today*.

3

THERE ARE FEW THINGS IN LIFE AS ANNOYING AS THE SOUND OF four hundred and seventeen pairs of feet stomping up wooden bleachers. Except for maybe the *smell* of the four hundred and seventeen teens attached to those feet, crammed into a stifling high school gymnasium that held a varsity wrestling match yesterday afternoon and the town rec program's Zumba for Expectant Moms before first bell this morning. Nothing could rival the smell of that blood on the derby track two weeks ago, but this is mounting a good case for second place.

"You ready?" Sibby asks, surveying the audience from our spot under the basketball net.

I nod. How could I not be? I said I would find a way to own this situation and I've hit upon the *perfect* solution. Plus, this is hardly our first rodeo. Or our tenth. This scene is both familiar and exhilarating.

There are two places I feel most like me: on the derby track and onstage at a rally. Roller derby is out at the moment, so rally it is.

I glance at my mother, who's here for "moral support" and is standing on the sidelines nearby, chatting with Miss Leekley, my art teacher. They catch me looking and Mom flashes the subtlest of thumbs-up signs, paired with a tentative smile.

"Who am I?" Sibby asks, drawing my focus back to her.

I grin. "You are the madwoman in their attic."

"And *you* are a rebel swamp forest goddess. We yield to no one and nothing. We bend all to our will."

Some rely on Kanye in their earbuds, some chug Red Bull. Sibby and I pump up for our speeches with our own special brand of affirmations.

Principal Kurjakovic raises her eyebrows at us and, upon Sibby's answering nod, strides to center court and taps the microphone. "Good morning, seniors! I'm sure many of you are wondering what the purpose of today's assembly is. For that, I'll hand things off to Sibilla Watson and Amelia Linehan. Please give them your full attention and respect."

I'm not sure we'll get either for long. Graduation is less than three months away, close enough that we can taste it, so attention spans are shot to hell already. And with college acceptances coming in earnest this week, those are basically all anyone can focus on. But for the moment my classmates' naked curiosity is keeping smuggled phones tucked in pockets and whispers quiet.

Sibby squeezes my pinkie one last time before stepping forward for the mic handoff. Everyone cringes at the scritch-scratch noise the speakers broadcast when she vigorously wipes the head of it with the edge of her T-shirt, which reads EXTRA AF. I doubt much blame is cast, though; our principal has a well-documented issue with spittle.

I force my shoulders back and my spine straight as I catch up to my best friend, accept the now-clean mic from her, and turn to face my classmates.

"Fellow Falcons," I begin. "We interrupt your morning to bring you an important call to action. A big thank-you to Principal Kurja-kovic for allowing us this platform."

Sibby tips her head toward the mic in my hand and says, "And we know you've come to expect this kind of stuff from us, but today's is bloody important so don't be a bunch of Tooligans."

This earns some appreciative giggles, even though the majority of my classmates have no idea what she's just said. Sibby collects Australian slang words like they're souvenirs from her annual trips back home and takes glorious pleasure using them in undiscerning ways.

I allow the laughter to fade away, then launch into the next bit of our speech. "We want to talk to you today about organ dona-tion . . . specifically why you should consider registering to be a donor. Your organs alone could save the lives of up to eight patients and help countless more. The numbers speak for themselves and, in fact, polling shows that ninety-five percent of people in this country support organ donation. The problem is that only fifty-two percent have taken the mere minutes required to register."

Sibby's hand covers mine on the mic and she raises it toward her. "Why, you ask? Because you American tossers are even bigger bludgers than us Aussies, that's why."

My classmates who recognize that she's now sworn—not once, not twice, but *four* times—within the first few minutes, and in plain earshot of half the school's administration, reward her with scattered cheers.

She silences them with a finger to her lips and waits for their full attention before dropping her voice low and sober. "There's nothing to applaud, friends. There's a severe shortage in the number of available *lifesaving* organs. Every ten minutes another person is added to the waiting list for one . . . and every day twenty-two people die while languishing there."

I purposefully reviewed this speech over and over so I could become immune to those numbers, although a shock wave still passes through me at hearing them reverberate through the gymnasium. I plant my feet and will it away.

Mental toughness, that's what Dr. Wah prescribed. *Which happens to be your specialty*, I remind myself.

Sibby is giving me raised eyebrows, waiting for me to speak my line.

I gather my breath and speak from my diaphragm. "Seven thousand patients in America alone could be saved each and every year if we had a more robust donor pool."

Here we go.

My stomach roils but I stare boldly at my classmates and state, "One of those patients saved could be me."

A ripple runs through them and I will myself to keep my chin high. Activism 101: There are two core components to every successful campaign—hit your audience with stats to drive home the problem, then give them a personal story to connect them to the cause. Today that story is my own. We've reached the "necessary evil" part of this rally and I just have to power through it.

Even so, this is the part I'm most apprehensive about. I'm telling them about my BA this way so I can own the narrative, on my terms, *and* turn a bad situation into positive action. I'm not doing it in dramatic fashion as a play for anyone's pity—that's the very *last thing* I want—but I've worried it could be seen as that.

I need to command their respect, not their sympathy.

I picture all my activist idols from Sojourner Truth to Emma Gonzalez, channel their fierceness, and exhale. "A couple weeks ago I learned that a disease I was born with, but that hasn't really affected me until now, is slowly turning my liver to cement. If I don't receive a transplant, eventually the liver I have now will go into organ failure."

My voice stays steady and strong and I'm proud of that.

Fear is not the boss of you; courage is.

The gym stills abruptly at my words, but I don't react. I'm reciting memorized lines, injecting calculated emotions, stopping any real ones from penetrating my armor. I don't dare glance at Sibby or, equally dangerous, my mother. Instead, I clench my jaw and force myself to return my classmates' attention.

I know what they see when they look at me. They see the same pink streak my hair always has. (Well, the color sometimes changes, but the streak itself doesn't.) They see the familiar necklace that spells out *Rolldemort* in loopy gold letters. They see yet another of my shabby chic/retro outfits. Today it's a white blouse with a Peter Pan collar, topped with a navy cardigan that has embroidered rosebuds marching up the button band, a bright yellow pleated skirt, and pink-and-white-striped socks that reach well above my red boots.

I don't know all four hundred of them personally, but I'm pretty sure I can guess what every last one of them is thinking: *She doesn't look like she's dying.*

Which is very true.

There are no outward physical signs that anything is the least bit off with me. If central casting put out a call for "Dying Girl," I would not—repeat NOT—land the role. For one thing, those trope-y kids are always baby-faced and angelic-looking, whereas my eyes, while perfectly fine as far as I'm concerned, aren't saucer-shaped enough to be described as "doe-like."

Also, Dying Girl is always "wise beyond her years." I'm pretty damn smart and happy to own it, and I wouldn't be sitting on an early admission to Amherst if I wasn't. But smart and wise are two very different things.

Oh, and I could never convincingly flutter my eyelashes and ask Dr. Only On TV Do Medical Professionals Look Like Me for a chaste yet still utterly age-inappropriate first kiss before I slip away to meet my maker on the gentlest of exhales. Especially since my first kiss ship sailed, well . . . a while ago. Hudson Fordham. Ninth grade. Maisy Tannenbaum's house. Maisy Tannenbaum's *mother's* peach schnapps. (For Hudson, not me. *I* was stone cold sober for the whole disastrous slobberfest.)

So pretty much the only X mark I'd get on the Dying Girl checklist of requirements is that . . . I might be dying.

As soon as I have the thought, I push it away. Harshly.

You are not dying. Do not *think like that. Ever.*

The whole point of this assembly is that I don't intend to let anyone *else* think like that either. I might be sharing my story with them now, but I want them to walk away with all the proof they need that I'm the same Amelia as ever: fierce and fabulous.

A cell phone rings deep in a backpack and there's a curse and a frantic rustle for it. Someone cough-shouts "Dumbass" and a few people giggle.

I embrace the comic relief, smiling myself before saying, "I want everyone to know that I'm getting good medical care and I'll be fine—I didn't share any of that to shock you or to have you worry about me, but because I want to put a face on this cause and make the point that you never know just who might need this lifesaving gift *you* have to offer. So, if you do decide that you'd like to register to become a donor, we're here to make it really easy for you. Some of you may have already declared yourself one when you got your driver's license."

I hand the mic to Sibby, who continues, "If you aren't sure, look to see if you have a little heart symbol on there. If you didn't know what that meant at the time or you've changed your mind since, you can sign up today and you'll get a card you can carry in your wallet."

She passes it back to me. "We have volunteers with materials from Donate Life on hand today. They'll be set up outside as you leave and they can answer questions and get you all taken care of."

I'm supposed to continue with instructions here, but Sibby tugs at the mic. I release my grip and a whisper of apprehension ghosts along my skin when I turn to her and see the two marks of red high on her cheeks. Those are Sibby's "I'm going to cry" tells.

Sure enough, her voice is choked with tears when she says, "Lia's story *will* have a happy ending. It will. I'd like to think you'd all form a long line if Lia needed a kidney. Actually, you wouldn't even need to, because she'd already have one of mine."

The sentiment is super sweet but . . . *no*. No, no, no. *Please don't, Sibby.* This isn't what we rehearsed at all; she's completely off script. She's supposed to be strong, like me. She can't get emotional. They'll take their cues from her and that's not what this assembly is for—it's for exactly the opposite. It's so that everyone can see I'm handling things just fine and even being proactive about using my experience for a greater good. This is me setting the tone and leading by example.

Sibby sniffles loudly into the microphone and pauses to run her sleeve under her nose. "But while we each have an extra kidney to offer, none of us has a spare liver. I get that."

My hands twitch, desperate to swipe the mic away from her. I know she's my best friend and I should be sympathetic to how this whole thing is affecting her—and I *am*. It's not like it doesn't twist my gut to see her crying over me. But how can she not realize what this display of hers is going to do? Maybe she didn't know she'd react this way until we got up here, and that's fair. Except now that she *has* lost it, she *should* be cutting things short and rushing us off the floor—not ad-libbing all this other stuff.

But she *doesn't* hurry us offstage. Instead she continues, "Since we can't offer up our livers, the least we can do is offer our names to that registry. I know we're all dreaming about breaking loose from this place and setting off on grand adventures, me included, and I wouldn't actively wish for anything terrible to happen to any of you. But the fact of the matter is that none of us knows what our futures hold and your very last act on Earth could be saving a life. *Lives*, even. Lives like my Lia's."

She throws her free hand around my shoulders and I'm too shell-shocked to do anything but play along. Does she really not recognize this has veered so far off message we're practically in another time zone?

"Save Amelia! Save Amelia!" someone chants.

Oh no. No, no, no. Please no. My story was only supposed to *connect* people to the case for organ donation—generic, anonymous organ donation.

I was never supposed to *become* the cause.

Half the class has taken up the refrain, ignoring the hand I'm holding up to stop them, before I manage to grab the mic from Sibby and plead, "No, please! *Please* stop!"

I can't believe Sibby is actually smiling at them, when *I'm* horrified. Positively horrified. I don't need them to *save* me. I don't need saving. Okay, yes, technically speaking I guess I actually do. But from a stranger, not from my peers.

I need everyone *here* to treat me the same way they always have.

I wave the last stragglers quiet. "Um, look. I'm fine. Please. This isn't about— What I mean is . . . whether you decide to be a donor yourself or not is totally your choice. If you do decide *for yourself and of your own free will, minus any guilt trip*, more information and sign-ups will be in the hallway outside the gym."

People crane their necks toward the exits and I rush out the last little bit of my script, desperate for this horror show to be over. "Also, make sure you tell your parents your wishes, because if you haven't turned eighteen yet, they still get final say and they should know what it is *you* want done with *your* body."

Sibby hijacks the microphone again, with my hand still attached, to say, "Take extra forms! Hand them out on the T, or at your next track meet, or at Comic-Con, for all I care. The more people we can sign up, the better odds Lia has!"

"Save Amelia! Save Amelia!" a lone voice from the back resumes and it's only by some miraculous blessing that everyone's now too absorbed in gathering things and talking to their seatmates that it doesn't get taken up again. Thank god. Maybe it won't be as bad as I'm imagining.

But then I happen to catch KellyAnne Littlefair's eye as she lines up to make her way across the bleachers, and she glances away quickly, like she's embarrassed to have been caught studying me.

KellyAnne and I swap Anatomy notes. We're not friends, exactly, but we're friends*ish*. I know she's not *trying* to be hurtful, but she's just confirmed my biggest fear.

I'm used to being noticed around school for being the girl always ramped up about a cause, or for playing roller derby, or for one of my more unusual retro outfits, or maybe even as one half of the

Lia + Sibby badass duo. All of those things are expressions of who I am, and I have no problem owning them.

But what if, from here on out, everyone only sees me as . . . Dying Girl?

Well, screw you, central casting, because I do not accept the role.

4 ❧

SIBBY HANDS THE MIC OFF TO OUR PRINCIPAL AND PROMPTLY
tackle hugs me.

"You were amazing—total baller to *my* sniveling mess," she says,
squeezing tight.

When she releases me, the corners of her eyes are still damp with
tears and the sight of them steals any desire I may have to confront
her here and now. I have to believe she has no clue she just threw me
under the bus.

So I fake a smile to match hers. "You were great too."

I don't know if I've ever lied to Sibby before—at least not about
anything real—and it churns in my stomach.

She grabs my arm. "Ready for Phase Two? I had them hold a table aside for us and you *have* to see the lime-green visors I got us off the Donate Life site to wear while we man it. They're *très* chic . . . by which I mean, they have zero fashion value. None. I love them. C'mon!"

I glance toward the gym's exit into the lobby. Most of my classmates are filing out the sets of double doors, but a few of our friends hang back, clearly waiting to talk to us. Well, to me, I'm guessing. I haven't told them a thing about any of this—not even my GI bleed—and I'm sure they'll want to know what gives. I make eye contact briefly with my friend Nells and she juts out her lower lip in an exaggerated sad face while crossing her hands over her chest in a long-distance hug that whooshes any bravado I had left straight out of the gym.

I can't be here. I can't let everyone gush about how tragic my situation is or spew "hang in there" platitudes at me—I'll never be able to keep it together. Dr. Wah said to do what I need in order to stay strong mentally and I know without a doubt that it's to get as far away from here as possible.

My mother approaches and I grab at the lifeline her appearance offers.

"Sib, I think—I think I might cut out with my mom instead," I say, hoping I look and sound casual. "I don't mean to abandon you but, um, this was a lot of, um . . . excitement . . . and so . . . would that be totally shitty of me?"

Her eyes go wide, then she shakes her head emphatically. "Of course not! You need to keep your immune system in tip-top shape—the last thing we need is you getting run-down because you're pushing yourself to do too much."

No, the last thing I need is to start using my biliary atresia as an excuse to get out of things, and I wasn't trying to suggest I was physically tired, but clarifying would mean getting into my emotional state more than I'm willing to, so I just nod and thank her for being so understanding and for doing the assembly with me. I bite back anything else I could add about how it didn't turn out at all the way I'd envisioned.

At all.

Mostly thanks to *her* actions.

I just want to go home.

Both Dad and his bike are propped against my mother's car when we emerge from my school.

"Hey, Sunshine! I thought I was only grabbing Mom. Luckily, I got an extra coffee just in case. Call it father's intuition," Dad greets me, sipping from his own travel mug. His smile is a little too bright to be natural, but I pretend not to notice that. Fresh air and a change of scenery are exactly what I need to help the last hour fade. At least I know I can always count on Dad to keep things easy and light.

He reaches behind him for the two mocha cappuccinos he's set on the car roof. I *would* ask how he biked here balancing three coffee cups, but he's been pedaling Cambridge's streets his entire life and could probably have managed it with six more, plus a random tuba on his back. He hands me one and I accept it gratefully.

"How'd it go?" Dad asks. I take a quick sip to buy time to formulate a decent yet uncomplicated answer, but immediately spit it out.

"Oh, blech! They forgot my sugar!"

"Whoops, that's Mom's."

He makes the exchange and I gulp at mine to wash away the bitter taste, before saying, "That just means they forgot Mom's, though."

I've known my mother's "three spoonfuls of sugar, heavy on the cream" coffee order since forever.

"I'm . . . trying something new," Mom says, avoiding my eyes.

"Your mother's sweet enough all on her own," Dad answers, cuffing her chin.

Uh, not especially true when I put the Cheerios back in the cabinet with a handful of stragglers at the bottom of an otherwise empty box, or when I accidentally leave my skate bag from practice in the back seat of her car over a summer weekend. But my parents are kind of gross and lovey-dovey this way (which I pretend to hate, but secretly don't).

"Should we blow this Popsicle stand?" my father asks.

I roll my eyes. "Dad, no one says that anymore."

"Then how do you explain me? Because I just *did*."

"There is no explaining you, weirdo." My sigh is appropriately exasperated as I round the car and pull open the door, but inside I'm thrilled we're having this totally normal exchange. Normal is all I crave these days. Especially *this* day.

But then I happen to turn my head as I prepare to duck inside, and I catch my parents having one of those private conversations that involve nothing more than locked eyes. Mom's face is so raw that it physically hurts my heart. Dad's hand reaches for her and my mother steps into him, but then glances over and catches me staring. She must whisper something under her breath because Dad's eyes jerk up to mine and widen slightly, before he schools his expression into a smile.

"Hop in, Sunshine," he says, sidestepping Mom and hefting his bike up and into the trunk of the car.

I follow instructions rather than acknowledge what I witnessed. The dismissal bell shrills across the courtyard as I buckle my seat belt and we pull away just before people begin spilling outside. Thank god for that. I exhale loudly, which Dad, turned sideways in the front passenger seat, catches. He raises an eyebrow. *I'm okay*, I communicate with my eyes.

Lie. I'm not okay, even though the distance we're putting between us and school is helping.

He turns back to Mom. "So, I never got an answer from either of you—how did it go back there?"

Mom catches my eye in the rearview mirror, indicating I should take this one. I have no idea what her impression of that assembly was and I'm a little curious to hear, but I also would love to never think of this afternoon again. Ever.

"Fine," I reply.

Dad raises that eyebrow again, but I simply shrug. He turns forward. "Okay, well . . . that's good. So what's on deck for the weekend?"

"Do you think we should find you someone to talk to? You know, like a therapist?" Mom blurts.

"What? Mom, no! I don't want to talk to anyone."

"I'm just saying, I think it could help. You've been processing this in a bubble the last couple of weeks but now that it's out in the open, it's, well, it's a lot to deal with."

"I'm fine. Dr. Wah said to go about life normally," I protest.

"And to stay strong *mentally*," Mom adds.

Yes, and spending hours on a couch exploring outcomes that are way too dark to even think about would really help with that. Or not!

I tamp down an annoyed reply because I'm not *trying* to be a bad patient; it's just that I don't really see the point of talking ad nauseam about something when doing so can't change anything. I'd still need a liver, and as a bonus I'd be hyperfocused on it.

Maybe I'm being obstinate, but I don't think so. It's basic human nature. We're all experts at self-preservation, right? We *all* purposefully choose to ignore the unpleasant things we don't want to acknowledge. We climb onto dizzy-fast rides at two-bit parking lot carnivals that weren't there the previous week and won't be there the next. We use the TV remotes in our hotel rooms, even after watching those *Dateline* specials where the hosts take black lights to them and expose all the poop germs left behind by the previous guests. We eat sausages, which . . . what the hell is in *those* anyway? And *if* we even bother to stop and really think about any of it, we shudder . . . and then push the knowledge away so we can carry on in denial.

My not wanting to put scenarios for my future under a microscope isn't really so different, the way I see it.

Besides, sitting around opening a vein on deep feelings is nothing I could ever picture my mother doing, so I'm not sure I'm loving the double standard here from Miss Cool and Collected.

"I'm *fine*," I repeat. And I will be too, as soon as I wash my brain of the remnants of today's assembly and get some of my mojo back.

Mom executes a left turn onto Mass Ave. "Fine isn't exactly an optimal state of being."

Dad turns to wink at me. "Leave her be for now, Nat. 'Fine' might be plenty good enough at her age. You remember eighteen."

Picturing my father on a therapist's couch is even harder than imagining my mom on one. I knew I could count on him to have my back.

"Most of what I remember about being eighteen was sneaking out to meet you in the alley behind the Coop," Mom answers dryly.

Right around the time Alex left for college two years ago, my parents stopped censoring themselves around me. Which is normally flattering and, in cases such as this, sometimes horrifying.

"Inappropriate! Child in the back seat!" I screech.

"What?" Mom's voice is all feigned innocence now. "We met to study."

"Yeah . . . chemistry," my dad murmurs to her, but not so subtly that it escapes my ears. I choose to ignore him.

Mom catches my eye in the rearview mirror again. "Funny how you insisted you weren't a child anymore when you were trying to convince us to let you drive to DC with Sibby."

The reminder of our abandoned trip stings, but I push it away. "I'm not a child when it comes to being able to handle myself with something like that, but consider me always one when it comes to hearing about parental sexcapades. Two words that never, ever belong next to one another, by the way."

Mom reaches across the front console to squeeze Dad's hand and I close my eyes briefly. My parents are giant dorks and sappy as hell and . . . it's everything. It's us and it's normal and it's uncomplicated. Three things I desperately need right now.

And then my mother ruins it again.

"If you don't want to talk to someone in a one-on-one setting, what about a group thing, because, you *know*, you just might—"

I cut her off. "I get that you've seen *The Fault in Our Stars*, but you are never going to convince me I might find my own hot cancer boy there, just waiting to whisk me away to Amsterdam. Nice try, though."

"Did you ever wonder why Amsterdam has more bicycles than people?" Dad interjects. "Is it because people need a spare or because some of the owners have died off and there's a slew of abandoned, homeless ones, or—"

"Not helping, Jeff," my mother says, but now she's hiding a small smile.

She seeks me out in the rearview mirror yet again. "Would you at least agree to consider it?"

If it will end this conversation, I will agree to bathe in habanero sauce for a month. I shrug in semi-acquiescence and both my parents return their attention to the road. My coffee isn't hacking it solo, so I rustle through my backpack for the spare granola bar I usually carry.

"Do you have a meeting tonight?" Dad asks Mom under his breath. It's clearly not intended for me to hear, but I perk my ears as I pretend to be absorbed in searching the depths of my bag.

"Weight Watchers?" my mom whispers. "Yeah. But I think I'm going to hit one before work in the morning instead. I'm kind of wiped."

I *was* wiped too, but now I'm wide-awake—intense shock will do that to a person. If you told me my mom was going to a meeting but didn't specify which kind, my first three guesses would be National Organization for Women meet-up, book club, or neighborhood association. My last three guesses would be Ultraconservatives of New England, Satan worshippers, or the American Association of Model Ship Makers.

Weight Watchers wouldn't even make the list.

And not because there's anything wrong with Weight Watchers, but because if there is *one thing* my mother is one thousand percent of the time, it's body positive. And while I completely understand and embrace that someone can have a healthy relationship with their body and also still have a desire to lose weight, that second part has just never, ever been my mom. She's always given me the message that I alone get to decide the weight where I feel most comfortable and powerful and beautiful. Her own might not be the conventional number a fashion magazine would dictate, but it's what she's always insisted was perfect for her and she owns it with pride.

So what's changed now? Is this what the new coffee order was all about?

We turn into our driveway and both my parents unbuckle, but I don't make any moves to get out.

"Why are you going to Weight Watchers meetings?" I ask.

My dad lifts his eyebrows and says, "Love you, ladies, but that sounds like my cue to leave. If you two need me, I'll be in my Fortress of Soli-Dude checking my March Madness brackets."

He disappears inside and my mother turns in her seat so she's half facing me. "It's not that big of a deal, really. I just thought it was time."

"Time for what? You've never wanted to lose weight before. And how come it's some secret between you and Dad?" I hear how accusatory I sound, but I can't help it. First Sibby went soft on me in the middle of a rally and now Mom's *dieting*? What is happening to regular world order?

"I didn't tell you because I wanted to avoid this discussion." My mother glances at me, then drops her gaze to her hands, which are fiddling with her car keys. "The truth is, I need to lose at least thirty pounds to qualify as your potential living donor."

Oh.

Oh no. No, no, no. My heart cracks in two.

"Mom," I say as gently as possible, "you know Dr. Wah doesn't support that in my case."

Some patients with liver disease can accept a partial liver from a living donor. In a side-by-side operation, a chunk of the healthy person's liver is sliced off and inserted into the sick person. Within a matter of months after the surgery, both the donor's liver and the recipient's will have grown back to a whole size. It's pretty cool actually. But it only makes up one half of one percent of all liver transplants.

"Yes, well, Dr. Wah's not the only hepatologist in Boston."

"Mom."

Her shoulders drop. "I know. It's a long shot. But I'm the only one of us who matches your blood type and *she* may not recommend the surgery but *I* can't support simply sitting around waiting for my daughter to get sicker and sicker while hoping, by the grace of god, some stranger with a heart symbol on his license decides to text while driving? Shit, Lia. I don't know how to do that."

I choke back a gasp. My mother never curses. And I don't remember ever hearing her voice tinged with despair, the way it is now. My mother is a force; I study at her feet. She has a long history of activism herself, and her work as an immigration lawyer is her way of turning that passion for bettering the world into something that can also sustain our family. Mom cares deeply, but she's got hard edges, honed by years of fighting to keep her clients from being deported. Sure, I've seen her emotional over losing particularly brutal cases, but on those occasions she's been angry or resigned or pragmatic . . . not despairing.

Tears press at my chest and I shove them back down. I don't know how to feel these emotions and stay upright. If I allow them to burrow in, I won't recognize myself anymore.

My mother clears her throat and reaches through the opening between our seats to tug lightly on a chunk of my hair. She's been doing that since I was a little kid, our private code for "I love you."

"I didn't tell you because I didn't want you to worry or think I was doing it because I felt obligated," she says. "This weight loss thing is something that's helping me feel like I have some measure of control over things, so I'm hoping we can leave it at that, okay?" She finishes with a heavy sigh.

I wrap my arms around my backpack and draw it to my chest. "Okay."

"Would it help if I promised not to force any green smoothies on you?"

She smiles and I know my cue here is to smile back, so I do.

But it doesn't reach my eyes.

5 ~

ONCE INSIDE, I HEAD STRAIGHT FOR MY BEDROOM AND DUMP MY
backpack on the floor before curling up among the throw pillows on
my window seat. My room has a turret window that is life itself. It's
home base.

I feel that way about our whole house. We're the third generation
of Linehans to live here, which is the only reason we can afford a
three-story behemoth on a tree-lined street in one of the most exclu-
sive zip codes in Massachusetts, only a short walk from Harvard's
famous ivy-covered campus. (Although in truth my parents still
probably sink the equivalent of a hefty monthly mortgage payment
into heating all the drafty nooks and crannies of this place.)

Dad grew up here and we moved back in when I was six, to

help my grandmother, Babi, after my grandfather died. Within two years Babi ran off with a visiting professor from Lesley and now she traipses around the world with him, coordinating his lecture tours. So we've slowly claimed the house as our own, although none of us wants to test what would happen if we were to disrespect her one rule: the quirks stay . . . every last one of them.

This house has *plenty*.

Some are amazing, like my turret or the secret drawer in the elaborate fireplace surround where several stock certificates of my great-grandfather's are still tucked away (unfortunately, they're from a company that went out of business sixty years ago; I checked).

And some are annoying: the loose wooden staircase spindle that falls out if you clomp past too heavily, the wide gaps between the floorboards in the kitchen where decades' worth of crumbs that even the strongest vacuum can't dislodge have fallen, the fact that the floors slope so much we have to screw some of our furniture to the wall to keep it from sliding away.

The giant irony is that my father supplies contractors all day long, and he's not exactly helpless with a hammer himself. Some of these "quirks" could be fixed in a matter of minutes. But we all accept that Babi would somehow *just know*. This theory has been supported countless times, most recently last year, when Dad thought he'd drywall over the weird telephone alcove in the front hallway so my mom would have a wall wide enough to hang the antique map of Budapest she'd found at a yard sale. He was literally holding the first panel of drywall in place with one hand and reaching for his nail gun with the other when the phone rang. Three guesses who it was. Not the first time that's happened either. And yes, all logic says the calls were just coincidences, but we're too scared of Babi's bark to test things again.

To me, there's a comfort in knowing nothing about this place will ever change. The oddities are what make it lovable and the constancy makes it safe. I'm totally up for adventure anytime, anyplace, but having somewhere familiar to curl up afterward is key.

Like my turret window seat. After a minute, the quiet becomes too loud for me and I pull out my phone. One glance at the screen reminds me that I never switched my ringer back on after the assembly. Crap. *Not the smartest move for someone waiting on an urgent lifesaving phone call, Amelia.* But luckily, all I've missed are three texts from Sibby and a notification from Words With Friends that my brother has played his tiles. (We mostly ensure the other is alive and kicking via an epically long series of online Scrabble, because we're nerds like that.)

Sibby's first text reads: Liaaaaaaa! We had heaps of sign-ups! I wish you could have stayed to see it. Plus I had THE BEST idea about how we can expand the campaign to catch the junior class too. Close your eyes and picture the posters for . . . PROM WITH A PURPOSE. Incredible, yeah?

I swallow and move on to the next: Hello?!?

Finally: Will try you after derby practice. I love you. XOXOXOXO.

So much for saving my mood. I don't even know the details on the prom idea she has, but already it sounds more than mildly horrifying. This is what I get for not being more honest about how today's assembly went from my perspective. The last thing I need is the entire school looking at me the way KellyAnne Littlefair did.

The casual mention of derby is also a stake in my side. *I* should be packing my skate bag and headed there right now too.

I'm so tired of feeling.

Screw it. The fastest path back to happiness has to be pajama bottoms and a decent Netflix binge. I text Sibby back a smiley-face emoji to avoid having to formulate actual words, play the word MOROSE in response to Alex, then drop my phone on my quilt and rummage through my drawers for my rattiest flannel pj pants.

I'm yanking them on when my screen lights up again, this time with my brother's picture. He *never* calls me directly, but Mom and Dad have been talking to him a lot more than normal the last couple weeks and I suspect they filled him in about the assembly scheduled for today. They might have even urged him to check on me. I absolutely *hate* the idea of all of them talking about me behind my back.

I push the FaceTime button and a giant chewing mouth greets me.

"Should I be reading anything into your word choice just now?" he asks, without bothering to swallow.

Gross.

"You could have waited to press Call until after you'd eaten, you know," I say, making a face as I pretend to be more disgusted than I actually am.

He pulls his phone away so I can see the entirety of his shaking head. "Not true. Got nine minutes between class and work study at the library and I had to fit in a stop back at my dorm to swap out my flip-flops, dinner, *and* a check on my bratty sister's day. How'd things go at school?"

The question is caring and kind, but that's sort of the problem. That's not normal *us*. Obviously I love him—he's my brother—but we're not at all mushy with each other about stuff. We fought like animals when we were little, mostly because I was always trying to get into his room or tattling on him and his best friend, Will, or he was pissed I was taking advantage of my "baby in the family" status to get away with something he'd never have been able to at my age. Now we either *pretend* we still can't stand each other or he tries to play the role of mature, protective older sibling, offering valuable life advice from on high to helpless little me. Too bad I'm not remotely helpless and that his version of mature includes showing me the contents of his mouth.

I raise an eyebrow. "You know, you *could* just carry your other shoes with you in your bag and shave off at least three minutes, dork."

He pushes the last bit of his sub into his mouth with his free hand, the middle finger of which looks suspiciously like it might be forming a rude gesture aimed at me. "I sense diversionary tactics."

I sigh and sink onto my bed, lying on my back with my phone held above me.

"It was . . . okay," I say. "A little different than I expected, but . . ."

"Whaddya mean? Different how?"

"Just . . . I don't know." I really don't want to get into all of this, not right now and not with Alex. Or anyone, for that matter. "More intense, I guess. It doesn't matter. At least there's a whole weekend before I have to go back there."

Alex makes a face. "If anyone's giving you crap and you need me to deliver sucker punches, I'm here for you."

"Oh yeah? Did you suddenly grow some muscles I don't know about?" I raise an eyebrow in challenge.

His eyes narrow. "Really? You wanna go there? Because I don't recall *your* muscles getting in the way of any of my wet willies, did they, *baby* sister?"

"Bring it, *big* brother," I reply, making air quotes around the word *big* as best I can while still holding my phone in place.

"Think long and hard on issuing challenges, Lia. I'll be done with classes in something like six weeks, which doesn't give you much time to bulk up."

"Maybe done in six weeks, but not *home* in six weeks," I say. "Believe me, I'd like to see you *try* to take me down, but attempting it from a boat in the middle of the Chesapeake adds a whole other obstacle to the mix, doesn't it?"

My brother is staying down in Maryland to spend the months of June and July helping with an environmental survey of the Chesapeake Bay. Not only is it his big passion, but it will look amazing on his eventual grad school applications, something Mom and Dad keep proudly harping on.

His eyes drift from mine and they don't return when he says, "Yeah, well. I'm thinking about bailing on that."

"What?" I bolt upright on my bed. "You've applied for that internship four semesters in a row! Why would you ever—"

I don't need to finish, though, nor do I need him to answer, because it's suddenly crystal clear.

"It's not that big a deal," he murmurs. "It'll still be there next summer."

And you *might not be.*

The unspoken words hang in the air between us.

Why did I answer the phone?

But just like I don't plan to live my life under this big cloud of what-ifs, I *refuse* to let anyone else around me do so either. What would he do here in Cambridge? Bite at my heels all summer, trying to soak up every second? Please. He'd be restless within the first two days and he'd drive me up a wall long before that. I don't predict any Hallmark moments worth savoring for a lifetime would come out of that scenario.

"You should stay there, T-rex," I state, as emphatically as I can, employing his childhood nickname (given by a kindergarten classmate who connected the last two letters in Alex's name with the dinosaurs they were both obsessed with at the time). Alex only barely tolerates it, which is precisely why I adore using it. Maybe the subtle reminder of what a pain in the ass I can be will keep him away. But just in case it doesn't do the trick on its own, I add, "I don't want you to come home."

I wasn't trying to hurt him, only to let him off the hook, but he winces. *Shit.*

I try to backpedal. "I didn't mean it like that—it's not like I wouldn't welcome the opportunity to wake you up every morning with my off-key renditions of the *High School Musical* soundtrack. I remember how much you loved me doing that in elementary school. Or maybe I'd be sweet and let you sleep in. Since that would give me ample opportunity to sneak your fake ID out of your wallet and introduce Mom and Dad to Finn Tucker of Bartimis Lane,

Timonium, MD. I'm curious—did you actually *choose* the name Finn Tucker?"

His response is part growl, part appreciative laugh, and I smile, relieved.

"Maybe you should come here for a visit, then," he says. "What about Preakness in May, if we can get Mom and Dad to sign off? The infield party's ridiculous—you'd love it."

I open my mouth to tell him I need to stick within a certain radius of Mass General, in case the call for a liver comes in. But I don't want to introduce any more reminders of my BA now that we're back on safe ground, so close it and nod instead. "Sure, maybe."

His head bobs too, but I think it has more to do with him trying to hold his phone steady while walking fast.

"What time do you have to work till tonight?" I ask.

He shrugs, which makes the camera bounce more. "Nine. But nothing really happens around here before then anyway, so it's no biggie. What about you? Got big Friday night plans?"

I move my phone to show off my flannel pajamas. "Oh, definitely. Me, a box of cereal, and a full season of something trashy."

Alex gives me a look somewhere between pity and amusement.

"What?" I answer. "I haven't figured out a new hobby yet to take the place of my derby practices until I can get back to them. I was contemplating underwater basket weaving—what do you think?"

"Sounds wet."

I groan. "Dude, you're too young to be turning into Dad."

"What about that mural thing you won?"

I make a face. "I would *love* to be working on that, but the design's done and approved. Not much I can do now until it gets warm enough for the paint to adhere to the wall. Dad says it needs to be at least fifty degrees for a few days in a row—not finding a lot of those temps in Boston in March."

"Another reason to come to Maryland; we hit near seventy today. Some warm front passing through . . ."

"And *now* the flip-flops make sense. Oh, *please* let that be coming here. I need spring in the worst way."

"Yeah, it doesn't suck. But seriously, you should call Sibby to hang out with you tonight." Alex's voice is slightly breathless as he hikes up a steep hill. I've visited with my parents enough times to gauge his spot on campus, and I like knowing exactly where he fits in time and space as we talk.

"Uh, yeah, except that *she's* at derby practice." I punctuate this by making a face.

Alex grimaces. "Right. I forgot she did it too."

I can never tell Sibby this; she prides herself on being absolutely unforgettable.

Catching my image in the small square at the bottom of my screen, I tuck a stray hair back into place before answering. "It's not like I don't have other friends. I'm not the weirdo you were in high school, glued to one person morning to night."

Not totally accurate. I have other friends, sure, but they're casual . . . nothing on the level of me and Sibby.

"Hey! I resent that," Alex says. "Will and I weren't *that* pathetic." He pauses, considering. "Okay, you might have a point. We *are* pretty tight. Anyway, listen, big brother advice—you ready? Whatever you do, do *not* let Dad talk you into picking up hours at the store. You've been officially warned."

Dad goes into a funk whenever we drop Alex back at school. I'm convinced it's got as much to do with losing Alex's college-boy strength in the stockroom as with missing his child. (I'd never admit this in front of my brother, but Alex actually does have a couple muscles.) Advil's stock probably goes up every September, when Dad has to resume inventory duties.

The hilarious thing is that I'm not far behind Alex in the strength department, but I'm more than willing to let down all of woman-kind in this particular instance by neglecting to point that out to my father.

And though I really didn't want to revisit the subject of my BA, I can't resist saying, "At least there's one advantage to all of this—no heavy lifting."

Alex's eyes widen and he gasps. "Oh, damn, Li. I didn't even think—"

I wave him quiet. "Sorry, bad joke on my part."

He closes his eyes briefly and my stomach twists. No! Please don't let Alex start treating me with kid gloves now too. I never thought I'd say this, but I actually *want* him to give me crap.

Stacks of books appear behind him on-screen, making it pretty obvious he's reached work. He hesitates, then says, "Hey, Lia? I gotta go, but hang in, okay?" Before I can respond, he adds, "Send me a pic of your green milk on Sunday."

Ever since I can remember, my dad has colored our milk on Saint Patrick's Day, and though the likelihood of Alex making a trip off campus to buy food dye just for one silly picture is probably pretty low, I answer, "Yeah, you too."

The heaviness settles again as soon as I end the call. No thank you. I've had enough of this. I attempt to literally shake it away, and if anyone walked in right now they'd probably laugh their head off at my arms and legs flailing. But it actually works. A little.

"Not gonna catch me," I tell the melancholy, sticking my tongue out as I tug on fuzzy socks and settle in for my date with the remote.

Words With Friends notification for AllHaiL(ia)TheChief:
QuitWithTheT-rex has just played ENDURE for 26 points

FOUR HOURS AND EIGHT MINUTES. THAT'S HOW LONG IT TAKES
for the first knock on our door.

"Lia!" my mother calls up. "Come here a sec!"

As I descend the stairs, I'm met by the upturned faces of my
former Brownie troop leader and her daughter, Annabel, who trans-
ferred to private school when we were in second grade—which may
also be the last time I've seen either of them.

Mom's voice is fake-bright. "Look who stopped by! Blast from
the past, right?"

(My mother has never quite gotten over the time Miss Lesley
told her, in response to Mom not being able to help us sell Girl Scout
cookies after school because she had to *work*, "Oh, well, of course I

understand if you have to put yourself first.")

I step off the bottom step and am promptly swept into Miss Lesley's arms and squeezed tight.

"You are simply the bravest thing, honey," she whispers before releasing me and continuing, "When Annabel saw everyone—all the old crew from Haggerty, this is—posting about your plight online, we just had to jump into action."

Annabel alternates between studying the floor and stealing glances at me. She's ditched the braids for a crew cut that I covet, but that makes her look like even more of a stranger from the image of a toothy eight-year-old I carry in my head.

"Now, I've arranged a sign-up page on Meal Train and it's filling fast, so this is only the first of many to come," Miss Lesley says, her chin indicating the plastic-wrap-covered sheet pan in Annabel's hands.

I blink, struggling to compose myself, when all I want to do is yell, *But I'm not an invalid!*

"This is really so sweet of you, Lesley," my mother says, covering for me as I stand thunderstruck. "And Annabel, of course."

Finally, I find my manners and echo, "Um, yeah. *Yes.* Thank you. So sweet."

Which it is. Here's the thing: it sounds incredibly bratty to complain about the fact that people care enough to rally around me and my family. I know that. I should be grateful to be surrounded by a sweet, generous community. But the words *everyone posting* and *your plight* run on a loop through my mind. Combined with the fact that two people I haven't seen in ten years are in my front hall with lasagna—it's all too unbelievable to be real.

How can this be my life?

It's just . . .

What I *really* need right now—far more than any pan of pasta—is to keep focused on the positive. Not to *forget*, per se, because it's not like that's possible, but also not to have the constant reminders in my face. It might look like an innocent dish of pasta and cheese, but to me it's a taunt. *You're weak, Amelia.*

I am *not* weak. I'm the same me as ever.

Why can't everyone just allow me that?

7

DING DONG.

I'm in my room late the next afternoon, gathering my supplies for work, when the doorbell rings.

Correction: when the *broken* doorbell rings.

It hasn't functioned properly for the entire twelve years I've lived here, and fixing it would violate Babi's Do Not Disturb rule. We embrace the chaos though. For my dad's birthday a few years ago, I found him a mat that reads *Doorbell Broken. Yell Ding Dong Really Loud* and it won me the coveted Best Gift prize (basically just bragging rights, but those go a long way in my family).

My chest tightens. *Another meal drop-off.* More awkward porch shuffling and stumbled reheating instructions, amid sideways glances to assess how critically close to death I might look today.

I'm the only one home and I consider pretending I'm not here either, but when it sounds again, and then a third time, I give in to curiosity over who holds this doorbell magic.

I clomp down the steps, yelling, "Coming!" The loose spindle wobbles free and clatters to the floor.

Oddly enough, our doorbell *does* work . . . sometimes. Well, technically speaking, it works all the time, but only for exactly two people in the world, neither of whom are around at the moment. One is Michael, our former mailman, who used to give it a quick single jab when he wanted to let us know he was leaving a package on the porch. The other is Will, my brother's best friend, which used to drive my mother up the wall because Will was such a constant in our house growing up that he was practically a Linehan. She would insist that his ringing the doorbell to come inside was as unnecessary as Alex or me doing it—not that he ever listened.

Michael went on disability last year, and while my brother and Will are still close, he hasn't been over in ages. Even when he and Alex are both in town at the same time, they meet up to go out; they're not hanging around here the way they did when we were little. Sure, Will stayed in Boston for college, but since my brother is currently a thousand miles away, it obviously couldn't be—

I freeze in the opening, grateful for the heavy six-panel door propping me up.

"Will!"

He's standing just off center of the word *Yell* on the doormat, and even with sunglasses obscuring his eyes, it takes only his familiar smile to render me fourteen again. That was the year I developed a totally clichéd—and unrequited—crush on the Boy Next Door (a few additional streets away geographically, but close enough).

I'm long over that now, but still . . . cringe, cringe, cringe.

Get it together, girl. You are a take no prisoners BAMF, so Will being on your doorstep doesn't get to fluster you.

"I . . . uh . . . Hey! Alex isn't here," I manage. Not the greatest, but serviceable.

"I know. I *am* Alex."

"Funny," I say, beginning to recover now. "I don't remember Alex being so—"

"Tall? Charming? Devastatingly handsome?"

I raise an eyebrow and say blandly, "Thai."

He's nonplussed as he casually slides his sunglasses up and props them on top of his head. His dark eyes, now that I can see them, flash amusement. "Well, I guess that does give me away, huh? Should've known better than to try to pull one over on you, Decker."

I fight a groan over a nickname I haven't heard in years. I may or may not have gone through a brief obsession with all things presidential when I was nine, and may or may not have begged Alex and Will to pretend to be my Secret Service detail, and, maybe, mandated they, at all times, call me by my designated code name: Decker. (So coined because I was hanging out at the hardware store the day I was trying to pick one and the first thing that caught my eye was a Black & Decker power drill.) The fact that Will has insisted on calling me this ever since is . . . I don't even know.

When I don't respond right away, Will jumps in with, "But the point is, I want you to *consider* me Alex."

I lean into the door frame, casually cool, even though my brain is whirling in overtime. *The heck?*

"What does that even mean?" I ask, more curiously than sarcastically.

His eyes soften. "Your brother called me last night. He's pretty worked up about not being here for you right now."

Will's voice is matter-of-fact when he says this, but my stomach drops out as I'm hit with several competing emotions at once. I could tell our talk yesterday shook Alex, but getting Will involved? Telling him everything? Alex had no right. He might have meant well, but why oh why can't anyone ask *me* what I need, instead of assuming they know what will help me?

Before I can fully process, Will continues. "As someone who is— was? is?—practically family, that makes me your practically brother, yes? I hope? So here I am. Reporting for big brother duty."

Inside I'm a mess, but externally, I fall back on my reliable cover: snark. "If I'm supposed to consider you Alex, my actual brother, how can you also say you're Will, my practically brother? Sorry, but that's splitting metaphors."

It's possible I'm not within the technical definition of that term, but I'm not too fussed. Will rocks back on his heels, studying me with a serious expression on his face.

"I concede. Ten points to Gryffindor," he finally says.

I narrow my eyes. "I'm a Slytherin."

He laughs and I have to fight to keep my face neutral.

"You've grown up, Decker," he says, with a note of appreciation in his voice.

Oh, so now *you notice?*

"It was incredibly nice of you to stop by, Will, but honestly I'm *great* and I'd really be happy if you could pass that message along to Alex—he doesn't need to worry about me.

"Seriously, I'm fine," I repeat to Will, when the first time garners no reaction. He tilts his head but still doesn't reply. To cover the silence, I ramble on. "I know my parents will be really bummed they missed you. Stop back when they're here sometime and say hi. But honestly, it was great to see you."

I wait for him to answer with niceties of his own and step off my porch, but he doesn't move. His still-present smile is bland, but grows into something that could maybe be described as slightly condescending, which emboldens me to be firmer, possibly even rude. "Well, I have to get to work soon, so . . . thanks again for coming by."

I'm not inclined to slam the door in his face or anything, but when he *still* doesn't move to leave or even say a word in reply, I begin to gently ease it closed, waving goodbye as I do.

The second it clicks shut, the doorbell rings.

Damn, traitorous doorbell.

I open the door with a partly exasperated but partly amused eye roll. "Yes, Will?"

"Sorry. No can do. I promised Alex an authentic check-in on his baby sister, so I'm afraid you're stuck with me for at least the next few hours while I complete my formal assessment."

I grind my teeth at the words *baby sister* and at his dismissal of my brush-off. Will's every bit as cocky as I remember. That once fueled my crush, to be honest. But that was then and this is now, and he's no longer under my skin.

"If only that was an option," I say, "but it's possible you didn't hear me say I have to go to work." I aim for sticky sweet and nail it.

"Oh, I heard you," he says. "Where are we working these days?"

I raise an eyebrow. "I can't speak for you, but *I'm* working at Lemondrop."

Will's eyes widen. "The bakery? Oh, damn, Decks, tell me they don't let you near the ingredients."

Another reason for me to be exasperated? This guy has years and *years'* worth of ammunition on me. I know he's referring to the time I mixed up the abbreviations in a recipe and added two *table*spoons of vanilla to the chocolate chip cookie batter I was making, instead of two *tea*spoons. Who would imagine that something as amazing as vanilla could taste so absolutely disgusting in large quantities?

"Nooooo." I huff out a breath that pretty clearly conveys my feelings on the matter, but it doesn't do much except make the corners of his mouth twitch. "I do the chalkboards."

"Come again?"

"The chalkboards. I hand letter their menu every week. You know, with chalk?"

"You mean like the signs you used to do for the hardware store?" Will asks, and I answer him with a nod. "They have you doing this on *Saturday nights*?"

I roll my eyes and face my phone's display to him. "It's barely five o'clock, not exactly primo partying hours. It's a quiet time for the shop and they like to have the new designs in place for the start of a fresh week, so . . ."

Will recovers quickly. "Fair enough. I'm always up for new experiences. Are we walking or driving?"

I blink at him. "Oh. No, you can't come with me."

"Why not?" He leans against the railing and crosses one leg over the other. God he's smug. He knows it too, but I bet he'd call it *charm*.

"Because! It's my place of employment. It wouldn't be . . . professional."

Will examines a fingernail. "Is the bakery open to the public while you do this?"

"Yesssss," I say, drawing out the word with suspicion.

"Okay then. I'll just be another customer, stopping in for—" He pauses, considering. "Do they have macarons? Or is it macaroons? Which ones don't have coconut?"

"Macarons." I grind out the word.

"Right. So do they have those?"

I close my eyes briefly before nodding.

"Perfect!"

I try to stare him down, but his answering look is pure innocence as he checks a nonexistent watch on his wrist. "Can you roll in whenever, or are we in a time crunch here?"

It turns out grown-up Will is no less infuriating than the little boy who used to flick Pokémon cards at my head while I read books.

Whatever. I can handle one night of walks down memory lane if it ensures Alex will get a clean report and prevent any further attempts to "help" me.

I hide my defeated sigh. "Now is fine. I'll just grab my stuff."

"Sure. Hey, but not too long! I don't want all the yellow macarons to be gone. Those are my favorite."

I close the door on his laugh, but just as quickly yank it open again and march myself eye to eye with him. "Just so we're clear, I don't want to talk about, you know . . . *it*. At all. That would be a dealbreaker, so tell me right now if you can't agree to my terms."

There are so many people in my life I wish I could extract this same promise from, though I know if I ask *them* they'll refuse to let me off the hook so easily. Especially Sibby.

But Will studies me quietly for a second, then holds three fingers up. "Scout's honor, the topic's off-limits."

I squint at him suspiciously, though given the fact that I have an actual visual of Will and Alex in those stiff blue shirts with the orange neckties, clutching their pinewood derby cars, I decide to give him the benefit of the doubt.

Returning inside, I take my time climbing the steps, dawdling while I set the spindle back into place. It takes me all of three seconds to finish collecting my work supplies, considering they only consist of an eighteen-pack of liquid chalk markers and my iPad, but I linger for several more minutes, in part to keep from seeming too eager and also to calm my swirling thoughts. I'm usually happy to roll with surprises, but this is a lot to spring on a girl already trying to regain her footing after the events of the last couple weeks.

Maybe I should find it sweet that Will cares enough about Alex to do him the favor of checking in on his kid sister, but it's also humiliating as hell. I don't want to be anyone's obligation, and I'm sure he has plenty of other ways he'd rather be spending a Saturday night. Why couldn't he have just taken me at my word that I'm really and truly *fine*?

Or at least that I will be, once this health crisis stuff is in the rearview mirror.

I collect a deep breath and channel my frustration into the fuel I'll need to prove to Will that I'm handling all this perfectly. With a determined bounce, I take the steps two at a time, lightly enough that all staircase components remain in place. I flash Will a smile to show him just what a good sport I'm about to be as I pull the door closed behind me and zip up my coat. "Ready when you are!"

He slides his sunglasses back into place and sweeps his arm toward the steps. "After you."

8

"SO ALEX TOLD ME YOU'RE HEADED TO AMHERST," WILL SAYS AS we begin walking. "That's impressive. Do you know what you want to major in yet?" Then he groans. "Sorry, that's the generic icebreaker for every college student on Earth. I hate myself a little right now."

"That's okay, I'm not jaded by it yet, so it's all good. To answer your question: everything!"

"Ah, so you'll be on the twenty-five-year plan, then?"

I'm grateful Will is abiding by his promise and talking to me about my future as if my BA doesn't exist. I step around a stray patch of ice on the sidewalk and say, "Whenever I look at the course catalog online, I want to sign up for all of them. *Everything* sounds interesting. That's how I landed on Amherst, because they have a liberal arts focus, so I can sample a little bit here and a little bit there."

"You're making 'undecided' sound strangely appealing."

I wrinkle my nose. "'Undecided' sounds terrible; I *hate* uncertainty. This doesn't feel like drifting aimlessly to me though, because I have a solid plan. It just happens to be a plan to try everything, like a big ol' college buffet. One helping of Anthropology of Food, one side of Introduction to Oceanography, one spoonful of History of Opera . . . I think it's more like 'overdecided.'"

I fill him in on some of the classes I've already bookmarked as we cover the blocks between my house and the bakery.

"Your plan does not sound boring," he says.

"Boring is the enemy."

"Yeah, I can see that." He gestures at my bright red boots, peeking out from under my long puffer. They have embroidered dragons climbing up their sides.

I purse my lips to hide my grin. This might be the longest non-BA conversation I've had in days, and it lets me feel like *me* again. We're reaching the business district now, where cute local shops line this stretch of road. I catch my reflection in one of the storefront windows and my posture is tall, my shoulders back, my stride easy.

A bubble of happiness catches in my throat. I might not be thrilled that Alex took it upon himself to send Will my way, but I have to admit it's not been *terrible* so far.

As we turn the corner, I steal subtle peeks at Will's reflection too. I used to be able to conjure him from memory, but the most recent glimpse I've had of him before tonight was probably a picture on my brother's Instagram feed from a visit Will made to Alex's campus for

Halloween. That photo clearly didn't do him justice.

Will was always on the skinny side, and though it's hard to tell just how much can be attributed to his winter coat, it looks like college has bulked him up. He's wearing his black hair a little longer than I've seen it before—I can't tell, but it *might* even have product in it—and unless his sunglasses are prescription, he's ditched the specs too. I always liked those, actually, but I can't help appreciating that he's done some growing up of his own.

"So, uh . . . ," he begins as the bakery comes into sight. The note of hesitation in his voice is so out of character that I swing my head to meet his eyes.

"Yeah?"

"I know I didn't give you much choice in my tagging along here."

"Oh, so you're willing to admit you bullied me?" I tease.

"Okay, maybe some would call it bullying, even if it was only with the best intentions. Although we both know you don't take BS from anyone."

I offer nothing more than my best Mona Lisa smile.

"But honestly, are you gonna get in trouble if you show up with me?" he asks. "Should I pretend not to know you or something?"

"How exactly do you plan to properly assess my state of well-being if you're pretending not to know me?" I respond, curious for his answer.

He scrunches his nose. "Yeah, I don't know. Body language?"

I can't help but laugh. *Welcome back, laughter! I've missed you!* "It's fine, Will. You can hang with me while I work. Lemondrop's mostly dead on Saturday evenings, so it's usually just me and this grad student, Jumoke. I'm pretty sure he requests this shift so he can log quality study time; he'll probably be relieved he won't be duty-bound to make small talk with me. Plus my friend Sibby tags along a bunch anyway. She would have tonight too, if I hadn't insisted I wanted some alone time."

That had more to do with my still not wanting to confront Sibby on the Prom with a Purpose stuff, but if my words have the added benefit of giving Will a twinge of guilt for being so intrusive, I wouldn't complain. No reason for him to know I'm warming to the idea of having him here with each minute I get to be Badass Amelia, instead of Dying Girl.

But also? I might have, um, oversold the whole concept of "job" a little. Can something you only do for a couple hours once a week count as legitimate employment?

"Of all your abandoned obsessions, I can't believe you stuck with the lettering one," Will says. "Although having heard you play the ukulele, I think you made the right call."

I elbow him for that and he yelps and rubs his arm. Whatever. He deserved it, although . . . he's not wrong. The aforementioned presidential phase was preceded by a passion for all things dog-related, until I finally grasped the reality that my parents were never getting me one of my very own (Mom's allergies and Dad's fear of what one would do to Babi's floors). After presidents came Percy Jackson fan fiction. Then there was the regrettable six months where I decided to take up the ukulele and became consumed with teaching myself to play using YouTube tutorials. Alex scored noise-canceling head-phones from my parents that Christmas.

Hand lettering was my middle school obsession and it turned out I had a hidden talent for being able to perfectly shape a letter by sight. Out of sheer boredom one day, I started "fancying up" the chalkboard easel my dad places on the sidewalk to advertise the daily bargains. It attracted the attention of some of the neighboring stores and a little side business was born.

"How long have you been doing this as a job?" Will asks, deliberately putting more distance between us as he side-eyes my elbow warily.

"A few years now. Most consistently for Lemondrop, but I sometimes get calls from other local places."

"It's pretty cool you get paid for your art."

I shrug. "Not that much."

It usually hovers around minimum wage, depending on the intricacy of the design and how much time it takes me to complete— but as far as quasi-jobs go, it's fun and absorbing and just creative enough to keep it from feeling like actual *work* work. Plus, I can easily fit it in around my more recent obsession of roller derby (which is already three years strong and counting). Though I guess "*used to* fit it around roller derby" would be the more accurate verb tense these days. The thought sends my BA to the forefront of my brain. No. Not tonight.

"But I won a grant to paint a mural on the side of a restaurant and it comes with a cash award, so that's pretty cool." I tell him this in part to redirect my own thoughts, but mostly to impress him, so I'm gratified when he whistles low and long.

"That's amazing, Decks. Seriously."

"Thanks," I murmur, turning my face from his so he can't see my blush.

As we reach the bakery I hold the door open, swatting him away when he tries to take it from me. "Just get in there."

He holds up his hands in surrender and steps inside. I follow.

Lemondrop is everything you'd want a tiny neighborhood bakery to be. The walls are white shiplap and the floor is also white planks, but enhanced by a pale yellow diamond pattern. A high shelf acts as a border along the tops of all four walls, displaying Martin and Miguel's impressive and colorful cake stand collection. A counter has been installed across the front window, with a handful of stools lined up under it. Other than that, there's only enough room for two café tables and a small wooden hutch that's been turned into a coffee prep station, because the massive bakery case takes up the rest of the space. The entire wall behind it (with the exception of the cake stand border) is reserved for an enormous framed chalkboard menu: my domain.

Jumoke flips a textbook shut and straightens behind the register. Catching sight of me, his posture eases from eager employee to friendly coworker.

"Hey!" he greets me. "Did you trade the Kiwi girl in for a new model?"

I raise my fist to meet Jumoke's bump, ignoring the teasing waggle he does with his eyebrows over the fact that I've arrived with a—*gasp!*—guy. He's not the least bit subtle about it and I catch Will's smirk from the corner of my eye.

"Sibby would kick your ass if she ever heard you mistake her for a

New Zealander. You know that, don't you?" I gesture to my tagalong. "This is Will. My *brother's* friend."

I make sure to overemphasize the word *brother's*. Will doesn't react, but Jumoke rolls his eyes at me, then turns his attention to the boy in question. "Nice to meet you, Will, friend of the brother."

Will gives him one of those guy nods as I squeeze past Jumoke and slip behind the counter.

"Where's the best place for me, so I won't be in anyone's way?" Will asks.

I point to a spot where the bakery case meets the wall, close to the far left of the chalkboard and Will drags a stool into place. He straddles it so that his legs fall behind him and his elbows prop on the top of the glass case. Jumoke takes his seat at the counter's far opposite end, untangles a set of earphones from his sweatshirt pocket, and slips them in. "Yell if there's a customer I don't notice," he murmurs into his textbook.

"Sure thing." I slide my chalk markers out of their box and drop them into a cup by Will's elbows.

"You did all this?" Will sounds impressed as he points to the menu board, and I bite back a satisfied smile as I sweep my eyes over it with pride.

"Thanks. Just trying to leave my mark on the world," I joke.

Truth is, Pinterest and Instagram provide most of my design elements, with only minimal tweaks from me, but I do like the approach I've taken recently. I've divided it into three sections and made the middle one the main menu, which I usually only update with different lettering every month or so. On the left panel I've been doing a quote of the week, typically something about baking or from a famous Cambridge resident. This week I have one about cake from Julia Child, who lived only a couple streets over from my house, so I'm checking both boxes at once. On the right panel, I do illustrations of the combination of ingredients that go into a particular recipe. It might be something like: milk bottle, plus sign, butter on a dish, plus sign, bag of sugar, plus sign, eggs, equal sign, cupcake.

I come around front to grab my own stool.

"I could have passed that over," protests Will.

"True, but I'm an independent woman," I shoot back, winking. I haven't flirted in ages. I don't even know if I'm flirting now, at least not with any particular goal in mind, but what I'm *not* doing is holding back from enjoying myself.

"Touché!" He laughs and it tickles my insides.

I climb up on my stool to bring myself to eye level with the top of the menu. The legs wobble a few times and I glance down to find Will's fingers twitching like he's fighting an urge to reach over the case and steady me. I prop an elbow on the wall and raise an eyebrow in challenge. "Can I help you?"

He rolls his eyes but adds a smile.

I use my chin to signal my messenger bag. "Actually, *you* can help *me*. Grab the iPad out. My password is my birthday: ten—"

"Twenty, oh-one," he finishes, before I can. Our birthdays are exactly two weeks (and two years) apart, and *I* remember this, but I'm surprised he does too.

"Uh, yeah. Right," I say. "It should have Pinterest open already. Can you turn the screen this way and kind of prop it up on that napkin holder, so I can see the design I'm copying?"

He does as I ask, while I uncap a white chalk marker and make a few light strokes to outline the art deco border I'll use on the top and bottom. I double-check my proportions, then get to work, trying not to be conscious of Will's eyes following my every move.

"Do you need to concentrate, or . . . ?" he asks after a minute.

"Nope. Just don't be offended if I'm not making eye contact."

"Right. So, uh, catch me up on all other things Decker. Are you still determined to be the first female president? Seeing as how the job title is, unfortunately, still up for grabs?"

I snort. "Ha! No way! I'm all for fighting the good fight and I wouldn't rule out public service of some kind, but I think that level of politics might have become too brutal even for me."

I move on to the lettering itself. Once done, my Julia quote will read *A party without cake is just a meeting.* The first *a* will form a tiny apple and the whole phrase will sit atop a cake stand.

"So what you're saying is that you *don't* have an inauguration speech written out and tucked into the bottom drawer of your nightstand?" Will asks.

"My nightstand is a hanging shelf I made myself. It's a thing of beauty, but . . . no drawers."

Zero need to confess my speech is actually in a shoebox underneath my bed, along with my other mementos from elementary school.

"Anyway, there actually *was* a female president for a little while," I continue. "Even if she doesn't get credit for it in the history books."

"What are you talking about?"

I spare him a quick smirk, then resume shading in the apple in green. "Yeah. In 1919, Woodrow Wilson had a bunch of strokes that left him partially paralyzed and almost blind, but he refused to step aside, so instead he had his wife, Edith, run things for him. People called her 'The Presidentress.'"

There's a smile in Will's voice as he says, "I see you still retain an impressive inventory of presidential trivia from your formative years."

"Equally cool, she was a direct descendant of Pocahontas," I reply, before acknowledging his statement with, "Never know when they might come in handy."

"Like right now, to impress a stranger from your past?" he asks.

"Hit me with another."

"You're not exactly a stranger, Will."

"Thank you for that."

I'm so surprised by how quietly he says this that I glance over at him again, but his expression reveals nothing.

To steer us back to safer territory, I quickly scroll through an inventory of presidential factoids taking up space in my brain, trying to settle on one Will would find funny. "Okay, here you go. Gro-ver Cleveland became legal guardian of his law partner's orphaned daughter when she was eleven, and then he married her when she turned twenty-one. So basically, he out–Woody Allened Woody Allen."

"Um, eww?"

"I know, right? Plus she had to kiss his Vulcan jaw."

Will coughs. "I'm sorry, what?"

I nod. "His jaw was partly made of vulcanized rubber after a secret surgery he had done on his friend's yacht."

"Why are they wasting time teaching us about cherry trees and boring 'cannot tell a lie' stories when there is genuinely interesting stuff like this out there? We're failing the youth of America, dammit!"

I raise my fist in solidarity and relish my buoyant mood. *I've missed fun and lightness and easy-breezy.* I exhale, testing the airiness in my chest and find it holds up. It's an unexpected gift, like that first day of warm weather, when you realize how much you'd been drawing your shoulders in tight all winter only after noticing what it feels like not having to anymore.

Using the dampened corner of a rag, I clean a smudge along the edge of the cake stand I'm drawing.

"Another," Will demands.

"Really? You want more?" *Yes, more. I will tell you a thousand random presidential facts and you'll keep on shielding me from reality. I am more than prepared to make that deal.*

"This is our country's *sacred* history we're talking about," he says. "As a first-gen, I'm duty-bound to put all you 'my relatives came over on the Mayflower' snobs to shame with my superior citizenship and knowledge of American history. Help a guy out, Decks."

"Ha! Okay, one more, but that's all you get."

Will's only response is to prop his chin into his hands and lean forward on his elbows.

"In the seventies, there were two assassination attempts on Gerald Ford in one seventeen-day span and both were by women," I say.

"Oh my god, my mother would love that one." He quickly

clarifies. "Not to suggest she's homicidal or anything. She just appreciates stories about interesting women."

"I miss your mom. How is she?" Will and Alex played soccer and baseball all through school and I used to hang in the bleachers with Mrs. Srisari whenever my parents both had to work, before I was old enough to leave home alone. She taught me to celebrate the boys' wins with her by cheering, "*Chai-yo! Chai-yo! Chai-yo!*"

"She's great," Will answers. "I'm sure if she knew I was seeing you, she'd send hellos and want me to make sure you're eating enough."

"Ha! Yes! Every time I used to see her she'd ask if I was hungry." Will grins. "And now you know what it is to have a Thai mother."

We're interrupted when a customer wanders in. After handling her transaction, Jumoke decides to take a study break and chat with us as I finish up the left panel and move on to the right side. It doesn't take me much longer to complete the design, and Will helps me gather my supplies as Jumoke packs him a complimentary box of yellow macarons for the road.

My mood is still warm and fizzy, even as we exit into a night that's way colder than it was earlier. The chill makes us walk briskly as I regale him with a description of last year's junior derby championship, trying not to be *too* effusive about my role in it.

"So . . . ?" I ask, as we near my street.

"So what?"

"Are you satisfied that I'm not on the precipice of any abyss? Does Alex get a good report?"

In response, he nudges my arm with his. "I don't think trivia and small talk necessarily counts as delving into the depths of your soul. But you seem like you're holding up okay."

I smirk.

Then his voice drops and he adds, "It was pretty shocking when Alex told me everything."

A prickle crawls along my neck and I increase my pace even more, forcing him to do the same. *No, no, no, no.* He'd been doing so well. Tonight let me completely forget for a few blissful hours and that's a relief I'm not even sure I can properly explain.

Please don't ruin things now, I telegraph.

He's quiet for a long minute and then he says, "Do you want to turn around and get some coffee or something, and maybe talk about—"

I cut him off before he can finish the thought. "Scout's honor, remember?"

I feel his eyes on me but refuse to look up. We're nearly in front of my house now and the light from the lantern at the edge of our walkway stretches our shadows.

Will sighs. "Right. I did promise, I'm sorry."

I pause at the bottom of the porch steps and force a casual smile to change the mood. "So, I'd say thanks for hanging with me tonight, but that might make it sound like I had any choice in the matter."

He answers with his own grin. "Tell your parents I said hi."

"And you let Alex know 'hey' from me. Also, warn the meddlesome prick he'll be hearing from me."

I shake my fist in mock anger, my real annoyance having *mostly* faded at this point.

Will laughs, then raises his box of macarons in salute. "Good seeing you, Decker."

"Back atcha, Will Srisari." I jog lightly up the steps and wave bye as I unlock the door. He answers the gesture and turns away.

For a second I wonder if he rode the T here and whether I should offer him a ride across the river; Mom's car is right there in the driveway. But I decide to let tonight end on this note and be happy with what it was: a chance to spend time with an old friend and, more important, with the missing pre-diagnosis Amelia.

Aside from the tiny hiccup at the end, as Saturday nights go, definitely not the worst one I've ever had.

Words With Friends notification for QuitWithTheT-rex:

AllHaiL(ia)TheChief played GALL for 14 points

9

FRANCIA, WHOM I'VE BARELY TALKED TO SINCE WE HAD COOKING class together in freshman year, is leaning over my desk in the minutes before English Lit starts on Wednesday.

"I'm sure he'd be happy to talk to you, if you want me to ask him," she tells me, referring to a great-uncle of hers who had a heart transplant in 1978.

1978.

My *mother* was barely even alive then, let alone me. I'm guessing the procedure has changed a teensy bit since. Also, Anatomy might not be my strongest subject, but even I know that a heart is not a bladder is not a kidney is not a liver. Pretty sure the operations differ a smidgen.

I usually pride myself on my witty comebacks, but I'm finding out fast that everything's different when the subject matter is so intensely personal.

Instead, I fumble an answer. "Um, thanks, but, uh, there's a private Facebook group of people who've had liver transplants, so I can, um, find lots of people to talk to there."

This is true. I even went so far as to request membership just after I got home from the hospital, before I changed my mind and decided being on there would not fit in well with my plan for keeping the darkness away, which consists of one step only: don't even look *sideways* at the darkness.

Of course, Francia doesn't need that extra info.

Bryan tips his desk on two legs to lean closer to us. "I saw this one episode of *Grey's Anatomy* where the guy has this liver condition, right? And—"

My friend Jemima turns around in her seat. "I never would have pegged you for a *Grey's Anatomy* fan, Ty."

"Shut up. I have sisters, okay?"

"No shame. Guys should be more in touch with their sensitive side," she replies. "So, which is it: McDreamy or McSteamy?"

Jemima winks at me, and I reply with a grateful smile. I don't know whether she jumped in specifically to save me or is simply gleeful about the chance to give Bryan crap, but man, I wish there were a thousand Jemimas to follow me around school and run interference.

Those few hours of relief with Will Saturday night are already a distant memory. I *know* my classmates are (mostly) well-meaning and sympathetic and curious, but it's been two and a half solid days of questions and anecdotes, and it doesn't seem to be easing up *at all*.

What might be worse are the conversations that stop the minute I come into sight.

Or the people I've known forever who suddenly can't seem to make eye contact with me. Like they're worried I'm contagious or something. Or as if I'm somehow to blame that they have to feel uncomfortable for the five seconds it takes them to pass me in the hallway.

How am I supposed to remain calm and optimistic when the entire world is conspiring against my plan to get through this the one way I can envision being able to handle it?

"I've been bingeing reruns of that show! McDreamy gives me life," Francia says. "What about you, Amelia?"

Sibby's books hit the desk next to mine with a loud CLAP! "McDreamy's a pig. All men are pigs. Screw the whole lot of them."

Bryan opens his mouth to mount a defense and Sibby snaps "Get stuffed!" before he can utter a word.

He and Jemima exchange glances, then turn around in their chairs just as the bell rings. Our teacher isn't in the room yet though, and I continue to stare at Sibby.

"What?" she asks, busying herself searching for a pencil in the black hole of her backpack.

I dangle an extra of mine in her face. "Uh . . . ? What do you mean '*what*'? Spill! What happened to bring on the mood?"

Please don't let it be worry about me. Please don't let it be worry about me.

Things between us are mostly back to normal, I guess, although

I still can't bring myself to share my real feelings about the assembly, partly because it doesn't seem worth getting into a big thing with her when I know at least some of my feelings about her role in it are irrational, and partly because it would mean reliving that afternoon. No thanks.

She swivels to face me, snatches the pencil from my fingers, and whispers, "It's that creeper Dormer. He gave me detention last period because my shorts are 'inappropriate.'"

I peek under her desk. Her shorts are noteworthy only for the fact that she's wearing them in March. In Boston. The freakish warm spell Alex talked about has miraculously made its way north to us this week and it has everyone dreaming of spring. I'm the one always cranking up the thermostat and even *I* couldn't resist wearing my favorite light-weight tee, bright orange with a tiny print of girls in sunglasses riding Vespas. While it's not bare legs weather per se, try telling that to an Australian beach bum.

"How are they inappropriate?"

"Oh, he reminded me coolly of the fingertips rule in the dress code, before telling me they were 'a distraction to my classmates' and giving me detention. Classmates, my arse. Perverted jerk."

My jaw drops open. "I'm sorry, what? He said that to you?"

She nods and her shoulders slump. Which is just . . . no. No way am I going to let her feel crappy over this ignoramus's comments.

"WTF, Sib!"

Mrs. Aguilar enters the room and calls everyone's attention to the front. "I know this change of temperature makes graduation feel all that much closer, but you're still mine for the next few months, so I trust you're all up to date on your *Anna Karenina* annotating. Bitter Russian winters are the perfect antidote to this cheerful spring weather, don't you think?"

Sliding a blank sheet of paper from my binder, I write in all caps:

WE ARE FIGHTING THIS!!!!!!!!!!

I angle it toward Sibby, who reads it and shrugs. I can guess how she's probably feeling: embarrassed and icky. She's likely still in shock. But that's gonna fade fast and when it does, I'll be ready and waiting to match an anger that's going to be epic.

Mrs. Aguilar clears her throat significantly and I glance up to find her eyes on me, so I spend the rest of class pretending to focus on her. But I smile inside when, in the edges of my vision, Sibby's posture transitions from slumped to sharp and her foot goes from still to jiggling.

And I scheme.

My motives are pure, but I'd be lying if I said I don't also welcome *any* opportunity to be consumed by something that has nothing to do with livers or prognoses or intrusive questions. It's different from the flirty fun I had with Will; it's the "take charge and handle shit" attitude I love and miss about being on the derby track—the one I *thought* I could recapture at the assembly.

That plan turned out to be . . . misguided. But this?

This I can *slay*!

I'm actually a little surprised we haven't had occasion to take on the dress code before the bitter end of senior year, but I'm all for getting it in under the gun. The minute the bell rings, I bolt from my seat and grab Sibby's arm.

"I have a plan. Come with me."

I'm reassured she's hit outrage level when she doesn't utter a peep of protest.

"Where are we going?" is all she asks, followed by, "Am I gonna miss Spanish?"

"Art room and yes," I answer, tugging her into the hallway.

"Don't you have Anatomy now? Isn't that your hardest class?"

"I would rather fail Anatomy than fail my best friend."

"How noble. You're not gonna be saying that when Amherst pulls your early admission." She gives me a look. "Also, you're full of crap."

I stick out my tongue as I dodge a locker door that swings open. "Okay, fine, I might not be *heartbroken* about missing Anatomy, but I can also be incensed on your behalf, can't I?"

"Which is why I love you so much. Hey, do you reckon Rindge is obligated to report any disciplinary action they take against me to Tufts, even this long after I submitted my application? If this one detention means I won't get my fair go with them, that'd be crap."

I pick up my pace, dodging a cluster of kids huddled around a cell phone. "I don't know, but it's not gonna reach that point, Sib, I promise."

She nods and quickens her pace to match mine.

We luck out to find the art room empty and a sign on the door instructing all students to meet behind the gym for outdoor classes today. Miss Leekley ("But you guys should call me Skye") is the kind of person you'd expect to live in one of those hipster tiny houses and uses words like "chakra" and "aura," so I'm not surprised she'd want to be one with nature on the first nice day of the year.

"Grab some markers," I tell Sibby. "If you can find fabric ones, all the better, but otherwise any will do."

I cross the room to the wall of cabinets in the back and yank open the far right one, where I know I'll find a bin of extra-large men's white T-shirts, which Miss Leekley keeps on hand for students who find themselves in need of makeshift smocks. I pull a bunch from the pile and shake them out, looking for those with the fewest wrinkles. When I have two viable candidates, I present them to Sibby.

"Voilà."

"Okay, I'm all in for this, whatever it is, but . . . *what is it?*" she asks.

This, dearest Sib, is a chance for us to take on the world on equal terms, instead of that lopsided dynamic at the assembly. A chance to get back to our regular relationship, with zero conflicted feelings.

I spread a shirt on the paint-speckled table in the center of the room and uncap a marker. It's green-apple scented, which reminds me of the one I drew at the bakery on Saturday and makes me smile. Well, that plus my scheme. I'm not going for aesthetics, but I have to confess my hand lettering skills come in handy as I shape the words WHY ARE YOU STARING AT MY LEGS ANYWAY? down the front of the shirt in loopy letters.

Sibby grins. "Ah. Got it!"

"We need something about the dress code for the back."

"VIVE LA RÉVOLUTION?"

I wrinkle my nose and she tries again. "DOWN WITH PER-VERTS?"

This time I hold my fingers an inch apart. "Maybe a teensy bit much?"

"Not where Dormer's concerned. Right then, have a go at OUR DRESS CODE NEEDS RE-CODING."

"Perfect! You're brilliant!" I block out the letters, then hand the tee to her with a triumphant smile. She drops her backpack and tugs it on over her outfit. My girl is tiny; it hangs almost to her knees. While she models, I write the same message in strawberry-scented marker on the other smock and pull it on. I'm not nearly as short and the skirts I favor are all vintage, which means they tend to run longer, so I have to roll my waistband several times to make my hem disappear underneath. When we're situated, Sibby and I clutch hands and giggle.

"Should I ditch my tights?" I ask. "Before you answer, I'm gonna mention that I haven't shaved my legs in a couple of days."

Sibby backs up and assesses me. "Nah, you look like an adorable chicken with the white shirt and bright yellow legs."

I sigh in mock despair. "No one ever said revolutions were glamorous."

Sibby snips a few fashionable little triangles out of our necklines, then drops the scissors into a bucket, where they hit the base with a clink. "Shall we go take on the patriarchy?"

I throw a fist in the air in solidarity. "Down with the patriarchy!"

It feels good. *I* feel good.

This is what I *thought* last Friday's assembly could give me—that sense of purpose that drives me. I love challenges and targets and feeling like there's a force pushing me on. I actually felt a tiny bit let down when I got into Amherst early admission because so much of my high school career up until then had been focused on building an impressive transcript for my college application and I wouldn't have that to occupy me anymore. I adore that pre-scrimmage derby locker room talk where we get each other pumped up beyond belief and fill our chests with fierce desire and motivation.

Obviously the assembly didn't go as planned.

And other than that doomed attempt, my only task lately has been waiting. Waiting for the call telling me they've found me a liver. Waiting for temperatures to be consistently warm enough to begin my mural. Waiting for high school to end so my future can begin.

Waiting to see if I get to have a future.

I brush that last thought away as fast as it forms.

Taking on the school's antiquated dress code policy can be my new purpose. I feel it! A gift to future generations of Rindge students!

Sibby heads for the door, but I grab her arm. "Hold on. Always come to battle armed with facts, right? We need ammunition," I say.

It may have been tough to recite the organ donation statistics at the assembly, but I can't deny: cold, hard figures have the ability to sway hearts and minds.

She tugs off her smock and tucks it into her backpack. "Definitely. Okay, we hit the library through the end of this period, conquer the internet, then storm the halls between bells when we'll get maximum exposure."

I gesture to her legs. "No pun intended?" I couldn't call myself

Jeff Linehan's daughter with my head held high if I let such an easy one pass me by.

Sibby groans appreciation, but then I catch her exhale.

"What?" I ask, trying to interpret the expression on her face.

She shakes her head and fixes her attention on tightening her backpack strap. "This coming weekend is when we were supposed to be driving to DC for the climate change march, you know."

"Yeah," I whisper. "I'm sorry."

Her eyes jump to mine. "No! I wasn't reminding you to make you feel guilty. For fuck's sake, it's not like you had any say in the matter, Lia! I was trying to say that I'm happy we're doing something like this. Together, I mean. It's seemed a bit like you—yeah, nah, that's it. Just . . . I'm happy."

I press my lips together with relief and nod several times. "Same."

"Well, c'mon then!" She gestures for me to shove my own smock-slash-protest-piece into my purse and links her arms through mine as we exit the art room.

While I would never wish detention on Sibby, I don't know why I didn't think of something like this sooner. I'd been praying for the next drama to pull everyone's attention off my BA; it should have occurred to me to *create it myself*. The attention will still be on me, but not as Amelia Linehan, Dying Girl.

Amelia Linehan, Sexist-Dress-Code Slayer, has a far, *far* better ring to it.

I am very okay with that kind of notoriety.

In fact, it gives me life.

We wait just inside the double doors of the library for a good ten seconds after the next bell rings, allowing the hallways to fill, before we simultaneously burst through them like the warrior goddesses we are.

There are some curious glances to start, but once we twirl to allow both sides of our shirts to be seen, our mandate becomes clear.

"You go, girls!" a boy calls.

"Shake it, sisters!" a girl from my French class last year says.

I relish the attention.

Two girls step in front of us to act as bodyguards, parting the crowds so our two-person parade can sashay down the hallways unimpeded. One of them starts a chant of "Down with sexist standards!" that quickly catches on and bounces off the walls.

Sibby and I make eye contact and her grin is every bit as wide as mine. We skip up to the first landing of the stairwell. But perched at the top is Mr. Dormer himself.

"Do you two need an escort to the administration wing or can I trust you to find your own way there? Immediately."

Sibby fixes a death glare on him, so I answer for both of us.

"We're good solo," I say, giving him my most angelic smile.

No big deal. All part of the plan.

I do miss the energy, though, once we're in the hushed cocoon of the waiting area outside Principal Kurjakovic's office, where we fidget in too-straight chairs well into the next class period, before she ushers us inside.

"Have a seat, girls," she says, waving at the couch along one wall. I move aside a needlepoint pillow that reads I AM SILENTLY CORRECTING YOUR GRAMMAR and plop down. My shirt rides up and exposes the bottom hem of my skirt and I have to fight my instinct to pull them both down. Instead, I let them creep higher. Sibby balances on the edge of the cushion beside me.

We've planned ahead of time to let Kurjakovic steer the conversation to start, so she'll think she holds the power. She must be onto us, though, because she simply leans back in her chair, waiting for one of us to speak.

Our game of chicken goes on for a good twenty seconds before she finally breaks down and asks, "Why don't you tell me what led to all of this?"

Her hand swishes through the air to indicate our shirts.

"Total humiliation," Sibby responds, and the principal's eyebrows rise. "It's utter embarrassment to have a male teacher give you detention and say that your shorts are distracting to your classmates because they're riding too high on your thighs. And it makes me wonder: Why was Mr. Dormer looking and where must his thoughts have gone for him to come to that conclusion? It's totally inappropriate."

I'm so proud of Sibby for getting all that out in a strong, clear voice.

Kurjakovic's face turns a little green and I almost giggle. I'm sure she's imagining how tiny Sibby's sweet, round face would play to cameras if we were to take this issue to the court of public opinion.

To her credit, Mrs. K recovers fast and her tone is measured when she says, "I'm hopeful Mr. Dormer didn't intend his remarks to be interpreted this way, which, of course, I'll clarify when I meet with him about this. In his defense, though, all of our teachers, male *and* female, are tasked with noting dress code violations, and in this instance the rule does say 'hemlines of skirts and shorts must reach to the fingertips of the wearer's extended arms.' It doesn't appear that yours do, Sibilla."

My turn to join in. "Maybe you haven't logged much time recently in stores selling clothes for girls our age, but we spent last class period online at H&M and Forever 21, and of the two hundred and seventy-one pairs of shorts they were selling, only four would pass the fingertip test."

"And those four were pretty heinous," Sibby adds.

Our principal stifles a cough that might have been covering a laugh, and I rush to continue. "Let's be honest, the policy only really applies to girls. No one cares how guys wear their shorts. The implication is that shorter hemlines *on girls* would create a distraction in the learning environment. We should call it what it really is: you people are worried about guys getting turned on. How about instead of policing *our* outfits, you spend that energy telling guys they need to stop seeing their classmates as sex objects just because we choose to wear shorts, because sometimes when it's hot outside we'd be more comfortable that way. Simple as that. My legs are for walking, not gawking."

I reach the end of my argument on the last air in my lungs and inhale deeply as Sibby bumps my thigh in celebration.

"We should have gone with that last line for our T-shirts!" Sibby whispers out of the corner of her mouth, and my lips twitch in reply.

I haven't felt *this* energized since my last derby game, when I broke through the pack and began racking up points. I try not to bounce in my seat, but adrenaline is flowing now and I have *missed* adrenaline. How I've missed adrenaline!

Mrs. K rubs her forehead with two fingers, like she's trying to soothe away a headache that just formed.

I am completely on board with being her headache.

"Look, Amelia," she says, "I know these have been trying times for you lately and I'm willing to excuse some acting out as a result, as I can appreciate something of this nature might be a welcome distraction for you."

My first response is a flash of indignant anger. But as the rest of her words sink in, I shrink back into the cushions, because even after my amazing soapbox speech she's smacking me in the face with the very thing I've been trying so hard to avoid: pity.

"Um, excuse me, but *I'm* not sick, so what's your brush-off for *me*?" Sibby interjects, before I can quiet my swirling thoughts enough to formulate a response. My heart squeezes with love for her. Why was I upset with Sibby again?

Kurjakovic leans back in her chair and tents her fingers. "What I was about to say is that I don't intend to discipline either of you for the scene you caused this afternoon, nor will I expect you to serve detention for the code violation, Sibilla. I won't be calling your parents either."

Sibby snorts. "I'm fairly certain my mum would be happy to hear from you about this. She'd applaud our initiative. Lia's too."

Damn straight they would.

Mrs. K studies us both for a long minute. "As do I. I know you probably see administrators as the enemy, so maybe you'll be surprised to learn this argument against our dress code is precisely what I represented to the board at our meeting earlier this year. Happily, they concur and are in the process of rewriting it, to go into effect this fall. A bit too late for either of you to enjoy, I'm afraid."

This news completes my deflation. I'm airless.

It should be a good thing; the dress code is changing. A mere two hours ago I didn't even know I *cared* about fighting the dress code, and as it turns out, I really do. But an hour ago I had a sense of purpose again, an actual goal to work toward. And now I'm back at square one.

People will talk about our hallway parade for the rest of today, maybe even into tomorrow, but once word gets around that it was a nonissue we were fighting, everyone's attention will swing back to my BA, and I will have nothing to do with my time and energy beyond fielding all their questions. Lose, lose.

Sibby looks between Kurjakovic and me, also at a loss for words. Finally she manages, "Well, that's a dazzler. You were two steps ahead of us."

Our principal's smile is conspiratorial. "Essentially my job description, girls."

"Right, so then I guess . . ." Sibby trails off, wiping her hand on the sides of her T-shirt and earning a green marker blotch on her palm as a result.

"You're both free to go," Kurjakovic answers, nodding to the door. "And rest assured I'll be speaking with Mr. Dormer."

"Okay." Sibby stands and holds out her clean hand for me. I

allow her to pull me off the couch, still a bit shell-shocked at how this all went down and very much at a loss for what to do next.

"Enjoy the weather today, you two," Kurjakovic offers in closing as we file out of her office.

We have to wait in line to get a late pass signed, and Sibby grins at me. "That was amazing, yeah? I mean, I never knew Mrs. K was such an ally. I was ready to burn it all to the ground, I really was, but I'm psyched we don't have to, because we're already going to have a ton on our plate organizing Prom with a Purpose. I already talked to the dance planning committee and they're on board with the theme change, after I said we'd take care of all the signage and lining up volunteers for the donor registration part. But I don't want to stop there. I was thinking we could go really big and create materials as we go along that we could share with other schools around the country so they could mimic our efforts, and maybe build a website to host everything, but then we're gonna need to fund-raise so we can buy a domain and—"

She stops when she runs out of breath abruptly.

I avoid her eyes. "Um, wow, Sib. That's— I—"

"Step forward, girls," the admin calls.

"To be continued," Sibby whispers, her smile easy and unconcerned.

I know I need to woman up before Sibby gets too carried away with this Prom with a Purpose stuff, but I also don't want to have to explain to her why I don't want to do it. The thing is, I want her to know why already because she knows *me*. Maybe that's not a fair expectation, but . . .

We collect our passes, and I notice Sibby is handed an additional sheet of paper.

"What's that?" I ask as we turn to leave.

Sibby glances at the slip. "Oh, whoa. They're letting me count the hours from the assembly and donor drive last week toward the community service hours we need to graduate!"

Before I can react, we're seized upon by a waiting photographer from yearbook as we exit the main office. He turns me around to get the back of my shirt alongside the front of Sibby's and I'm grateful to be saved from having to force a smile.

Because, great.

I am now an *actual* charity case.

10 ~

WHEN I WAS EIGHT I LANDED IN THE HOSPITAL OVERNIGHT FOR about the most embarrassingly ridiculous reason ever—I had an ingrown toenail that got pretty badly infected before I brought it to anyone's attention (primarily because nail clippers were my sworn nemesis and I was more terrified of them than I was worried about my toe). I vividly remember my mom cradling my head and Dad having to practically sit on my legs to keep me still while the nurse cut out the offending nail.

That was the last time *both* my parents accompanied me to the doctor's.

Until lately.

Today's visit is a regularly scheduled appointment, but it's also the first check-in I've had in a couple weeks.

"Who was John Lennon's assassin?" my dad asks, chewing on his pen cap as he studies the crossword puzzle in his lap.

"Chapman," my mother answers, without lifting her eyes from the *Cooking Light* she found on the seat next to her. A month ago she would have gone straight for *O* magazine, and I know her diet has to stop bothering me (especially since she's not complaining), but I just hate that she's doing it because of me.

"Nope," Dad says. "Four letters, ends in a *P*."

"Mark," Mom replies, flipping a page.

"How did you manage to earn a law degree with those spelling skills? Mark doesn't end in a *P*."

My mother glances up at me and mouths, "Wait for it."

A few seconds later, my dad grimaces. "Crud, the *P* is wrong. This is why I should never do crosswords in pen." He begins scratching out boxes. "Okay, how about a four-letter abbreviation for price hike, starting with an *O*?" Before she can answer, he adds, "Hey, have you ever wondered . . . why is the word abbreviation so long?"

"Why are there five syllables in the word monosyllabic?" my mother counters, turning another page of her magazine and pretending not to notice that Dad's pen cap has fallen out of his mouth as he gapes at her.

"Woman, I have literally never adored you more than I do right this second," he says.

"Amelia Linehan?" The nurse's query breaks up their lovefest and we all stand, gathering our things. "Right this way," she beckons.

She leads us down a hall and opens the door into a small room, telling me, "Dr. Wah's just going to review your blood test results with you, so you can stay dressed. She'll be in shortly."

The paper covering the exam table I'm seated on crinkles as I shift into a more comfortable position and it's the only sound in the room as we wait, until Dad asks, "Did you ever wonder why doctors work at a practice? Wouldn't you rather it was an 'already skilled' or something less unnerving?"

I groan. "Where do you get these? You're like a meme come to life."

He shrugs. "Mostly online. But c'mon, you have to admit they shine a light on how ridiculous we humans—"

A light rap on the door interrupts him.

"Amelia?" Dr. Wah nudges into the room. "Oh! Whole gang's here again!"

She exchanges pleasantries with my parents, then settles onto her stool and turns her attention to me. "How you holding up?"

"I'm good."

She studies my face carefully before nodding. "Still feeling fine physically? Any changes? Any more bruising?"

I shake my head. "Nope. Same."

She smiles. "All right then, that's good news. But remember, I don't want you to be alarmed if you start to experience more fatigue or see signs of jaundice . . ."

"And you'd tell us right away, wouldn't you?" Mom asks me.

"I think you'd notice if I had dragon eyes, Mom."

Dr. Wah's smile is sympathetic and covers all three of us. "I know these situations aren't easy on a family, and it's tough to handle the uncertainty, but try to remember my advice to focus on living life as normally as possible in the meantime."

Ha, ha, ha, ha, ha, ha. Oh, was she not joking? What is "normal" again?

She swivels her stool to face a small computer setup and begins to type. Mom and Dad both tense when the doctor sighs at the screen, and I pull the sleeves of my shirt into my palm to keep my nails from digging in. What could a sigh mean? Nothing good, I know that much.

Dr. Wah scoots her chair closer to me again. "I gotta be honest, I'm not loving your blood test results, Amelia. You remember how we talked about MELD scores?"

I nod. "It's the number that determines how urgently I need the transplant."

"In large part, yes. It's a figure derived from a formula that takes into account your values for bilirubin, creatinine, INR, and sodium. Usually, if someone's MELD score is twenty-four or greater, we determine the patient is a candidate for a transplant. Yours was a twenty-one last month when you came in, but your GI bleed factored into my decision to petition for you to be placed on the list at that time."

My mother beats me to the question. "And what is it now?"

The dread in her voice echoes what I'm feeling; it's like a Dementor has entered the room.

Dr. Wah's face is somber. "It's twenty-four, which isn't alarming in and of itself and far from a critical number. As I said, it's typically where we'd just be beginning a process we already have underway."

She addresses her answer to me, despite my mother having been the one to ask the question. I've always liked that about Dr. Wah, although in this instance I wouldn't mind my parents swooping in and taking charge of . . . well, everything. Instead of reacting, I study my hands.

The more I stare at them, the more convinced I become that the skin around my wrists looks slightly yellow, in a way it didn't before now. *It's psychosomatic*, I tell myself. *Your brain is playing tricks on you.*

"What does that mean? The fact that it shot up like that?" Dad asks.

"It means your liver is worsening," Dr. Wah tells me. "Which is exactly what we know and expect will happen, but I was hoping it would do so more gradually, to give us as much time as possible to find a match for you. You're nowhere near critical, though, and I'm not alarmed, so much as . . . wary. I'd like to bump your bloodwork panels up to weekly checks, so we can monitor things more closely."

"At what point do you become alarmed?" Mom asks.

Dr. Wah sighs. "Sorry. Poor word choice on my part. But once the MELD number is hitting the low thirties, that's when we'd really want or need to see a transplant happen within a couple of weeks. But your score could sit in the twenties for months, or longer. It could even go down."

Except I jumped three points in less than a month, and a mere six points is all that separates me from the low thirties. It becomes hard to swallow. Hard to breathe. Real. This is feeling too real and I can't let it in. *Won't* let it in.

Fear is not the boss of you.

I steel my shoulders and glance up to find Dr. Wah's eyes on me. They flicker with sympathy before she says, "There are a few other paperwork things we need to address today. Please don't read too much into it; they were on my list before I looked at your scores, okay?"

I nod, trying to swallow.

"I'm going to assume by the fact that your parents have been accompanying you to these appointments that you're comfortable continuing to involve them in your medical care?" she asks.

"I—what? Yes. Yes, definitely."

"Now that you're eighteen, you'll need to sign a health care proxy to empower them to make medical decisions on your behalf should you become unable to do so. It will also allow me to legally share information with them in that event."

"I mean . . . they're my *parents*, so . . ."

My hands clasp and unclasp and Dr. Wah reaches over to lightly cover them with her own. Her touch is gentle and so is her voice. "I know. But in the eyes of the law you're an adult now, so they don't get an automatic say, the way they would if you were a minor under their guardianship."

But I *am* under their guardianship! They house me and feed me and care for me same as ever, regardless of my reaching some random date on the calendar that arbitrarily determines I'm all grown up. Yes, I've been ridiculously excited to be out on my own in the world, to go to college, to be independent—not just in mind, but finally in body too. (Ha! In body. What a joke.) But I could never imagine facing all of this without them.

Yet again this disease seems determined to erode not just my liver but everything I relish so much about Badass Amelia. All my confidence. My moxie, as Sibby loves to call it. Instead I'm left with this hollowed-out version of myself who wishes so hard she was five again, so she could curl up with a stuffed animal and suck her thumb, take a nap, and wake up to a world where everything makes sense.

"We'll make sure it gets taken care of," my dad says.

That's what I want. I want my mommy and my daddy and the nice doctor to fix everything so I don't have to worry about any of this. I want them to make it all better.

I'm the hollowest shell of myself and I hate it.

Fear is not the boss of you. Fear is not the boss of you. Fear is not the boss of you. My mantra becomes a soothing chant as I inhale and exhale deep, quiet breaths.

"There's something else we should talk about," Dr. Wah says, interrupting me mid-inhale. I jerk my eyes up only to meet another of her tender looks. "I know you're planning to start college in the fall, but I want you to give some consideration to deferring a semester. Even if you were to get a new liver tomorrow, there are frequent follow-up appointments after the operation and it's very common for transplant patients to be readmitted within the first year for complications. You'll be, what, an hour and a half away?"

"Closer to an hour forty-five. Before factoring in Boston traffic," my mother injects.

Dr. Wah must register the horrified expression on my face at her suggestion because she smiles gently and says, "Maybe I'm being premature. I do have patients who've proven me wrong and I'm always happy for that."

"That'll be me. *I'll* prove you wrong." I set my jaw and dare her to argue.

If she can tell that just underneath my resolve I'm a puddle of goo, she's kind enough not to acknowledge it.

"I hope you do," she replies, walking her stool back to the computer and making a note in my chart. "But the more time that goes by, the more I want you to think about exploring your options. If not a deferment, maybe at least a reduced course load."

Goodbye, college buffet.

I nod at the back of Dr. Wah's white lab coat and avoid eye contact with my mother as I keep my jaw set.

Dr. Wah lets her gaze take in all three of us as she asks, "What other questions can I answer for you?"

"Last time you mentioned a scope to monitor her varices following her ligation?" my mother says.

"We'll give it another few weeks and then, yes, I'd like to check that the elastic bands we placed are holding. I'd also like to set up an appointment for you to meet the surgical staff, since one of those doctors will be performing any transplant and it's always nice to be able to put faces to names and have a chance to chat with them. It tends to help everyone be a little more relaxed when the time comes."

I appreciate that Dr. Wah uses the word *when*, never *if*. I allow myself to be lulled by the back and forth of my parents' questions and my doctor's calm, measured responses. A few minutes later, she's bidding us goodbye and squeezing out of the exam room, probably on her way to patiently reassure some other terrified family down the hall. How does she do this job day in and day out?

Dad helps Mom into her coat, then holds mine up for me. He gives my shoulders an extra squeeze as he settles the jacket over them. "Love you, Sunshine," he whispers. I want to say it back but I can't form words over the lump that forms in my throat, so I just nod.

My mother is already five strides ahead of us, beelining for the front desk to make my next appointment, entering the reminder into the calendar on her phone with angry jabs. She's prickly efficiency and my dad and I trail her to the elevator like obedient ducklings. She summons it with a forceful button punch and we all face the doors, waiting for them to slide open.

"When we get home, I think we should call the admissions office at Amherst and—" Mom begins.

"No!"

"I just meant so we could get their take on—"

"Mom, please, no! Dr. Wah said that's premature."

"Well, she—"

"Nat, let her be for now," Dad interrupts, in a quiet but sturdy voice. From the corner of my eye, I watch them exchange glances, then my mother exhales a breath that registers as half annoyed, half resigned, but she doesn't pursue the conversation.

Instead we enter the elevator mutely and all turn to face the doors. I press the button marked Lobby and we begin our descent. We watch the numbers light up with each floor we pass, until Dad breaks the weighted silence with, "Hey, did you ever wonder how you can be overwhelmed or underwhelmed, when there's no such thing as whelmed?"

I manage a small groan of appreciation and my mother just sighs.

What I'm actually wondering, though, is: *Why is all this happening to me?*

11 ~

WE DROP MOM BACK OFF AT THE LAW FIRM, THEN DAD POINTS his car toward home, both of us quiet as we put distance between us and Dr. Wah's office.

"How you holding up, Sunshine?" Dad asks.

"I'm okay," I reply.

I'm not okay.

He doesn't push the issue, though, which I love about my father. But he doesn't drive straight home either. Instead, he parks in front of Linehan's Hardware.

"Do you need to grab something?" I ask.

He shakes his head and smiles. "I thought you might."

When I return his look with a blank one of my own, he adds, "I peeked at the ten-day forecast and it looks like the sun might finally make a return by the end of the week. Thought it might cheer you up to shop for some supplies to—"

"Start my mural!" It doesn't wipe out my dark mood, but it does give it a tiny lift.

I trail Dad around the store, pointing to tarps and debating brushes with him. I've never worked with paint as a medium before, so I'm glad to have his guidance. I'm even more grateful for the family discount—the arts commission gave me a budget to work within and I'm going to blow them away when they see how far under it I'm staying.

If only it hadn't rained earlier today. I would love to work out my frustration over my MELD score by slapping paint all over a brick wall right this second. But that's not an option, so we head back home after finishing our mini spree.

"Sox preseason game starts soon. Wanna watch with me?" Dad offers as we enter the front hall.

I shake my head and retreat to the safety of my room, where I attempt to immerse myself in finding a new chalk design for Lemondrop. Although I update the left and right side every week, tomorrow will mark four Saturdays since I changed the center menu and it's due for a refresh.

But all I can think about as I scroll through Instagram is how different my life was the last time I worked on that panel. Has all this really only been going on for less than a month?

Stop it! Focus on the menu design.

But I can't get there; I need a plan B.

I eye the pile of laundry in the corner of my room. Maybe a change of scenery will help. Balancing my iPad, sketchbook, and colored pencils on top of my hamper, I drag the whole thing into Mom and Dad's walk-in closet, where they'd (shockingly) scored permission to relocate the washer and dryer from the basement after going a bit heavy-handed on the pours of Babi's favorite wine during one of her visits home a couple years ago.

I shut myself inside the small closet and start a load of whites before plopping down on top of the remaining pile. I don't even care that it's not the most hygienic of seats; it's a cozy cocoon in here and this isn't the first time I've used the space as a makeshift art studio. The washer fills with a whoosh as I prop my pad on my knees and begin to sketch a menu board.

I'm still buzzing from the appointment, so I don't get lost in my drawing the way I often can, but with effort I manage to keep my thoughts from spiraling. I pause forty-five minutes later only to transfer my first load to the dryer and start a second one before picking up my pencils again. It's soothing: the scratching on the paper, the clicks of the machine working its way through each cycle, the rhythmic thumping of my clothes, the *ping!* that makes me jump whenever the metal button from my jeans hits the dryer's spinning ceramic drum.

What if this is one of the last times I hear a washing machine churn water back and forth?

The sentence flits across my brain before I can stop it and I chide myself immediately. *Who would miss something so random? WHY ARE*

YOU ALLOWING YOURSELF TO HAVE MORBID THOUGHTS?
Shouldn't they be over the possibility of missing something more, I don't
know . . . normal? Like Christmas morning or a new Billie Eilish song
on repeat or buying school supplies or the slippery rocks under your toes
at Lake Winnipesaukee or an unexpected snow day or nailing the perfect
hair color on the first attempt or stepping off an airplane in a different
time zone. The smell of sunscreen. The texture of Sibby's curls. Trying to
make a box of Milk Duds last the whole movie. Laughing so hard you
snort your drink through your nose.

BUZZZZZZZZ! The dryer signals the completion of its cycle
and jerks me back to the present. I try to calm myself as I shovel the
entire load of laundry into my arms, but a vise in my chest holds my
breath hostage. *Why is it so claustrophobic in here?* I struggle to free a
hand to turn the knob, then knee the closet door open and stumble
to my parents' bed, leaving a trail of clean clothes on the floor in my
wake.

I dump the surviving armload in the middle of the comforter,
grab Mom's pillow and tuck it between my legs, bending at the waist
and trying to force big gulps of air.

Dad's footsteps sound on the stairs. *Crap!*

He can't see me like this.

I straighten and stuff the pillow back into place, frantically pulling the sheets up over it. I'm petting the top third of the bed in long
strokes to smooth out any wrinkles when Dad walks in.

"Sunshine, do you want to—uh, what are you *doing*?"

"Laundry, why?"

I offer a small prayer of thanks that my scramble to appear ordinary has somehow loosened the fist in my chest and my inhales are halfway normal again.

I snap the creases out of my MOTHER OF DRAGONS T-shirt and fold it in neat thirds. Dad squints at me, obviously confused by my behavior, but doesn't comment further. He collects my discarded items from the floor and places them on top of the pile on the bed.

"Okay, well, I was just coming up to see if you wanted to get subs from Alfredo's for dinner. We've got about six different dropped-off lasagnas in the freezer, but I'm not sure I can handle another one tonight, and I thought maybe we could take advantage of your mom working late to indulge a little—wouldn't want to *guess* how many thousands of Weight Watchers points are in a meatball deluxe. But I figure if we take the trash outside and open the windows to air out the smell she won't be tortured by any evidence when she gets home. Whaddya think?"

"Um, sure."

What if it's the last meatball sub from Alfredo's I ever eat?

STOP IT! I scream at my brain.

The news about my MELD score rising three points is doing a total number on me.

I force a smile. "I mean, that sounds like a solid plan, Dad."

"Mmmm" is his only response. He can definitely tell something is off with me. But instead of probing, he reaches for a towel and begins helping me fold my laundry. I subtly dig around the underside of the pile to make sure he's not going to encounter any of my underwear. But it's not a bra he holds up a second later—it's the smock from Miss Leekley's art room. "What's this?"

The marker faded a ton in the hot water, but the words WHY ARE YOU STARING AT MY LEGS ANYWAY? are still visible.

"Nothing, as it turns out." I grimace and fill him in briefly on Sibby's and my brief and futile dress code protest.

"You never fail to amaze me, Sunshine. I'm in awe of all you've been juggling these last few years trying to beef up your college application, and you're still making time to devote to worthy causes. Proud of you, kiddo."

"Well, I mean, I'm already accepted into Amherst, so taking on the dress code wouldn't really have been in addition to any of that other stuff I was doing before."

It wouldn't have been in addition to *anything*, which is precisely the problem.

"Even so," he says. "You're passionate. Your mother's daughter, that's for sure."

I flush at the compliment and cradle a warm towel against my chest for an extra second before folding it. "Thanks."

"Thing is . . . ," he begins, pausing to take a big breath. The blush on my skin turns to goose bumps. I hope he's not going to try some earnest heart-to-heart talk here, because I'm barely recovered from whatever was happening to my body a few minutes ago and I don't think I can handle anything upsetting right now.

But no. He wouldn't, right? My dad and I don't do deep discussions; no one in my family does, but most especially not the two of us. We do smoothie challenges. We do Father Daughter Restaurant Week. We do carpool karaoke on road trips.

"You should see your face right now! You look like a deer in headlights!" he says, chuckling. "Take it easy there. I was just going to tell you the same thing I'm always saying to your mom, which is that it's okay to ease up sometimes. You're allowed to just *be*, without having any end goal in mind."

I'm a little offended because, yes, I love making plans of action and a lot of my hobbies involve reaching a particular goal, but that doesn't mean I'm high-strung. I'm proud to be a blend of both my parents: Mom's drive *plus* Dad's playful nature.

I struggle not to sound overly defensive when I reply, "I know how to relax."

His eyebrows go up as he aims his gaze meaningfully at my hands. They're fisting the sweatshirt I'm holding so tightly it's turning my hands red. I grimace and force my fingers open, allowing the shirt to drop onto the bed.

Luckily Dad simply shrugs. "I'm just suggesting maybe you take some time to goof off for the sake of goofing off every now and then. Escape the chaos, you know? Get lost in the moment."

If only he had a clue how constant my quest for that has been these last three weeks. Not necessarily the goofing off part, but the escape? Yes, please. Any heartbeat that doesn't contain thoughts of biliary atresia or transplants or . . . not getting a transplant . . . is one I'd like to stay lost in for a good long while. Preferably until a liver is located.

Dad's quiet for a second, then a smile tugs at the corners of his lips.

"What are you plotting?" I ask, suspicious.

"Alexa, what time is it?" he asks the Echo on his nightstand.

"Six forty," replies the disembodied voice.

"Dad?"

He grins. "Plenty of time to fit this *and* meatball subs in before Mom gets home. Speaking of your mother, you can never tell her I did this. I promised her I wouldn't the night we moved back into this house."

Now I'm really curious. I can't even begin to imagine what could be so mysteriously off-limits about a structure whose every nook and cranny I've explored, so I follow him down the hall toward my brother's room.

"If it's Alex's hiding spot for his pot stash, that's old news *and* it's empty."

There's a tiny crawl space that connects Alex's closet to the attic, which served many illicit purposes throughout our childhoods.

Dad halts and spins around. "You think I'd *smoke pot* with my high-school-aged daughter?"

"I mean, no, I guess not really, but you did say not to tell Mom, and then we started walking this way, so . . ."

"Alex had a secret pot stash? That little shit."

I smile. "If you think that's bad, wait until I tell you about his—"

"La la la la," Dad says, sticking his fingers in his ears. "Don't say anything else to disparage my favorite son."

"Dad, he's your only son."

He looks over his shoulder and grins. "So the competition isn't exactly fierce."

I groan. "You're so cheesy."

"You love my cheese."

I really do.

We zoom straight past Alex's room and descend the back staircase that leads into our kitchen, but Dad stops us on the landing halfway down.

"Might need a hand, this window sticks," he says, making room for me beside him. We both tug at the hundred-and-something-year-old frame until it finally budges with a scraping noise that's worse than nails on chalkboard.

I wince, but the promise of an adventure—a forbidden one at that—chases away any unpleasantness.

"After you," Dad says, sweeping his hand out the open window.

"Have you lost it? We're almost two stories off the ground!"

"There's a ledge. It's narrow, but it'll hold us both."

He smirks at my look of doubt, drops a foot through the window frame, and bends at the waist to fit under the raised glass. A second later, he's standing outside.

I barely hesitate before scrambling out to join him. "This is incredible!"

We're around the side, near the back corner of the house, where the narrow yard between us and the tall stucco wall edging our property is all scrub, meaning I haven't spent much time down there. Never enough to notice the small ledge beneath this window.

"Have a seat," Dad orders, and we gingerly edge onto our butts. It's disconcerting to dangle my legs over the side and peer across at eye-level tree branches, though admittedly intriguing.

While the night air isn't exactly warm, the breeze has a fullness to it that promises the spring that arrived on the calendar this week will soon be here in more than just name. Nonetheless, I shiver, and my dad responds by shucking his fleece and wrapping it around me. It smells like his aftershave and the supply room at the hardware store. Like safety.

"Your mom and I snuck through this window for the first time when we were your age, but we practically lived out here when she was in law school. Talk about stressed! I'd make her count stars until the tension left her shoulders."

"Really?"

"Well, that and sip whiskey from a flask. But I maintain it was the stars that did the trick. Feel like testing my theory?"

"Um. Okay? Sure?"

I tilt my head to the sky and squint through the empty branches of the maples ringing our house.

A few seconds later I say, "Done."

"Oh, come on. You can't expect it to work that fast. Give it a little—"

"No, I mean, I counted all the stars I can see."

Dad peers at the sky and his brow wrinkles. "Damn light pollution. It's gotten so much worse since those days."

I snuggle into his chest. "It's okay. It's still early; I'll bet more will come out as it gets darker."

He rubs my arm in acknowledgment and we sit quietly like this for a long time. At first I'm okay, listening to my dad's heartbeat through his shirt, but it doesn't take long for my brain to return to the closet and the thoughts that swirled there. The yawning vastness of the indigo sky presses into my rib cage and my breathing turns shallow again. I shift away from my father's hold so he doesn't notice.

"You get a butt cramp?" he asks.

"Uh-huh," I manage, but the hum in my ears is now a roaring and the neckline of my shirt is tightening at the base of my throat and the thing that started in the closet, which I'm guessing might be my first ever panic attack, is beginning again and—

I scramble to a standing position, nearly edging my dad off the ledge in my haste.

"Whoa! Are you trying to kill me?"

"Sorry," I squeak. "I need—"

Not air. We're already outside, surrounded by endless quantities of that. I gulp some in, forcing it by sheer will into my collapsing lungs as I struggle to look composed on the outside. "I mean—I just remembered something I forgot to do."

I slip one foot, then the other, back into the house, touching down on the landing before Dad can situate himself enough to see me clearly.

"Mentally running through your to-do list is not what I meant by relaxation, Sunshine," he calls after me. Then, "I'll call you when Alfredo's delivers?"

"Sounds good!" I yell back, nearly to my room now.

I flop on my bed. Too late, I remember that my iPad is still on the floor of my parents' closet, but I need noise this very second so I turn up the volume on my phone as loud as it will go and find the playlist Sibby and I sing along to on our way to derby practices. I pull my knees in and rock back and forth as I count to a hundred in my head and wait for my vision to clear at its edges.

Eventually, I feel a little less like I might pass out, and a little more like my normal self, so I creep down the hallway and transfer my second load of laundry into the dryer, leaving the closet door wide open and the music blasting from my pocket. I carry my folded clothes back to my room and put them away, all the while silently repeating *You're okay, you're okay, you're okay.*

What if I'm not okay?

Dad might be very right that I desperately need to relax, but, unique as it was, his idea of how to go about it is not going to cut it for me. I need people, activity, noise, laughter. I need escape from the norm. I need to forget for hours upon hours, the way I was able to when I was hanging out with Will at the bakery last Saturday.

The thought sticks against the side of my brain.

Could *that* be a solution? Not the bakery, but . . . Will?

My dad calls up the stairs, "Food should be here in about ten!"

"Okay, perfect!" I answer.

I retrieve my iPad from the closet. My home screen is a picture of Amherst's campus in full autumn glory that I copied and pasted from their website. I click off it as quickly as possible, not wanting the reminder of what might *not* be waiting for me this fall, if Dr. Wah or my mother push the matter.

When I open Notes, it's still there and I blow out a breath.

I hadn't spotted the words until Wednesday, because I hardly ever use this app, but when I'd gone to make an entry about a homework assignment, the lined page that popped open already had two lines of text, reading: *Use it anytime, Will,* followed by a phone number that began with a 617 area code.

My iPad had been right next to him the whole time at the bakery; he must have typed it in while I'd packed up my chalk supplies.

Last Wednesday I had no intention of ever dialing this number. As far as I was concerned, Will had fulfilled whatever obligation he thought he owed my brother and I wasn't eager to be anyone's pet project.

But desperate times call for desperate measures and Will kept his Scout's honor promise before, except at the very end. Besides, I *might* be able to endure a few sympathetic looks if, in exchange, it meant hours of relief from a terror that keeps encroaching, ever-faster and ever-stronger, past every barrier I put up to keep it away.

I enter Will's number into my contacts and open a new text message.

Downstairs, someone knocks on the front door, and the echo of Dad and the delivery guy exchanging niceties drifts up through the floor vents as I type out a quick message.

"Sunshine?" Dad calls.

I hit Send and tuck my phone back into my pocket.

"On my way!" I answer.

Words With Friends notification:

QuitWithTheT-rex played SNITCH for 12 points

12 ～

DING DONG.

Four days have passed since the night on the window ledge with Dad, and I finally get to test out my new plan.

"What the—" my mother says. "Was that the *doorbell?*"

My chair legs screech as I push back from the table, Dad mutters a eulogy for the wood floors, and Mom beats me out of the kitchen.

"Will?" she exclaims, pulling open the door.

"Hi, Mrs. Linehan," comes his low, disembodied voice.

"Will!" She tugs him inside and wraps him up in her arms. He embraces her in return, and over her shoulder, he catches my eye and offers a slight waggle of fingers.

Mom disentangles from the hug but keeps hold of Will's

shoulders. "What on earth are you doing here?"

Dad adds, "Alex doesn't have a surprise visit up his sleeve, does he, because if so, you ruined it. Wanna hide in the coat closet to keep him from realizing? We're happy to aid and abet."

"No, I'm afraid Alex isn't on his way. I'm actually here to grab Amelia."

"Oh?" Mom asks. She looks from him to me, her eyes narrowing as she sharpens her gaze on mine. "You, missy, are not acting like someone who hasn't seen this guy in forever."

I fix a casual expression on my face. "Will stopped by the other weekend. We hung out while I did the Lemondrop chalkboards."

Braced for the slew of questions I imagine will follow, I'm surprised when she simply raises her eyebrows and offers a mild, "Hmm. You must have forgotten to mention that."

"Must have," I say, as my dad and Will do that one-armed hug slash back pat guy greeting thing.

"How *are* you?" Dad asks him. "School's treating you well? Your parents good?"

"I'm fine, Mr. Linehan. It's good, they're good."

"Still can't convince you to call me Jeff after all these years, huh?"

Will shakes his head and grins. "Can't. Goes against how I was raised."

My father grins at him. "Well, no case to be made against that then, is there? Do you want to join us for some dinner? We were already underway, but we've got enough to feed an army and it just keeps coming."

I wish Dad wouldn't bring up the meals being dropped off—it

skirts far too close to the reason *why* they're landing on our doorstep. I exhale when Will says, "No, thank you, sir. I already ate on campus."

"Mr. Linehan is one thing, but I'm going to have to draw the line at 'sir,' Will. You—"

"I was basically done eating," I interrupt. "Will and I were gonna head out for a bit. Is that okay? Can I borrow one of your cars?" I turn to Will. "Assuming you took the T here . . ."

"Yup. Too much hassle to have a car on campus."

My parents exchange a glance, but Dad hands over the keys from his pocket. "Where are you headed?"

I shake my head, my eyes twinkling. "It's a surprise for Will—we won't be late, though."

Mom says, "I hope we can lure you here another time for a proper catch-up?"

"That would be great!" Will answers.

I grab my coat while Dad sticks his head outside and peers around the corner at the doorbell. He presses it several times, garnering nothing but silence, then mutters something under his breath and ducks back inside.

"So," I begin, once we're in the car and zooming down Memorial Drive. "Thanks for agreeing to this."

"Anytime," he says.

I was vague when I texted, merely asking if he might want to hang out again. I was amazed how quickly he said yes, though it might be because he considers this an extension of his promise to Alex and truthfully, I almost hope it is, so I don't have to feel guilty about the fact that I'm kind of using him too.

"Scout's honor rules still in effect," I remind him.

"Whatever you say. When do I get to learn where we're going?"

I call on my Mona Lisa smile again.

"Welcome to Jordan's," the greeter says a half hour later.

Will mutters a reply, then crashes to a stop just inside the revolving doors. His jaw drops. "This is not real life. This is a *furniture store?*"

I step daintily around him and grin. "Have you really never been here?"

"No, and I'm currently questioning all my life choices. If I had a clue what I was missing . . ." He sweeps his arm to encompass the cheerful Jelly Belly store, the Fuddruckers restaurant with a hallway to an IMAX theater just behind it, the ice cream stand, the wall of thirty-foot water fountains, and the reason we're here . . . an indoor ropes course.

If you never made it past the warehouse-sized lobby, you wouldn't even know you'd come to a furniture store. The only pieces visible from our vantage point are a slew of café tables and chairs set up in the area between the Richardson's Ice Cream counter and the wall of water. The six fountains lined in a row are lit from above and below with a rainbow of colors, and shoot forceful arcs toward the ceiling in a synchronized choreography timed to the Beach Boys medley that blasts through the whole place. And everything, from a forty-foot-wide banana split perched atop Richardson's to the café tabletops to an enormous replica of Boston's State House, is covered in glued-on jelly beans. Twenty-five million of them, to be exact. It's every preschooler's dreamscape.

I point at the ropes course. "So? Is this the best or what?"

Will casts a doubtful eye at the ceiling far, far above us, which the top level of ropes nearly touches. "Uh. I might have to answer 'or what'?"

I do a double take. "Wait a minute. Do not tell me—no. Not possible. You're not scared of heights, are you, Will Srisari?"

He cringes and nods slowly.

"*You're* scared of heights?"

"You don't have to sound so shocked."

I stifle a giggle. "I'm sorry. It's just . . . you're always Mr. Smooth. Okay, I'm gonna soak this up for one little second and then I'll be appropriately sympathetic."

Will pushes his finger briefly against the bridge of his nose, which must be a leftover habit from years of nudging his glasses back into place. The gesture is endearingly familiar and makes my heart squeeze with a sudden tenderness as I picture him at age ten, all knees and elbows and giant frames spotlighting his eyes.

"Okay. Nice me is back. Look!" I point at the few figures on the course. "You're in a harness and clipped into a track the whole time! It's impossible to fall."

"Uh-huh," he says, not sounding the least bit reassured. Is he genuinely scared? Like, *scared* scared?

I touch his arm and wait for him to turn his attention back to me before saying, "I only picked this because it was something different. If you'd rather see what's playing at the IMAX or—"

"No! If this is what you had in mind, we're doing it." He cracks his neck left, then right, like a boxer stepping into the ring. "I'll be fine."

To prove his determination, he beelines for the check-in booth and, above my protests about paying, buys us both passes.

"You can treat for the ice cream when we're done," he says. "And just so you know, in my mind, I've already skipped over this part and am several spoonfuls into a sundae."

I grin. "Whatever it takes, dude."

We hang our jackets on the hooks provided and help the attendant feed our arms and legs into harnesses. She buckles them across our chest, grabs for a thick black belt attached to the front of Will's, and reaches above her head to fit a silver bit at the end of the belt into a track in the metal beam that runs above us. She does the same with mine, though I notice she doesn't linger nearly as long. She also primarily addresses Will as she gives us a few quick instructions and steps aside, but not before sending a flirty look his way.

Will doesn't notice because he's too busy craning his neck at the course above us.

The fact that it's a school night in prime suburban territory must be keeping most people at home, and we have the course almost to ourselves. There's a family with two little kids on the upper level, but otherwise it's just us as we climb the stairs to the lower one.

The first platform has four options for obstacles, spoking out in each direction. One has a rope ladder strung horizontally, with another rope above to grab for balance. Another is also a horizontal ladder, but with thicker rungs and guidelines at hip height on either side. A third has netting hung vertically and the fourth is a long, straight wooden board the width of a balance beam.

"You choose," I tell Will.

He turns to me. "You know, I just had a thought. Should you be doing this? Healthwise? What if it's too physical for you with your, um, thing that I promised not to mention and that I swear I won't again after asking this?"

Instead of answering, I cross my arms and stare pointedly at the tiny kid crossing the balance beam obstacle a level above us. She can't be more than five or six. If *she* can handle it without breaking a sweat . . .

He sighs. "Point taken."

Defeated, he pivots his lead into the track that feeds across the wider of the two bridge obstacles. His hands grasp so tightly to the ropes on either side that his knuckles turn white. One toe edges toward the first rung.

"Wait," I say, tugging on his shirt to stop him. "Seriously, Will! Tonight was just supposed to be casual and fun. If you're genuinely freaked out, we should—"

"I'm *fine*. It's just a matter of getting my brain in line with logic. Mind over matter, right?"

Oh, do I ever know a thing or two about that. *Welcome to my life, Will.* While I never meant to torture the poor guy, I have to confess it's kind of nice to focus on someone else's drama instead of mine. *Does that make me a terrible person?*

"Okay, then, if you're sure," I say. "Let's see whatcha got."

He takes two steps this time, before halting. "I might need you to distract me."

Hello, irony.

"Talk to me," he says. "About anything. Gimme some of those oddball presidential facts of yours."

I laugh. "On it. Okay. Um . . . lemme see . . . oh! There's a rumor Andrew Jackson taught his pet parrot to curse, which everyone found hilarious until the bird had to be removed from Jackson's funeral when he wouldn't stop letting go with f-bombs."

Will's eyes are fixed ahead as he progresses forward slowly. "Is that true?" he calls back, never turning his neck.

"Dunno. That's why I said it's rumored."

"Still. I'd buy it. Everything I've read makes him out to be an asshole."

"Uh, *yeah*," I agree as Will covers three more rungs, tentative but determined. "Total loofah-faced shit gibbon. Racist. Homophobic. He used to call James Buchanan and his boyfriend 'Miss Nancy and Aunt Fancy.'"

Will nearly stumbles as he whips his head around this time. He catches himself and clutches the ropes on either side of him more tightly, if that's even possible. "Did you just call someone a shit gibbon with a loofah face? Because that is oddly specific. And, more important, are you telling me that in addition to already having had a female Native American president, we've also had a *gay* one? Why isn't that common knowledge?"

"Jackson deserves worse. As for Buchanan, yeah, probably. Most historians think the evidence is fairly conclusive."

Will faces forward again and takes two more steps to reach the small platform. He visibly relaxes and I scoot across to join him.

"Fist bump! One down and only, like, twenty more to go. It's not terrible, right?"

He turns pale at the mention of the number of obstacles to come, but taps my outstretched fist with his before staring along the next one.

"Keep talking," he orders. "Elaborate on the evidence, please and thank you."

I laugh. "So, there's a lot of it. Buchanan's the only bachelor president we've ever had, but he lived with a senator from Alabama for more than ten years, even though both guys were plenty rich enough to not need a 'roommate' to swing their mortgage payments. There's also a letter he wrote that says something about going 'a wooing several gentlemen' but not getting lucky with any of them."

"He used the words 'getting lucky'?"

"I'm paraphrasing."

"You paraphrased and came up with 'a wooing'?" Will asks.

I huff out a breath. "No, I think the letter actually said that. You're kind of a pain in the ass, you know?"

Will turns to me with a proud grin. I don't know if it's because he's just reached the next platform or because he got a rise out of me.

Another horizontal rope ladder awaits us, with rungs spaced farther apart but more netting on the sides. This time Will doesn't even hesitate before tackling it and I actually have to rush a little to keep up.

"See? These aren't medieval torture devices, right? You're doing awesome. Maybe you're cured. What do they call it when you expose someone to their fears to help cure them?"

"Would you be referring to *exposure* therapy?" he asks, barely bothering to muffle his snort.

"Duh. Right. That . . . makes a lot of sense." I puff my hair from my eyes.

"People die from exposure," he says dryly before stepping onto the next rung. We've now covered more than a third of the second level and Will's footwork becomes sure and steady. He doesn't seem to need my trivia diversion anymore, so I keep quiet as we work our way through the rest and turn back toward the stairwell.

When we reach it, I bounce on my toes. "You were amazing!"

The family with kids is tromping down the stairs from the third level and the little girl gives us a perplexed look at my effusiveness.

"He's a big scaredy-cat," I tell her, pointing at Will, who groans good-naturedly.

Her eyes are balloon-wide and she nods somberly. "My brother was too." She gestures behind her at a boy who looks a year or two older than she is. "I showed him how easy it was."

"Little sisters for the win," I say, slapping her hand.

Her mom smiles at us as they pass. "Good luck up there," she tells Will, gesturing with her chin.

The girl adds, "Yeah! We'll cheer you on once we have our ice cream."

Will slumps against the stair railing. "Great. Now I *have* to go up, don't I?"

I sneak a look around him at the girl, who has reached the bottom step and is unbuckling. She waves. "Uh, yeah. Unless you want to be put to shame by a six-year-old."

"Probably wouldn't be the first time," he grumbles, switching his lead into the track heading up.

I smirk and follow suit. He's cute. Too bad the last thing I need in my life right now is the kind of complications cute boys can cause.

Will got some of his swagger back on the obstacles below, but now that we're up in the ceiling, I giggle quietly to myself when I hear him whisper, "Don't look down."

"Do you need more presidential facts?"

He shakes his head. "No. I just need to confront it head-on. Like I said, it's more a matter of making the logical side of my brain talk to the illogical one."

"You just have to give it a stern talking-to."

"Even if it's screaming at me that I might die?"

I nod forcefully. "Especially then."

Will's eyes jump to mine, and I'm frozen as I replay our exchange in my head. He examines me quietly for a long beat before opening his mouth to say something, but then seems to catch himself and snaps it shut again. Instead he drops his eyes, then curses. "Dammit! I just broke the first rule of not puking. I looked down."

I'm flustered, so it takes me a second to catch up with the conversation change, but when I see the expression on his face, I nearly laugh in spite of myself.

"Poor Will," I say, reaching out to rub his arm in exaggerated sympathy.

He snatches it away. "Go ahead and be smug, Decker. Someday the tables will turn and it'll be you squirming. In fact, let's plan another outing right now. What fears do *you* have? Snakes? Ghost stories? Line dancing?"

Ever heard of MELD scores?

As he talks, he steps onto the rope bridge and edges forward.

I scoff. *"Line dancing?"*

"Is that just me? Although that might be less a fear and more a strong aversion."

"Never been line dancing, so I can't say for sure there, but we did do a square dancing unit in gym class in middle school and I lived to tell the tale. Besides, if I did have a fear of it, I wouldn't need a Boy Savior to rescue me, thank you very much."

He reaches the next platform and calls back, "How does you gloating about exposure therapy maybe curing my fear of heights not make *you* a Girl Savior? Isn't that hypocritical?"

"Whatever," I answer, skipping across the rungs. "There's nothing more awesome than a lady saving the day. Um, hello? Wonder Woman?"

He hangs his head. "Damn, I have no comeback. You're totally right."

"See? Now you're acknowledging my superior intellect *and* coming around to my way of thinking."

Teasing Will is fun. Inhabiting the skin of Before Amelia is everything. Dad was definitely onto something with the whole "relax and just be in the moment" advice.

"Lia!"

The voice is distinctive, even as it travels three stories into the air.

"Amelia!"

The voice is also tinged in hysteria.

Will clasps the pole beside us tightly before venturing a peek down. "Is that—your mom?"

I don't even have to look. "Yeah, but I don't—what's she *doing* here?"

"Lia!" she yells again, over the noise of the fountains and the blaring Elvis song they're pulsing along to.

I gesture to her that I'm coming down. To his credit, Will keeps right on my heels as we quickly work our way back to the staircase. She's waiting at the bottom when we reach it and my stomach clenches at the expression on her face.

"Mom! How did you—"

"Track you down? I used Find My Phone." It wasn't hysteria in her voice, I now realize; it was fury. Will must assess the same thing, because he politely pretends to be absorbed with shucking his harness, helped along eagerly by the same employee who flirted with him before. I slip out of mine on my own.

"Why? You could have just—" But then I glance at my jacket, hanging on the hook. "Oh, ugh. Sorry." I grab it and begin patting the pockets. "We've been on the course and I didn't think to bring my phone up with—"

"You won't find anything there. It wasn't *your* cell I tracked, it was your father's. And you're damn lucky he left it charging in the console of his car, young lady."

She holds out a palm with my iPhone inside it. "Because you left *yours* on the kitchen counter!"

I accept it from my mother with wide-eyed horror. *Damn it!* I want to offer myself for a voluntary flogging.

The ropes course girl looks skeptical that a cell phone could be the cause of so much drama. I'm tempted to snap, "It is when you're waiting on a lifesaving organ!" but of course I don't. She finishes hanging the harnesses in place and retreats, tossing a final glance over her shoulder at us. Will understands right away, though, judging from the breath he sucks in.

"Did . . . did it ring?" I unlock the screen, but it's devoid of any notifications.

"No," my mother says, slumping against the wall as some of her adrenaline wears off. "But *what if*? What if the hospital had called and you weren't there to pick up? Yes, I'd have answered or they'd have called the house next, but how would I have known where to find you, if not for sheer luck—you never told us where you guys were going. I left Alex ten voice mails trying to get Will's cell number before Dad remembered leaving his phone in his car."

She seems to deflate in front of my eyes. She's quieter when she says, "We talked about this, Lia. You never, ever, *ever* let this thing leave your side. I thought that was standard practice for teenagers anyway. Is it really that hard?"

"I know! Mom, I know! I didn't mean to—I was driving, so I didn't have it out, and then when we got here we came straight to the course, and I—I never even realized it wasn't on me."

I can't bring myself to do more than glance quickly at Will, who's still standing off to the side, visibly uncomfortable. As much blame as I accept for this screwup, I'm also majorly embarrassed he's witnessing this.

"But Lia," Mom says, "you *have* to realize. You have to plan and be *vigilant*. Do you know what happens if they find a liver for you, but they can't get assurances you'll make it to the hospital in time to accept it? Do you?" Her voice breaks and Will offers me a sympathetic look, which I duck.

"They move on to the next person," she finishes, barely breathing the words.

"I know," I whisper. It's not just that I'm embarrassed because of Will; I'm also ashamed I put my mother through this, on top of everything else she's dealing with that's out of our control. This wasn't. "It was so incredibly careless of me. I'm so, so sorry."

I stare at the phone in my hand, avoiding eye contact with either of them.

"Not wanting to talk about it, pretending it's not happening, that's one thing. But I'm not going to allow you to be deliberately obtuse about this. That's not you, baby."

I dart a quick glance at Will, who's pointedly studying the ground now. Keeping my voice low, I say, "Mom, I know. I get it. I'm *really* sorry."

Her answering look is equal parts anger and disappointment. She shakes her head slowly and says, "No, I don't think you do. I don't think you get it at all."

She steps away from me and turns to Will. "Sorry you had to witness this. The situation we're in doesn't bring out the best in us, I'm afraid."

He's quick to jump in with a flustered, "Oh, no, please don't apologize!" and she squeezes his shoulder.

"That dinner invite still stands, okay? We'd love to see you. Jeff will make meat loaf; I seem to remember you inventing excuses to stay whenever that was on the menu."

"Was I that obvious?" he asks, following with what he probably wanted to be a light laugh, though it's clear he's shaken by what just went down. "Your house was one of the only places I got to sample quintessential American food growing up. Meat loaf is hardly ever on a restaurant menu, so it was such a big deal to me when you guys made it."

Mom's smile also still holds tension, but she replies, "That's really sweet."

I stand silent throughout this exchange, trying to absorb the turn of events and the way the whole Scout's honor thing blew up, with only myself to blame.

"Will, do you mind if I pull Amelia aside for a second?" Mom asks.

Couldn't she maybe have suggested that in the first place?

He straightens. "Oh, yeah. Of course. I'll just, um—check out the fountains."

Mom offers me another lingering half-annoyed, half-sad look as Will slides from sight. "I'm trying really hard to treat you like an adult, Lia, I am. But . . ."

I study the floor and nod sharply, caught between wanting to argue back to save a little face and knowing I have no ground to stand on.

She nods her head toward the fountains. "You and Will—is this a *date*?"

"Mom! No!"

She holds up her hands. "All right, all right, just making sure because Dad is pretty shaken too and I think he'd really love to have you safe and sound with him, sooner rather than later. So how about if I offer Will a ride back to his dorm in my car and you take Dad's home?"

Oh, sure. Not at all embarrassing. This may not be a date, and yes, there was a time when Will used to treat my mother like a second mom, so I know it won't be awkward for him to ride with her, but still . . . *What a perfect way to cap off the night.*

I nod, avoiding her eyes, and slip an arm into my jacket.

I'm humiliated.

And defeated.

Two seconds before she arrived, I was actually feeling giddy. Giddy! But *every single time* I get the slightest glimmer of hope that there'll be a break in the rain cloud hovering above my head, it starts to pour instead.

Every.

Single.

Time.

13

FLUORESCENT LIGHTING MAKES EVERYONE'S SKIN LOOK YELLOW,
right? Right?

I curse the overhead bulbs in our English classroom and steal a
quick glance at Sibby's arm, lying across the desk next to me. Hers
looks yellowish too, I think. Maybe.

I compare it to mine, even though I know I'm probably just
being paranoid because it's been a week since my last appointment
with Dr. Wah, which means I'm due for another panel of blood tests
this afternoon. Other than the GI bleed, I still haven't had any real
symptoms, but I'm dreading the results anyway. What if my MELD
score climbed again? I know I should be grateful I don't feel sick, but

the idea that terrible things could be happening inside my body right this second and I can't even *tell* is . . . disconcerting. No. Screw that. It's a mindfuck. A terrifying mindfuck of epic proportions.

All I want is to continue pushing away any and all scary thoughts of BA, but if it *is* coming for me, then maybe a little heads-up would be nice? Or not? I don't even know.

As if in answer to my request for physical symptoms, a hard knot appears in the center of my chest, twisting and tightening. The roar starts in my ears again, just like it did the other night on the roof with Dad.

No. I can't have a panic attack in the middle of English Lit. Please, please, no. This'll put me in the spotlight even more and that's the *last* thing I need.

"Psst," Sibby hisses, glancing at me. "You okay?"

I'm wide-eyed, but attempt a nod, which she doesn't buy for a second. She holds up a finger to me, peeks at Mrs. Aguilar in the front of the classroom, then cups one hand over her left nostril and shoots the other into the air.

"Mrs. Aguilar? I think I'm having a nose bleed. Can I go to the nurse?"

"Sure."

Sibby's halfway to the door when she lets her backpack clatter to the floor and adds a second hand to cover her nose. "Bloody oath! This is a bad one. Can Amelia carry my bag for me?"

Mrs. Aguilar probably doesn't buy the theatrics and it would be easy enough to bust Sibby by simply requesting she take her hand from her face, but it's almost April and most of our teachers have about given up on imparting any further knowledge to a restless senior class.

"Just go, you two," Mrs. Aguilar says, waving to the door. I grab my things and race to follow, scooping Sibby's backpack from the aisle on my way.

Sibby's waiting around the corner, her (notably clean) hand held up for a high five. At least if a panic attack had to threaten, it had the decency to do so during the one class I share with my best friend.

"Let's chuck a sickie," she says.

I don't even need to consider whether or not to ditch. We breeze right out the front doors, daring anyone to stop us. No one does.

We go two blocks out of our way to walk the scenic route through Harvard's quad and it's still only fifteen minutes later that we're seated in Mr. Bartley's, a kitschy burger dive across from the university campus that has the best frappés in Massachusetts. It's barely eleven a.m., so the communal seating tables are wide open, which almost never happens.

"Way preferable to examining the theme of marriage in *Anna Karenina*," Sibby says, slurping from her s'mores frappé. She drops her voice, even though there's no one around to eavesdrop on us. "Wanna talk about what was going on with you back there?"

"Nope."

If she's gonna ask, she's gonna get an honest answer. I stab my straw into my strawberry shortcake frappé and avoid her gaze. But as I feared, when I lift my eyes again, she's still staring at me. I don't even know if they have Girl Scouts in Australia, but I do know my best friend and that she'd never agree to any Scout's honor pact to back off on the tough stuff or to not make me psychoanalyze it.

It's the reason I haven't confessed my feelings about Prom with a Purpose or told Sibby anything about my last appointment and my MELD score rising. I'm used to dumping the contents of my brain into my best friend's lap without a second thought (and vice versa), and I hate being guarded around her.

But she's on to the fact that something was happening to me back there in English class, and I know she won't back down, so I sigh and shrug before offering a little something to appease her. "I've got a silly blood test at the doctor later today."

Even admitting my nerves out loud makes me feel like a traitor to my mantra. *Fear is not the boss of me.*

"I'll come with!" she volunteers instantly. "I can hold your hand when they stick you with the needle."

Great, yes. Let her believe it's the needle I'm worried about, not the results.

"Thanks, but you have derby practice. My mom's taking me, so I'll make her do the hand-holding."

Sibby considers for a second, then shrugs. "Okay, fine, but if I can't be there in person, I'll come along in spirit. When we finish our burgers we can head to CVS and find you some ridiculous Band-Aids to put on after that will make you laugh and think of me. Sponge-Bob? Or are you more the Power Rangers type? How do I not know this essential detail about you?"

"Power Rangers were Alex's favorite. Mine was Dora the Explorer."

"*¡Qué bueno!*" She tips her milk shake at me. "Hey, speaking of Alex, have you? Talked to him, I mean?"

I exhale, grateful we're moving off the subject of what happened in English class so easily.

"A few texts and our regular Words With Friends games. I know he's waiting for me to bring up the fact that he sent Will to check on me, but I still haven't decided how much crap I want to give him for it. I wasn't having the *worst* time with Will, up until . . . you know."

MELD score, no. But Will? Sure. Sibby knows all about him, up to and including the whole saga of how the night at Jordan's ended. She nods sympathetically.

"So I'm taking the passive-aggressive approach with Alex," I continue. "I've been playing only words related to 'annoyed.' Vexed. Nettle. Gall. I have to keep using cheats to swap out my letters for the ones I need, but I crushed a huge win yesterday with a triple word square *plus* a bonus for using all seven tiles when I played 'umbrage.' And before you call me out on the cheats, he has access to the same ones I do, so the way I see it, it's an even playing field."

Sibby pushes her chair back, stands, and gives me an ovation that attracts stares from the guys working the grill.

I grab her sleeve and she plops down again, stuffing one of my onion rings into her mouth and speaking around it. "Seriously, though. *Are* you okay?"

I should have known she'd circle back.

"That . . . *whatever* . . . back there in English was a fluke; I'm okay." Her expression makes it clear she isn't buying it, so I revise to say, "I'll *be* okay."

This she accepts a little better, nodding and passing me a fry. As I chew, she says, "Hey, do you want to take some time this arvo to sketch out a to-do list for Prom with a Purpose? I had some ideas for the website fund-raiser I wanted to run by you. . . ."

I buy myself time by taking a long sip of my frappé. "I was sort of thinking on the walk over that maybe I could get going on my mural. I'm already feeling behind because of all the rain lately, so if I could squeeze in a few hours today, that would really help."

She avoids my eyes. "Sure, of course. That makes total sense."

My heart twists. I'm the worst friend ever. Why can't I just talk to her about this Prom with a Purpose stuff and clear the air between us? Why does it feel like doing so will be opening Pandora's box and that everything else I'm trying to keep at bay will come crashing in? Sibby has the power to break through all my defenses and I just can't go there. But I also hate the distance I sense between us—we're tip-toeing around each other and we've *never* done that before.

I cast about for a compromise. "But maybe first . . . I'll bet there'll be people at the chess tables, since it's so warm out. Wanna hustle some smug old men?"

Sibby's aunt back in Darwin taught her chess when she was a little kid and she can hold her own with the best of them, including a majority of the dudes who camp at the outdoor area in front of the Out of Town News kiosk that functions as part gathering spot, part tourist attraction.

Sibby puts her chin in her hand. "Do you *really* need to ask?" Her eyes light up and she adds, "Maybe I can win us enough to cover some of the website costs."

I hope my smile is less like a grimace than it feels as I reply, "Sounds like a solid plan."

Words With Friends notification:

AllHaiL(ia)TheChief has just played FAVORITE for 35 points

You won!

AllHaiL(ia)TheChief 440 vs QuitWithTheT-rex 336

Top-Scoring Word

AllHaiL(ia)TheChief: DWEEB (64)

Your Stats:

Longest Word: FAVORITE

Total Tiles Played: 50

Bonus Tiles Used: 19

Rematch?

Words With Friends notification:

QuitWithTheT-rex has just played BRAT for 17 points

14 ~

I REFUSE TO GIVE MY BROTHER THE BENEFIT OF MY LAUGH, EVEN
if he's not here to hear me, so I stifle it and close my phone.

"Do you think you could drop me back at my mural, Mom?" I
ask, adjusting my seat belt.

Turning my attention to it after doctor's appointments is becoming
something of a trend, but unlike last week I won't be using my art
to help get me out of a funk—exactly the opposite, actually.

"I *could*, but I have something else in mind to help us celebrate
and I think you might like it even more," she says, glancing over with
a smile.

Bring it. Today may have started out like crap, with the almost
panic attack in English Lit, but it went everywhere good from there.

First, there was ditching school with Sibby for the afternoon. Obvious highlight. Then there was *finally* starting on my mural. I got half of the background painted in just a couple hours. I know it will slow down once I reach the actual design, but it's amazing to have it underway at all, after waiting out all the crappy weather this spring has started with. And then came the best part yet: my MELD score went down. Only by a point, to twenty-three, but after it'd jumped so quickly last time, I'm flying high to see it move in the opposite direction.

"What'd you have in mind?" I ask Mom, who's clearly elated too.

"Mmm . . . maybe a quick skate?"

"Skate?" Now I'm confused.

Her grin is mischievous. "Okay, I have a confession. I didn't really have to run back into Dr. Wah's office because I'd forgotten to get my parking ticket validated. I wanted to get her opinion about letting you attend derby practices—I know how much you've been missing them. Dr. Wah thought it would be perfectly fine, as long as you continue to feel physically up for them."

"Mom," I breathe, stunned.

The familiar landmarks along the route to Themyscira (our nickname for the warehouse in Medford where we practice) begin to whizz by out my window, but I still can't bring myself to believe her. "This isn't an April Fools' joke, is it?"

"April Fools' Day isn't until Monday, babe. And just how cruel do you think I am?"

I shake my head in disbelief, then freeze. "I don't have my skates! Or my pads or my helmet!"

"Check the floor behind you." The grin on her face makes it obvious she's loving this. "I put them in there this morning, thinking this would be a way to cheer you up, but I'll take celebrating instead!"

"You sneak! You said I couldn't adjust my seat because you had bags of clothes for one of your clients on the floor back there."

"Which is the truth, just not the *whole* truth. You seem to have forgotten, I'm a lawyer. I can spin anything."

I contort myself to reach my skate bag, which is indeed hidden under a bunch of other stuff. I drag it into my lap and slide one of my Riedells out, cradling it lovingly. I flick the wheels with my fingers. "Yeah, well I'm a skater. I can spin too."

"That's what I'm counting on, sweetie."

Themyscira smells the same as ever—a mixture of damp cinder block, sweat, and the upholstery foam that, along with old blankets, forms the padding around the support columns. I inhale deeply. Just before pushing open the door I'd had a brief moment of worry that being back in the same atmosphere would trigger some kind of PTSD anxiety, but instead everything feels friendly and safe.

The three-hour practice is well underway, so I expect to find the makeshift track, created by duct tape and rope, crammed with skaters. My nerves give a sudden jump because I haven't seen anyone from my team—other than Sibby, of course—since that day at the arena, and I know I'm going to have to endure some uncomfortable fawning before I can get back to the business of skating. But if that's what it takes, I'm prepared for it.

Except the track is empty, as are the handful of camp chairs scattered around the perimeter. Instead, everyone is clustered into a bunch facing the back corner of the warehouse and there's the distinct sound of giggling, followed by shushing noises.

Immediately, my stomach drops. Mom must have told them I was coming and they've got some big "welcome back" thing planned, which is really sweet, but not what I need. I just want to get out there on the track with them; that's all the welcome back I care about. One glance at my mother, though, lets me know she's not in on any surprise.

I'm about to alert them to my presence when Sibby skates out from the bathroom, rubbing her hands on her bicycle shorts. She's facing away from me, toward the group, and she calls, "Hey, what's going—"

"Congratulations!" my teammates all scream at once.

"You guys!" Sibby exclaims.

What is going on?

"T-U-F-T-S, T-U-F-T-S, hurrah! Hurrah! For dear old Brown and Blue!" they chant.

Sibby got into Tufts?

"You learned the Tufts fight song for me? I don't even know what to say." Sibby has her hands on her hips and is skating slowly toward everyone.

"You'd better too, if you plan to represent your college well," Hannah teases.

Everyone piles onto my best friend with hugs as my skates nearly slip from my fingers.

Sibby got into Tufts? But . . . I only left her a few hours ago.

Why didn't she text me right away? Why would they know before her best friend in the world?

"Rolldemort?" One of my teammates, Hazel, catches sight of me over Sibby's shoulder. "Holy crap, Rolldemort! You're back!"

Everyone's attention immediately turns to me and they squeal and start in my direction. I leave Mom's side and step onto the track, plastering on a smile to cover my swirling thoughts.

"Couldn't stay away," I tell them, when they reach me a second later.

Sibby is right on Hazel's heels. "I can't believe you're here!"

She looks guilty, though. Busted. Her eyes skitter past my face instead of sticking to my gaze.

"I'm glad I was just in time for the big celebration," I say, trying to keep any accusation from my voice or eyes, well aware that we have a crowd of onlookers.

How long has she known? We spent the entire *afternoon together— why wouldn't she have told me this enormous news, which we've both been waiting on forever?* I texted her video of me opening my email from Amherst about two seconds after I recorded it. I told her before I told my *family*.

On the way here, I'd been looking forward to practice as the perfect way to extend my good mood, but now I need it so the burn in my muscles can replace the burn my best friend just delivered.

"How *are* you? Are you sure you're okay to skate?" Hannah, our team captain, oozes sympathy as she rests a hand on my arm. "Sibby's been keeping us up to speed, but, god, the last time we saw you, you were . . ." She trails off and shudders. "That was intense."

I need to shut her Mother Hen act down before everyone takes their cues from her, so I pop a hand on a hip and wink. "Why don't we run a few three-on-ones and I'll show you how good I'm feeling?"

"Damn but we've missed you, lady," Desiree says, grinning. A few others nod enthusiastically.

"Your girl over there's made sure every last one of us is registered as an organ donor," says Hannah. "*And* she handed out brochures to the opposing team at the last bout; she's on a mission for you!"

I watch my best friend, now off to the side chatting with my mother, and plant yet another cheerful smile on my lips. "She sure is."

Hazel starts to butt in, but Coach interrupts her. "Hey! Chat all you want when we finish practice. Let the girl lace up!"

This earns Coach a grin I don't have to force, and Hannah says, "Okay then. Whaddya waiting for, newbie?"

"All right ladies, let's start with some lateral work," Coach tells us.

I grab my skate bag and head to the bathroom to change. Gearing up is a routine as familiar to me as getting ready for school in the mornings or prepping a chalkboard surface for lettering: I tug on padded shorts, sports bra, T-shirt, and knee socks that I cover with ankle guards; tighten my skates and check my toecaps; slip on knee, wrist, and elbow pads; snap my helmet into place; and, lastly, pop in my mouthguard.

Everyone else has already logged time on skates tonight, so it doesn't take them long to get back up to speed—literally—but I purposefully seek out the end spot as I join in a drill where we form a long line to skate in one direction around the track, leaning to the left through the turns, then transition to reverse direction so we're leaning right into them. It's a basic drill, but even though I've run it hundreds of times, it feels good to be back out here. If this stuff with Sibby hadn't happened, I'd probably be approaching pure bliss right about now.

When we finish, the others begin weaving around cones set up in an S shape, but I edge to the wall on my own to run through some stretches. Just the one drill has my out-of-practice body beginning to protest, and the last thing I need is to miss more derby over something as small as a pulled muscle. I'm carefully balanced in a figure four—one ankle on top of the opposite thigh and squatted down like I'm about to sit on a chair—when Sibby appears at my side.

"Are you upset?" she asks. "You are, I can tell."

I wobble in my pose and grab the wall for support. "When did you find out?"

She ducks her head. "I got the email this morning before homeroom."

Homeroom. She's known all *day and didn't tell me?*

Reading my face, Sibby rushes on. "I tried to find you right away, but then the bell rang and perv-o Dormer was roaming the hallways, and *then* he interfered again by keeping a couple of us after History to talk about this awful group project, so I was two steps behind Mrs. Aguilar coming into English, remember? I didn't want to tell you once class started, because we wouldn't be able to properly freak out together, and then you know what happened next, so—"

"What happened next is we spent the *entire afternoon* together!"

She ducks her head. "Yeah, I know, but you were so freaked out about your doctor's appointment and I didn't want to be the arse jumping up and down insisting on a parade when you were dealing with that."

I drop my pose and stare at her. "*Sibby.*"

"*Lia.*"

We blink at each other, and though I'm glad to have an explanation . . . it still *hurts*. It hurts that my BA got in the way of my being there for her when she wanted to share her excitement with me, but it hurts even more that she didn't think I could put my own stuff aside long enough to celebrate her good news. She *knows* I'm her person. Of course I would have done that. Truthfully, I would have been thrilled to focus on someone besides me. To enjoy good news for a change, and *life-changing* good news, not just temporary good news like my MELD score dropping by a single point.

But mostly just to be there for her.

I hate that we've both started keeping things from each other. I hate that there are fraying edges to a friendship I thought was rock solid.

"I just wish you hadn't felt like you needed to protect me," I tell her.

"But I'm your blocker, luv, that's what I do," she jokes.

I muster a small smile and she sobers. "I know. I wanted to tell you, like, *at least* a thousand different times." She grabs my arm. "Hey, but you know about it now and *holy hell*, you're at derby practice and that is frickin' amazing!"

I try to let her enthusiasm rope me back into the pure excitement I'd felt heading in here. The feelings I've cycled through since arriving are hard to shove aside, but I don't want to ruin tonight when Sibby's right—she got into Tufts and I'm on skates again. I always believed she'd get off the wait list, but I didn't think the second thing would happen so soon, and I should be savoring every minute. With my best friend.

Coach's whistle blows. "Line up. You know you love it. You know you've missed it. It's the 27-in-5!"

Loud groans greet her. The 27-in-5 is a lap test the Women's Flat Track Derby Association uses as an endurance benchmark for skaters. You have to be able to complete at least twenty-seven laps in five minutes as one of the minimum skills required for clearance to play in sanctioned bouts. We've all jumped that hurdle already, obviously, but Coach likes to keep it in the training rotation.

It's a ballbuster.

It's also my favorite because I'm *fast*. Like, really fast. And the 27-in-5 lets me revel in it. My personal best is thirty-six laps, but our pivot has done 41-in-5 and I'm determined to match her. I don't care that she used to be a competitive speed skater with Olympic aspirations.

It won't happen today, of course. I'm well aware that I've been off the track for a month and haven't kept up with any training regimen, so I'm not seeking to break any records here. But finishing twenty-seven under the whistle should be no big deal.

I shove in alongside my teammates and surge forward with them the second Coach blows her whistle.

A mere ten laps in, I know something's wrong. I'm winded. Like, really winded. Winded like I'd expect to be at the very end.

Get it together, girl!

Sibby peeks over her shoulder at me as I reluctantly dial back a bit on my speed. I flash her a small thumbs-up and she smiles and turns around again. I match my pace to one of our workhorses, Vivi. She's powerful, and an amazing blocker; she's just not known for her quickness.

Even Vivi is lapping me by the time Coach blows the whistle to indicate five minutes have elapsed. I'm on lap seventeen.

"How many'd you get?" Sibby asks, passing me en route to her water bottle. I shake my head because I'm too out of breath to speak, and she smirks and resumes skating. Her reaction lets me know she has no idea how badly I struggled out there and I hope no one else does either, though I'm sure some of my teammates noticed I was the one getting lapped, when it's always the other way around. I had to wave off Coach's concerned look several times, so I'm guessing she has a clue.

I coast to where Mom is tucked into one of the camping chairs, paging through a work file. The fatigue I'm experiencing is different from anything I've ever felt before. It's like my *bones* are tired, that's how deep it goes. I'm out of shape from my month off skates, but this isn't just that.

It's because you have a disease, *jerk*, my brain taunts.

Shut up, shut up, SHUT UP! I tell it.

There's another hour of practice left, but I don't even have the strength to pretend I'm capable of another drill. I lean close to my mother and whisper, "Do you think you could invent some kind of after-hours lawyer emergency?"

She peers up at me, surprised. "Are you ready to call it quits already?"

I bite my lip and nod.

She must see something in my posture because her only follow-up question is, "And you don't want them to know it, because . . . ?"

I simply shake my head and fix her with a pleading look. Mom studies my face for a second, then grabs her purse from the ground beside her and stands. "I think I just remembered a very important, very *urgent* client call I need to make back at the office."

15

I WAIT UNTIL THE NEXT DRILL IS UNDERWAY BEFORE TELLING
Coach we need to leave and waving goodbye to everyone from the
sidelines. Sibby's eyes go wide and she holds a pretend cell up to her
ear. "Call me later!" she mouths.

The car is completely silent for the first couple minutes of our
drive home, and I stare out my window at the streets crammed with
multifamily houses.

Eventually Mom says, "No one expects you to be able to keep up
right now, you know. You could have been honest with them."

I stay angled away from her. "I'm already one of the newbies on
the team; I don't want them to see me as weak."

Although what will they think when I don't show up at the next practice? Because I can't imagine my fatigue is going to get any better from here—not until I have a new liver inside me.

I wish I'd never gone tonight. In English class this morning, I'd actually half hoped for symptoms so it wouldn't feel like this disease was eating me up inside so mysteriously, but now I regret ever thinking that. Being oblivious makes everything easier to deny, makes it easier to cling to positivity.

"I can't say I didn't feel the same way about being seen as weak when I was starting out at the firm, so I get it. Although I think maybe under these circumstances—"

"Mom, can we please not talk about this right now?"

There's nothing but her small sigh to indicate she heard me. I catch myself fiddling with my Rolldemort necklace, in the same absentminded way I do a lot, but this time the metal feels heavy in my fingers. I slip a hand underneath my hair and slide the clasp to the front of my neck, but I can't work the catch free without two hands, which would attract Mom's attention, so I tuck it out of sight under my sweatshirt instead. I'm not Rolldemort right now. I don't know *who* I am.

I can't believe this roller coaster crested again. I was riding so high mere hours ago and now I'm in a gully. I wish it didn't have to be like this: all or nothing. I wish I didn't have to chase highs to try to banish the lows. I wish normal could be good enough. But there's no such thing as feeling regular these days—I'm either fighting off the darkness or exhilarated to find a few moments of sweet oblivion from it. Up, down. Up, down.

I'm running out of new options for the highs though, since

everything I attempt backfires on me. The dress code protest. Sketching in my spot by the dryer. Hanging out with Will.

The mural is a tiny bright spot, but it will go by fast now that it's finally underway.

Derby was my shining beacon of hope. For the last three years, the track has been the place I've felt *most* like me. It takes guts to endure the elbowing and it takes showmanship to keep the crowd engaged and cheering when we're basically looping the same endless circle. But now, for the first time, it holds bad memories. Not just from my GI bleed but my feeling so physically incapable tonight and the slap in the face of Sibby not sharing her biggest news with me before she told anyone else.

As if she can read my mind, Mom breaks the silence. "Hey, you didn't tell me Sibby got into Tufts."

The car slows as we hit a red light and I sense her turn to me. I steal a glance at her.

"Oh," she says softly.

"Oh, what?" I snap.

"You didn't know? Wow, my plan for tonight certainly didn't pan out the way I'd hoped. Oh, honey. I'm so, so sorry."

"The light's green," I state, a half second before the driver of the car behind us lays on the horn.

Mom hits the gas pedal and I pull my knees up, leaning them into the door. Short of hanging a "Closed for Conversation" sign, I can think of no better hint I could send her. I know none of this is her fault, but I'm too raw for compassion tonight.

She's quiet through several more lights, then I nearly topple over when she swerves the car into a hard right turn and screeches to a stop. I blink and look around; we're in the empty parking lot of a closed flower shop.

"Mom, I really don't want to talk about—"

She waves me quiet, reaching across me to unhitch her glove compartment. "Neither do I."

She pulls her iPad out, then opens her door.

"We need to get in the back for this," she orders, sliding from her seat. A second later she's behind me in the second row.

"This is weird, you know that, right?" I say, ignoring her route and climbing through the opening between the front seats.

I settle beside her and wait for whatever is coming next, though I suspect I'm not going to like it.

"Look," she says. "You are very clearly wound to a tick trying to keep all these emotions bottled up inside you."

"Mom—" I start, but she stops me with an upheld hand.

"Just wait. I'm not going to make you talk to me about it. The offer of a therapist is evergreen, but I'm not even going to force that, because, quite honestly, I know you're a lot like me and neither of us are very good about putting ourselves on the line like that. But. You're a shaken soda can and we need to crack the lid just a tiny bit and let some air escape. Skating was my attempt, but since *that* didn't go so well, here we are."

"Here we are . . . at a shuttered florist?" I ask, aiming for a little levity to gain control over this strange turn of events.

She ignores my question and asks her own. "Did I ever tell you about the first case I lost?"

"What? Um, I don't think so."

"My client was a mom who had three little kids, all born here, so all citizens themselves, but she was from Peru. I'd been so sure I could win the judge over to my side when he saw the little ones, so I had them lined up right behind their mother in the first row of the courtroom. When the judge ordered the woman deported, the oldest—she was maybe eleven—wailed and raged beyond anything you can imagine. It was heart-wrenching. I was so stunned by the loss that I was numb. I barely reacted."

Mom fiddles with her wedding ring as she talks. "Afterward, my boss could not shut up about how impressed he was that I was able to keep my emotions in check so well in the midst of that scene and he awarded me an even bigger case right on the spot."

She snorts. "Message received, loud and clear. Tamp down the drama, lock the ooey gooey away, earn everyone's respect."

"Okayyyy," I say. I can probably guess where she's going with this story as it relates to me, but I'm still not sure what's up with the iPad or why we're in the back seat.

She sighs deeply and reaches for my hand. "The thing is, I'm afraid I might have passed that strategy on to you by example, without making sure you also knew one critical piece of information."

"What?" I whisper, wary.

"You can only bottle it up for so long before it catches up with you. I learned that the hard way when I broke down crying during a different—equally brutal—hearing. But I needed to find a solution, because I knew that keeping my emotions in check wasn't just about earning my coworkers' respect; it also let me be the best ally possible for my clients. They're already terrified and they need to know that they have an ally who is solid and steadfast." She collects her breath, then says, "So . . . I found one."

"A solution?"

"Yup. With special thanks to the brave men and women of our military forces." She turns her iPad to me to display YouTube's home screen. The video queued up is titled "Soldiers Coming Home, Most Emotional Compilations #26."

Mom gestures to the screen. "This sucker is guaranteed to have you sobbing your eyes out in two point five seconds, and if it doesn't, I have a slew of others bookmarked."

I shake my head in disbelief. "You want me to watch sappy videos with you?"

I'm relieved it isn't anything worse than that, but also a bit skeptical.

"I want you to let steam out of the pressure cooker. By crying over sappy videos, yes. The trick is, you can keep it from being personal; the tears don't have to be about you. You just have to release what's in there. Okay?"

I glance around the back seat. "I—okay. Yeah, I guess so."

Mom smiles. "Good. And then when we've cried all the tears, we switch to epic fail compilations and laugh our heads off. Sound like a plan?"

"How often do you do this?" I have a sudden image of my mother parked in the breakdown lane of the highway, blotting her eyes when a lieutenant emerges from a stuffed bear mascot at his kid's football game, then clutching her gut as some asshat attempts to use his sloped roofline as a ski jump.

She bites her lip and peeks at me from under her lashes. "Let's just say I recently upped my data plan."

I blink at her. "You are an interesting woman, Mom."

"Takes one to know one," she says. "Now come here, baby."

She angles herself so I can fit my back against her chest and props the iPad on my lap. Her chin tucks into my shoulder and her vanilla bean lotion invades my nostrils.

She presses Play.

We're only twenty-eight seconds in when the first fat tear spills over. By the three-minute mark I have to pause the video to wring out the cuff of my sleeve and Mom laughs around her own sobs. It should feel terrible to cry this hard . . .

But it doesn't.

16 ~

RING, RING.

My pulse jumps.

Ring, ring.

Literally everyone I know texts, so if my phone is ringing—

Oh god. Can't breathe.

The caller ID is a string of numbers, no name.

Slide to answer, you jerk!

"Hel— Hello?"

"Hi there! This is Suzy from Travel Discounts and I'm calling with some exciting news! You may *already* be the winner of a four-day, three-night cruise to—"

"Fuck off, Suzy!"

Suzy is not offended.

Suzy is a robot.

Suzy doesn't have feelings. She doesn't have a heartbeat to regain control of or a stomach to unclench.

Suzy doesn't have a liver to fail.

Which one of us might be the lucky winner here, Suzy? Cuz I'm thinking maybe it's you.

Click.

17 ~

MY PLAN FOR THIS ENTIRE SUNDAY IS TO PAINT UNTIL I DROP.

Things have quieted down ever so slightly over the last week. Heart-pounding robocalls aside, letting the pressure out of the steam cooker helped some.

So does the fact that April vacation week starts next Friday and everyone at school is focused on that instead of me. I guess my not frothing at the mouth, or bleeding from my ears, or doing anything else interesting to indicate I might be on the verge of imminently checking out of this world, means everyone can relax around me. Continuing to ask the kid on the organ transplant list if anything's changed since the last time you asked must not be all that exciting when the answer remains, "Nope. Nothing at all."

No news isn't actually good news where my liver is concerned. My MELD score climbed a point again at my appointment last Friday, which puts it back to twenty-four, but I've been here before and had it recede, so I'm trying to remain optimistic.

As for the rest, well . . . *avoid, distract, ignore. Stay strong.*

Today, distraction gets top billing.

I step back to admire the first bits of lettering applied to the brick wall and soaking up the sun's rays. Once done, my mural will span an entire side of a restaurant that's currently under renovation and scheduled to open in early May.

"Pardon me, miss," a voice behind me says. "I hate to disturb you, but I heard this weird rumor that President Obama once had a pet porcupine, and I was wondering if you might be able to confirm or deny?"

I push my sunglasses up the bridge of my nose and don't bother hiding my grin as I turn to face Will.

"Well, if it isn't my surrogate big brother. This is a surprise. I didn't realize we had another unscheduled check-in today."

Neither of us has reached out to the other since the night at the ropes course nearly two weeks ago, but that doesn't mean I'm not happy to see him now.

He smiles. "Well, by definition unscheduled *wouldn't* be on your calendar, now would it?" I stick my tongue out at him, but he ignores me and continues, "But that's not what this is."

I hadn't thought it made sense to arrange another "playdate" for us, given the way the last one ended and how it essentially obliterated the ability to be Badass Amelia around him, but . . . maybe I jumped to conclusions? Because I'm feeling decidedly banter-y just at the sight of him.

"No? What is it, then? Wait, if my father sent you to make sure I'm not up on the ladder without a spotter, I will—"

Will holds out a hand. "Easy, Decks. This is . . . Here's what this is. This is: it's a beautiful spring day and I was in my dorm room messing around online and feeling crappy about not going outside to enjoy it, but also a little wrecked from staying up way too late last night, and then I saw something on Tumblr about Snoop Dogg considering a run at the presidency in 2020 and knew immediately who I wanted to laugh about it with."

I hold up my hand. "Snoop Dogg *cannot* be our next president. We're all in agreement on this, right?"

Will contemplates. "Three guesses what substance he'd legalize nationally with his first executive order. And think of the trivia potential." He laughs when I roll my eyes. "Anyway. It felt like a sign that I should ditch the dorm, venture out into the sun, and track down this interesting person I know. So here I am. Well, after stopping at your house first and getting pointed here by your dad. He didn't mention anything about a ladder, by the way, but he did give me this for you."

Will holds out a bottle of sunscreen.

"Of *course* he did," I say, accepting both it and his explanation with a smile.

"I got to your house just as he and your mom were taking off for the Sox game. How'd they score tickets to one of the first of the season?"

I squirt a dab of sunscreen on my fingertips and smooth it onto my cheeks as I answer him. "One of the store's customers couldn't use his, so he gave them to my parents."

Will whistles. "For *opening week*? Sure hope that guy never has to pay full price for a box of nails again."

"Pretty sure Mr. Ventresca has been getting hefty discounts since back when my gramps was alive."

"Still," Will murmurs.

He steps back and takes in my wall. "So, because you couldn't join them, you painted an homage to the Green Monster?"

I groan. The paint color I chose for the background *is* a very similar deep green to the landmark wall behind the outfield at Fenway Park, but I hadn't made the connection.

"Totally unintentional and now I won't be able to unsee that—thanks a lot!"

"You're welcome," he says, grinning. He gestures at the wall. "What's this gonna look like when it's done?"

"Better than it currently does!" I promise.

The building that will house the bistro is actually cute. It's set back a bit from the street, which leaves room on the sidewalk for an outdoor seating area that, according to the renderings displayed in the front window, will have hanging fairy lights and the same bright red umbrellas that dot Parisian cafés. Inside, the design plans read "cozy chic." It's all perfectly adorable . . . except for the ugly, poorly paved abandoned parking lot abutting the place.

What the owners of this vacant lot are doing sitting on the cash potential of commercial space this close to Harvard Square is beyond me, but it's none of my business. What *is* my business is stealing approaching patrons' attention away from the half acre of littered asphalt and onto something more aesthetically pleasing.

"Do you have any sketches?" Will asks.

I pull out my phone and show him my design. The quote I've just started lettering is by Maya Angelou: *We are more alike, my friends, than we are unalike.* Ringing it will be a riot of all different flowers, forming a colorful border.

"Wow, that's really beautiful. Would I redeem myself for the Green Monster comment if I offered to help?" Will asks. "I mean, if you have any tasks an artistically challenged person couldn't possibly screw up."

The words are barely out before I'm striding to the ladder I left tucked behind the building. "How are you at spotting?" I call over my shoulder.

I'd be a fool to pass up this opportunity. I'd planned to stick to the quadrants I could reach from the ground today, then hit Sibby up tomorrow, assuming she's not too sore from today's derby bout and even knowing it might mean finally having The Talk about Prom with a Purpose. It hangs like a constant mist between us, though she hasn't mentioned it once since we made uneasy peace about the whole Tufts thing at the disastrous practice last week. This would let me avoid that a bit longer.

Will is quick to respond, lending a hand as I situate the ladder against the wall. He waits for me to climb near the top, then steps both feet on the bottom rung to stabilize us and lifts the paint can.

"You might get some on you," I warn, dipping my brush. "Is that okay?"

I peer down and watch him check to remind himself what he's wearing. Ah, boys. So clueless when it comes to clothes. I could have told him without looking that he has on a plain black T-shirt with a small V-neck and faded khaki cargo shorts that are frayed and trail threads at the hem.

He shrugs. "No biggie. Hey, you never did confirm the Obama porcupine rumor, you know."

"Did you make that up on your way over here?"

"Mayyyyybe."

I flick the barely wet brush at him, spattering his arm with tiny droplets of yellow that stand out against his light brown skin. "He didn't have a porcupine, but he did have an ape," I tell him.

"He *what*?"

I dip my brush again and lightly trace the outline of a poppy flower. "Yup, when he was a kid in Indonesia. He named it Tata."

"Oh, okay, but it was in Indonesia, not the White House. That makes it a little more understandable."

I glance down at him and laugh. "Yeah, well, Calvin Coolidge had two pet raccoons and they *did* live at the White House. Rebecca and Riley. No! Reuben. Rebecca and Reuben. And Hoover's son had two pet alligators."

"Bet that kept the fence jumpers away."

I grin. "There's some debate about whether they lived on the grounds. FDR was so obsessed with his dog Fala he made him an honorary army private during World War Two."

"By the way, how does it feel to be an unending fount of useless presidential trivia?"

I jerk my arm out, threatening to flick paint at him again. "It's entertaining *you*, isn't it? That makes it use*ful*, thank you very much."

I've spent the week feeling washed clean by the tears and in a slightly better place emotionally. But "slightly better" doesn't compare to "light and effervescent," which is how I feel right now, with my disease far—or at least farther—from my mind, my mural underway, and Will nearby to bat around insubstantial nothings with me and to make me laugh.

As if he received the directive, he calls up to me, "Maybe we can get Snoop Dogg a porcupine as an inauguration gift."

18

"GET STUFFED, YOU PIECE!"

Sibby's curse echoes through her apartment and beckons me
down the hall. Whatever she's doing in her room, she's not too happy
about it, and I can't help wondering what's waiting to greet me—with
Sibby you can never be sure. I edge the door open and am immediately smacked in the face with something small but hard.

"What the—!"

"Cripes, I'm so sorry!" Sibby's eyes are wide, but then crinkle
with amusement. "I had no idea you were out there."

"What *was* that?" I ask, massaging my cheek.

Sib glares at the offending object on the floor by my feet, which
appears to be a harmless marker, as she sucks on the pad of her index

finger. She has to speak around it to inform me, "Nasty bugger pinched me when I closed it."

I roll my eyes. "Need me to call an ambulance?"

Immediately I regret my words, because not so long ago she was screaming for someone to do exactly that for me. Luckily she doesn't seem to make the connection, because she merely pats the spot next to her and orders, "Come. What are you doing here?"

"I couldn't let my best friend take off for a week in New York City without a proper goodbye from her favorite person."

It's only Thursday night but tomorrow's Good Friday, so school vacation week gets extended by an extra day at the beginning this year. Sibby's mom—who's the director of partnership at the American Repertory Theater—is planning a summer trip to New York for their donors and her insanely lucky daughter gets to tag along this week to help scout which Broadway shows and restaurants to include on the itinerary. I mean, really.

Except Sibby does not look like someone who will be stepping onto a train in a couple hours. I allow my field of vision to expand enough to take in the rest of the scene. She sits cross-legged in a small clearing in the center of her rug, while the rest of her floor looks . . . well, like a craft store exploded. There are at least five piles of poster boards and dozens upon dozens of markers, colored pencils, and crayons flung about.

Sibby's room is always artfully messy, which complements its boho-chic vibe, with the tapestry-covered walls and beaded chandelier and ceramic elephant collection. But while this mess is art-*related*, it's nothing close to art-*ful*.

"*What* is going on here, Molly Jacques?" I tease.

Sibby examines her wounded finger more closely. "I just told you. Bloody marker pinched me." Then she looks up. "*Who* did you call me?"

"Molly Jacques. She's this illustrator I'm obsessed with—you'd love her stuff."

Even in its current state of chaos, this space is cozy and familiar and safe, and I step over a pile of neon-orange poster boards to join her in the center of her overdyed rug, our matching crisscrossed knees bumping as I settle in across from her. "But really, whatcha doin'? I know it's not school-related, because no one's assigning homework over April vacation. Unless—Dormer wouldn't dare, would he?"

She reaches around me to a different pile and turns over the poster on top.

GIVE, SO SOMEONE CAN LIVE! it reads.

"Prom with a Purpose," she adds needlessly.

I school my expression to neutral as the prickly-but-also-somehow-empty feeling I've been experiencing lately resurfaces. So much for Sibby's room being safe, at least not from BA reminders. Although really, practically *nowhere* is, except maybe when I'm hanging out with Will.

I stifle a sigh and pull the stack of completed posters—maybe ten or so—into my lap, flipping through them slowly. Despite the dip in my mood, I can't help but laugh a little at what I see. "Sib, I love you, but these are *terrible*. Is this supposed to be an *I* or a *Z*? And you misspelled *transplantation*."

I continue giggling softly, until it sinks in that I'm at a party for one; Sibby is most definitely not amused. She snatches them back. "Yeah, well, some of us haven't spent the last five years perfecting hand lettering."

I shrug off her snippy tone. "You should have called me to help."

Sibby waits for me to meet her eyes, which have a spark of challenge in them that makes my stomach twist. "I think we both know why I didn't."

"I don't, actually," I insist, feigning ignorance. I'll admit I haven't exactly sprung backflips any of the times she's floated the concept of Prom with a Purpose by me, but I've also never been able to bring myself to flat-out say, "I hate the idea," so from her perspective I'm still on board with things.

Her exhale contains a scoff. "I'm not dense, you know. It's hard to miss you clamming up any time I bring up the subject."

I shrug as I stare at her carpet. "You could have asked. We *should* hang out as much as we can while we have the chance."

Glancing up in time to notice the color drain from her cheeks, I replay my words in my head before gasping. "I wasn't suggesting— I just meant before we both go off to different colleges!"

I don't add that I'm aware the fact we haven't been spending more time together lately has been more my fault than hers. Just like I also don't tell her that *my* enrollment might be on shaky ground. There's so much I'm keeping to myself these days, but confessing the doctor's recommendation to Sibby would mean acknowledging it as a real possibility, and I'm not prepared to go there either.

Ignoring my words, she reaches around me again for a blank poster board and begins outlining letters with a marker. I have to fight the urge to yank it from her when I see how haphazard she's being about it. No snap lines to keep the wording straight, no pencil sketching first to ensure even spacing between letters or that everything will fit. Instead, I sit on my hands and absorb the irritation coming off her.

Irritation at *me*. Maybe more than irritation. Maybe full-on anger.

Sibby and I are both "feisty," as my dad terms it. Neither of us is afraid to be loud and proud. Sure, we might take down an obnoxious derby competitor, and I'm not saying we haven't discussed a few evil plans to exact a fitting revenge on Mr. Dormer before graduation, but . . . those are different.

When we confront something, we do it together and we have fun with it. We rant about the most recent *Doctor Who* casting or reviews that don't put spoiler warnings in the first paragraph. We rage about spammy Instagram ads; those who are old enough to vote and don't; people who refer to themselves as "pet parents" to their dog or cat; tourists who walk around here saying, "Hey, I really did just pahk the cah in Hahvahd Yahd!" like they're the first to ever make that joke (although it honestly wouldn't surprise me if that honor went to my dad).

I could go on, but I won't.

Fight *together*? Always. Fight *with* each other? Never.

We're both painfully silent as she pretends to be consumed with her poster making and I pretend equally hard to be absorbed with watching her progress.

Finally, with her head still bent over her work, she says, "I *should* be packing."

As much as I want to avoid any kind of escalation of whatever awkwardness this is, I chafe at her words. "Okay, but it's not like *I'm* keeping you from doing that."

She huffs a piece of hair out of her eyes. "Yeah, well, it's not like I asked *you* to prance down the hallway in an art smock to protest the dress code. I didn't *have* to ask. You womaned up because that's what we do for the other person; we fight their battles with them, no questions asked! So why wouldn't you expect me to do the same for you when it comes to your need for a liver?"

Her words are sharp, but they immediately soften my own defensiveness.

I swallow away the lump that forms in my throat and say, "My BA isn't a battle, Sib, it's a waiting game. It's something that's just . . . happening . . . and that will continue to happen, up to the day they find me a liver, no matter what we do or don't do. Until that call comes, it really isn't something you can fight with me. It isn't even something *I* can fight. Trust me, I *hate* feeling helpless about it, but it is what it is."

"That's a load of crap!" Her voice is as loud as mine was quiet, and I cringe at the thought of her mom overhearing us. Sibby obviously doesn't care about that, though, because she continues at top volume. "I'm stopping strangers on the sidewalk to ask them if they're organ donors. I signed up my mum's dry cleaner, our UPS guy, the girl who fixed my laptop at the Genius Bar. That boy we love at Mr. Bartley's—the one who adds extra ice cream to the frappés!"

She takes a deep breath. "Okay, I can't keep this in anymore. I'm going there."

Her warning sounds up and down my spine and I taste acid in my mouth as I wait for her to continue.

"I'm trying *so* hard to be a good friend to you and to push my feelings aside to give yours top priority," she says. "You think it was easy for me to stand next to you and listen to you tell everyone in our class how you needed a transplant to live? Or hold in my news about Tufts? I'm busting my *arse* trying to get this Prom with a Purpose thing off the ground on my own. For you. Meanwhile, *you're* just . . . what? Hanging from a ropes course with some fuckskillet who suddenly reappeared in your life? Ignoring anything that has to do with your condition? Fuck me dead, Lia! Where *are* you in all this?"

Her accusations, delivered in shouts, make my fight-or-flight reflex kick in big-time. My skin is too tight and my chest collapses and I don't know how to act normally or breathe normally and ohmygodIjustwantoutofthisroom.

I brace my hands on the floor and wait for the sensation to pass, taking several deep inhales. Avoiding eye contact and keeping my voice low, I somehow manage, "I'm right here, same me as ever. That's the whole point. I'm fighting to *stay* the same Amelia as ever while I wait for this to resolve itself."

Sibby collapses backward on the rug. Her sigh is epic and I can see her anger draining away; I allow my stomach to unclench ever so slightly.

"Okay, help me understand," she finally says, in a much calmer voice. "How would you not be the same Amelia as ever if you took action with me on this? Taking action is what we do."

"Because. Offering myself up as a sob story to tug at people's heartstrings makes me out to be some sad sack, woe-is-me pity case. And I can't let myself own that role. That's not me! I'm just like you. We're bold. And brave. We're not afraid to get rough on the derby track, we're always up for adventure. We're feral swamp goddesses and descendants of witches that couldn't burn, right?"

My own voice shakes now too, but not with anger. With . . . I don't know what with. Righteousness? "I'm not giving any of that—of *me*—up just because I have a crappy liver that's busy deteriorating inside of me, *which I can barely feel happening*!"

I hate that my eyes water as I choke out the words.

Sibby stares at me for the longest time. Long enough that my heartbeat slows to normal again and the air in the room expands.

She struggles to a sitting position with her legs still crisscrossed. When she's upright, she wiggles her knees right in against mine again and studies me for a second, before reaching over with both hands to gently slide the clasp of my necklace around to the back. Keeping her eyes fixed on my neck, she settles the Rolldemort letters into their proper position, centered beneath my chin, and says, "I'm really sorry I spat the dummy at you."

"I'm really sorry you spat the dummy at me too," I reply, and her lips twitch.

"You're super bad at apologizing."

My lips tick up now too. "Well, partly because I don't really know what that means, so . . ."

"Dummy. Pacifier. Spat the dummy's like . . . 'threw a tantrum,' in Aussie-speak."

"Oh, well, in that case, I'm still really sorry you spat the dummy at me." I smile, then add, *"And* I'm sorry I didn't tell you how I felt about Prom with a Purpose before now *and* I will help. Except . . . maybe can we make my role more of a behind-the-scenes one?"

Why didn't I just say all of this to her long before now? It wasn't that terrible and it would have been even less so if I hadn't let it reach this point.

Sibby examines the poster she's been working on. I think it's supposed to read YOU'RE SOMEBODY'S TYPE but the *y* and the second *s* in *somebody's* are stacked on top of the *d* where she ran out of room. She draws a lewd graphic over the letters and says, "You don't have a choice about helping. Turns out my poster-making skills are sweet fuck all."

My laugh dissipates the last of the tension from the air. "Reporting for duty."

Sibby salutes me, then picks up the pile of posters next to her. "Okay, I'm gonna trash the ones I messed up on and start over. Help me spell 'transplantation'? And then maybe help me redo every one of these using your perfect lettering sorcery?"

I stretch my arms wide and begin pulling markers toward me. "Lettering *is* my jam."

We wiggle out of each other's way so the poster making can resume in earnest.

"I'll outline the words and you're in charge of coloring them in, okay?" I ask.

"Yes, ma'am."

I grab my phone and pull up my Pinterest board of hand-drawn fonts. While I begin on the first slogan, Sibby crawls around her room, collecting all the writing utensils and organizing them by color and type. We're quiet as we set to our respective tasks, but this time it's a comfortable silence, not a tension-laden one. Sibby even starts humming something under her breath.

I'm just about to pass the first completed slogan over for coloring when she giggles.

"What?" I ask.

"I was just thinking what a good 'get' on my part the UPS guy was. He *always* has a giant bag of cheese puffs on the seat next to him in his truck. Talk about a heart attack waiting to happen."

I laugh, but then catch myself. "I don't think it's good karma to actively cheer on anyone's demise. Especially not a death-by-cheese-puffs."

"Did I mention he also listens to Robin Thicke on repeat?"

"Oh, screw it, then; he's beyond our compassion."

Sibby laughs and plops down next to me. "Sorry I called Will a fuckskillet."

"You did! I forgot that!" It was lost on me in the moment because I was so overwhelmed by the fact that *Sibby* was yelling at me.

"I don't actually think he is one, if that helps. At least, based on what you've told me, since I have yet to meet this mystery boy. Hint, hint."

"He's definitely *not* a fuckskillet," I say, hiding a smile.

"You have the worst poker face ever. Do you *like him* like him?"

I glance up from my poster and catch her conspiratorial wink. "It's not like that," I insist.

"Mmmm-hmmm," she singsongs.

"No, really. Hanging out with Will is just easy—we're flirty, but I honestly don't think either one of us is flirt*ing*. You know?"

"So, do you think this is still about a favor to Alex on his part? The reason he keeps hanging around?"

"He doesn't *keep* hanging around. I'm the one who texted him and invited him to Jordan's. This past Sunday was the only other time he initiated anything, and it was super casual. He said he was looking for an excuse to be outside."

"What about you? What are you getting out of it?"

Escape.

For some reason, I can't say this, though. I don't want her to think I need to escape *her*. I look for another way to phrase it. "I dunno, it's just fun to banter with him. Low-key."

She studies me for a few seconds and I sense the mood change. I'm already on guard when she says, "Since we're being brutally honest with each other tonight, can I ask you something you're probably not gonna want to answer?"

My gut clenches in warning, but I merely shrug. "Sure. I guess."

"Is it low-key because you know he won't call you on your shit?"

"What? *No*." I retrace a letter I've already outlined and avoid looking at her.

But I hear her inhale, and brace for her next words. "The thing is," she says. "That stuff we say about being fearless swamp goddesses and daughters of witches to pump ourselves up is—"

I cut her off. "You don't think we're fierce?"

She holds her palms up. "I do! But I think that's only one aspect of who we are. I think we have quieter parts too. I think all of us have parts that are a little bit chickenshit." She holds her fingers up to indicate a small amount, then drops her eyes and whispers, "Especially you."

"What?!" These are the last words I ever thought Sibby—of all people, Sibby who's my *person*, who claims she has my back always in all ways—would say to me, and indignation rushes in to take the place of any other emotions. "Excuse you, but you're right next to me on the roller derby track! And who just took on the school administration on the dress code, thanks very much. The way I *own* my zany outfits? You're saying I'm not brave? Fear is not the boss of me; courage is. What about that? Those words aren't just some empty chant we do before games. They're kind of my mantra these days!"

Sibby shakes her head. "I'm not trying to take away from any of those things, Lia, because they're amazing. *You're* amazing. But . . ."

"But what, Sib?" I demand.

She settles her eyes on mine. "What you're describing isn't bravery; those are examples of bravado. Two different things."

"Explain," I order. I'm somewhere between defensiveness and shock. *How long has she been holding this in?*

"Bravado is boldness, it's cheeky swagger, it's having front. Bravery is . . . it's more . . . putting yourself on the line."

"I put myself on the line!" *What is she even talking about?* "What do you think I do every time I elbow through a row of blockers?"

"I don't mean physically!" She composes herself and sighs. "I mean emotionally."

"I have zero idea what you're saying." I love Sibby and I trust her and maybe she thinks she's telling me these things to help me, but she's just flat-out wrong about this.

She points at the poster by my knees. "Exhibit A."

I'm lost and my look conveys it.

Pointedly, she unlocks my phone and hands it to me with Pinterest displayed on the screen. "Your art is beautiful, but it's not *you*. It's someone else's."

"I wasn't going for art, Sib! They're freaking slogans for a rally!"

Her smug expression makes me suspicious that I've walked right into a trap she's set. Confirmation comes when she asks, "And your mural?"

"What about my mural? I designed that!"

"Babe, I say this with love, but . . . did you? Or did you take elements of other people's designs and mash them together?"

"You are literally describing ninety-nine point nine percent of all artistic expression. Everyone pulls inspiration from what's already been done."

"And then they add their own unique vision to it, to make it say something personal about them. I'm not saying you didn't do that, except that maybe I am a little. I mean, Maya Angelou is the queen, but those are her words, not yours, yeah?" There's a flash of challenge in her eyes and it sends a new jolt of anger through me. *Who the hell does she think she is?*

"What do *I* have to say that could match Maya Angelou's wisdom?" I argue. "I'm a kid—I haven't *done* anything yet. What sort of inspirational wisdom do you expect me to impart, exactly?"

"It doesn't have to be profound, Li. You can tell me to bugger off but it's gonna be your signature on that wall; it should be *your* voice there too. That's all. I'm not trying to piss you off. Trust me, I'm sure I have *loads* of my own issues to work on, and I'm counting on my best friend to call me out on all of them. You can even start now if you want. Ready? Go!"

"I don't *want* to throw all your flaws in your face—I want to support you, the way we always do for each other. I don't understand why we're back to arguing. Have you just been *trying* to pick fights with me tonight?"

"No! I've been *trying* to get through to you. You don't seem to want to talk about *anything* real these days, you just want to pretend like none of this is happening and push it all away. Well, guess what? IT *IS* HAPPENING! To you. To me. To everyone close to you. It's *happening*!"

"See, *this* is why I didn't want to tell you I hated the idea of Prom with a Purpose, because you'd ask all kinds of follow-up questions and analyze my every response. This might all be happening, but I'm still *me*—I haven't changed."

Sibby's eyes search the ceiling before she looks back at me and sighs. "Lia. Come *on*."

"Come on, *what*, Sib?" She's talking to me like I'm some child she has to school and it's pissing me off.

"Babe, you've got this shit disease and, as much as it hurts to acknowledge it out loud, your future's a bit of a question mark right now. Like it or not, that's gonna do a number on your head. No matter what happens from here, this experience *is* gonna change you, Li. You can't avoid that. That's why they call these things life-*changing*."

I raise my chin and set my jaw. "I *really* don't appreciate the lecture, Sib. Just because I'm not reacting to this diagnosis the way you think I should doesn't mean I'm wrong! What's so bad about not letting myself wallow in everything? Huh? What *exactly* is so terrible about refusing to be Dying Girl?"

I forget about her mom somewhere in the apartment because my voice rises with each question. But Sibby's only reaction is an eyebrow lift that reads as condescending, whether she intends it that way or not.

"Who the hell is Dying Girl? Of course you shouldn't be her, whatever *that* means."

"What then?" I snap. "What is it you think I should be doing that I'm not?"

"You should be . . . I don't know." She throws her hands up as she casts about for words. "You should be furious! Aren't you hella pissed? *None of this* has to be happening to you! Not if there were enough organs to go around! What the fuck do these people think—that they can take 'em with them? Where is your anger? Where is your fire?" Sibby puts her hands to her head and yanks at her hair. "I don't know what you should be doing! I just think you need to . . . let it in!"

If this were any normal day, I would counter with, "I'd rather let it go," which would inevitably lead to Sibby singing "Let it go, let it gooooooo," and I'd join right in, and in five seconds flat we'd be channeling Idina Menzel on all the high notes of the *Frozen* soundtrack.

But nothing about this exchange is regular Lia + Sibby.

"Let *what* in? The fact that my best friend, who I thought I could count on to love me through anything, is being a total shit to me?" I counter. "*You're not brave at all, Lia; that's just bravado. You don't have an artistic voice, Lia. You're doing this all wrong, Lia.* Well, guess what? You have NO CLUE what it's like to be in my shoes, so step the hell off!" I take a deep but shaky breath. Then I lower my voice to deadly calm. "How about I skip letting it in, and let myself *out* instead?"

Her eyes, already wide at my outburst, open bigger, but before she can answer me, I jump up, grab my bag, and rush from her room. I duck my head low the whole way through her apartment, not wanting to encounter her mom because she'd undoubtedly report back to Sibby about the tears now streaming down my face.

It's not until I fly down two sets of stairs and reach the lobby that I crash to a stop and slump against the wall. Between shuddering gulps, I listen closely for the door to Sibby's apartment to click open, for footfalls on the steps that will let me know she's coming to tell me how sorry she is about everything.

Instead the silence is earsplitting.

19

I STUMBLE HOME FROM SIBBY'S TO FIND BOTH CARS IN THE driveway and a bunch of lights on, but no sign of my parents.

"Hello?" I call but receive no response.

I'm about to abandon my search and collapse in my room when I hear voices through the open kitchen window. Of course. I should have known they'd be in the backyard now that spring has finally sprung.

My hand is on the knob of the mudroom door when I catch Dad's words. "—been wondering whether we should bring Alex home. I know he only has three weeks left before exams, and he turned down the summer internship, but . . . do you think we should consider it?"

Turned down the internship? When? *Why didn't he tell me? We talked about this! He knows I don't want that.* And leave school in the middle of the semester? What?! I step away from the glass panes and flatten my body against the wall, out of sight.

"Maybe," Mom answers, her voice small. "It would be nice to have us all under one roof. I've been debating handing a few of my cases off to Jeremy."

Mom *hates* Jeremy.

"You hate Jeremy," Dad says.

Exactly! Tell her, Dad!

Mom sighs. "When we were at Dr. Wah's the other day, waiting for the blood test results, I felt so guilty that all I could think about was getting back to my files."

"Honey, you're doing important work and you love your job. There's no shame in that. It's probably really healthy that you have a place to escape from all this."

"None of that's why I wanted to get back, though. It was because—"

She takes a shuddering breath and I hear some rustling and a scraping of a chair. I lower myself carefully to the floor, in a crouching position, and waddle carefully to my right, positioning myself in front of the door so I'm hidden behind the solid lower half. Slowly, ever so slowly, I raise myself up a few inches to peek out the section that's glass. My parents are facing one another, their chairs close enough that Mom's forehead rests against Dad's, and their hands are clasped in her lap.

My heart is in my throat and I can't bear to watch anymore. But I also can't bear to walk away. Instead, I slump onto my butt.

"Because why?" Dad asks. His voice wavers.

"I think . . . I think somehow I've convinced myself that if I can help this group of refugees earn asylum status, that's twelve lives I'll be more or less saving. And twelve lives saved has to equal one for Amelia, right? God—or whoever it is out there—can't argue with those terms, can he?" Mom's tone is pleading.

"Sweetheart—"

"Because I will save a thousand people, Jeff. A million. I will, I swear. I will work eighty-hour weeks until I'm a hundred and three, if it means—"

She breaks off and it's silent for a long time.

I want to steal another peek, but I'm frozen in place. Between the fight with Sibby and now this . . . I'm scrubbed raw.

Then Mom speaks again. "The rational side of me knows it doesn't work like that. The same way I know I'm doing this Weight Watchers thing all wrong, denying myself even when I have plenty of leftover points. I know I need to lose these pounds the healthy way so I'm a viable candidate once I reach an acceptable weight, but it's taking too long! What if we don't have 'too long'?"

There's a pause and then Mom asks, "Does this all sound insane to you?"

"No! Of course not!" Dad pauses and adds, more quietly, "You want to talk about insane? The other day at the hardware store, I was helping a customer with grout options when a siren passed by and my first thought wasn't, 'I hope everyone inside that ambulance is okay.'" His voice drops lower. "My first thought was 'I hope whoever is in there dies and he's a match for Amelia.'"

I squeeze my eyes shut and let my head fall against the door.

"It was horrible. I beat myself up for it the rest of the day." I think Dad might be crying. I can hear it in his voice when he says, "But the truth is a tiny part of me genuinely still wants that person dead, if it means she—"

My pulse throbs in my veins and I desperately want to move, to leave. But I'm paralyzed.

"I think it's time to consider Tennessee again," my mom says, after a long stretch of quiet.

"We said we wouldn't decide anything about that until her MELD score hit thirty," he answers.

What are they talking about?

"I know, but what if we could have all this behind us before that even happened? The odds of getting a liver in Region Eleven are *three times* better than they are in ours. Stats like that make it hard to justify sitting things out up here."

Wait, what? They want to move us a dozen states away?

"Except for all the reasons we debated," Dad says, his voice stronger now. "Dr. Wah is the best of the best. We don't know anything about what the care is like down there. And Amelia's so close to graduation, it would be cruel to pull her out of school and move her away from her support system."

As angry as I am at Sibby right now, the thought of not having her mere blocks away . . .

I hold my breath for Mom's answer. I want a new liver for me just as much as they do, but these are drastic measures they're talking about. Are we really at that point?

"Crueler than what could happen if we don't?" she replies. "She'd have *you* as a support system."

"But not you," Dad murmurs, so softly that I have to strain to hear him. "Could you really bear to be away from her right now?"

Mom is silent for a long time, but finally says, "It's impossible to think about, but what choice would we have? I have to stay as a full-time employee so we can keep my insurance. If we switch to the store's, we'd already be bumping up against your policy's benefits cap and her operation would bankrupt us."

The word *bankrupt* punctures my lungs. *On top of all the pain I'm causing them, my liver could result in their financial ruin too. How much more of this am I supposed to be able to bear?*

"I can dial back my caseload, though, and still be considered full-time," Mom says. "And I could use family medical leave to be there between my court dates, which would be farther apart with fewer open cases. Babi's not going to let us defer her offers to come home and help much longer; maybe she could go with you and be a second set of hands. I—I know it's not an ideal situation, but . . ."

"There *is* another choice," Dad replies. "We stick to our original plan to stay put unless she worsens."

Please. Please say yes, Mom.

There's more rustling, followed by another long silence, and then my mother instead says, "Jeff, what if we lose her?"

Her voice is practically a whisper, but it travels across the tiny patio and straight into my cracking heart. "What if we actually lose her?"

Go! Run! Get away! my brain tells me, and finally *finally* my body parts unstick and I can respond. I crawl from the mudroom into the kitchen and lean heavily on the counter as I clamber to my feet. I climb the back staircase sluggishly, as if there are boulders in my shoes, ignoring the window on the landing that has taken on new significance after that night on the ledge with Dad.

I'm on an entirely different kind of ledge now. The one between sanity and a tumble into an abyss.

I reach my room and burrow under my covers, pulling my knees to my chest. The only noise in my room is a steady *click* as my flip clock counts up each minute. *Or is it counts down, in my case?*

Click.

Click.

Click.

I am floating in nothingness. This day has emptied me out.

Click.

Click.

My parents are going to find me like this. They're going to know I heard everything. Or I'm going to have to fake normal, so they don't realize I did. I don't know which option is more hellish. I have to get out of here.

Click.

Click.

Click.

I heave my legs over the side of my bed, a plan forming. It's a little unglued—*I'm* a little unglued—but it's all I have. Maybe it can let me find solid footing again, even just temporarily. Buy me enough time to figure out where to go—*how* to go—from here.

I throw a few items into a duffel, pull the blanket off my bed, and attempt to fold it, before giving up and crumpling it into a ball under my armpit.

I creep downstairs, using the front staircase this time, far away from the back patio. Taping a note to the banister, I grab my mother's car keys from the pocket of her coat and slip outside.

I escape.

20 ~

WILL'S DORM DOESN'T HAVE A DOORBELL.

It has a sign-in desk, where he's already waiting for me. "You found it okay!"

I hold up my phone. "Your directions were solid."

His smile is as easy and relaxed as ever, his stance assured. *Yes, give me playful Will, who will hold my attention on him and demand full-effort flirting in return.*

Stepping in, he examines me more closely and says, "Hey, are you okay? You seem a little . . ."

He doesn't finish his sentence, but I laugh as if he's said something hilarious. Even to my own ears, I sound manic. Unstable.

Get it together, Amelia. You'll scare him away and be left with no distraction.

"I'm fine! Totally fine! Just keyed up for our adventure, that's all."

He hesitates for a beat, but then his shoulders relax. "I have to admit I'm curious. This is turning into a pattern, you luring me out with the promise of adventure."

If I could get on an airplane right now, I would. Going anywhere, it wouldn't matter, though my preference would be somewhere exotic, like Morocco or Istanbul or Nepal, where nothing looks or sounds or tastes like real life. Like *my* real life, at least.

But, as frantically reckless as I'm feeling right now, I can't go full-on unhinged. I'm lassoed into a particular radius from the hospital, constricted by the mere hours of viability a healthy recovered liver has to reach me, anchored by the very people whose pain I desperately need to escape tonight.

So I've set my sights smaller. Adventure might be overselling it, but I needed Will to come along because doing this myself would be pitiful and desperate. Having someone else there makes it spontaneous and funny. *Right?*

"Do I need anything?" Will asks.

"Just your coat. I'm all set otherwise."

And I am. On my way to Will's campus, I stopped at our hardware store and used the keys on Mom's ring to let myself in and "shopped" its aisles for a bucket, shovels, an umbrella. Everything needed for a day at the beach.

The fact that it's neither day nor remotely beach season is irrelevant . . . because I say it is. When I was a kid, spending an afternoon digging holes at the surf line, tunneling my feet under sun-warm sand, splashing in the waves, was as close to idyllic as it got for me. I need a dose of idyllic in the worst goddamn way and I am going to make it happen. This minute.

There are a dozen quintessential New England-y beaches within an hour's drive of Boston, but I steer the car to Revere Beach instead, by sheer basis of the fact that I can reach it in under twenty minutes—fifteen if I feel like speeding a little.

I feel like speeding a lot.

"Easy, Danica Patrick." Will's laugh as we zoom through the Callahan Tunnel tells me he's okay with it, though, as does the fact that he turns the volume up on my Fever Ray playlist.

When we park and Will gets a peek at the contents of my trunk, he lets out a bark of surprise. "Um, are you sure we need all this gear?"

"We do if we're going to have an old-fashioned day at the beach," I tell him.

His laugh is wary. "Okay, when we pulled up, I was thinking moonlit stroll—a bit early in the season, but unexpected and different. This, though, is . . . next-level."

"I don't half-ass things, Will. You should know that about me by now." My words are light, but there is an edgy undertone to them, daring him to disagree, to call me out on how my abrupt actions and out-of-the-box concept for tonight are less "adorable manic pixie dream girl" and more "just plain manic."

To his credit, he seems down to roll with things, whether out of concern or cluelessness, I don't know, but his voice is light when I hand him the umbrella. "Pretty sure sunburn hours are eleven to three, Decks." He peers at the dark sky. "I think we're out of the danger zone."

Something he sees in my expression shuts him up, though, because he hoists it under his arm without further comment and grabs the buckets and shovels with his free hand. I scoop the blanket from my bed into my arms and lock the car.

Revere Beach has a reputation for being a little . . . cheesy. It was once home to a seaside amusement park that rivaled Coney Island, but that closed in the sixties and there's no trace of it now. There's still plenty of amusement, though, provided by the catcalling pot-bellied old men in Speedos showing off their ink to the walking clubs of elderly women in velour jogging suits. People set up their lawn chairs in the parking spots and actually turn their backs to the beach to watch a steady procession of muscle cars cruising the strip, ignoring the fact that right behind them, separated only by a short sea wall and a wide sidewalk, is a flat stretch of sand and endless blue-gray water.

But at eight o'clock at night, off-season, there are only the low-flying planes lining up to land at Logan and the dim house lights of Nahant—far across the water where the land forms a horseshoe that circles back on our wide cove—to remind us where we are. It feels like we could be on any beach, anywhere.

"Down there," I decide, pointing at a spot halfway between the street and the cresting waves.

We have the place entirely to ourselves, with the exception of one person shouting-distance away, who I can only make out as a shadow as they repeatedly throw something for their dog to retrieve. We shuck our shoes and leave them lined up on the retaining wall.

I smell the damp sand, taste the salt on my tongue, and hear the crash of the waves hitting the shore. It isn't Morocco or Istanbul, but none of these sensations are part of my normal day-to-day and that's entirely the point.

Neither is Will. Again, the point.

We walk in relative silence for a bit, our only conversation having to do with the biting wind and the frigid sand oozing between our toes. It was sixty-five degrees this afternoon, and at home, a few miles inland, the night air still felt balmy, but here on the coast's edge, with the wind whipping off the water, it's downright cold. I clutch the blanket closer to my body, but remain steadfast in my quest.

When I notice Will staring at me, I point to a spot in the distance where the crescent beach begins to curl in on itself. "President Roosevelt—Theodore, not FDR—once delivered a speech at a hotel up there."

"*And* she's back!" Will says.

I squint at him. "What does *that* mean?"

"You've just been acting a little . . . different . . . tonight, that's all. But that was a hundred percent Decker thing to say!"

We're only halfway to the vague destination I'd indicated, but I drop my blanket. "Here looks good."

I don't address his comment. Contrary to the presidential trivia that slipped out unbidden, I have no interest in bringing Decker to the party tonight, nor any other version of regular me. Tonight's me is dangerous and mysterious and a little bit off-balance, and Will needs to roll with that, because he's not getting anyone else.

Not tonight.

Fortunately, he follows my lead and deposits his gear next to the blankets. I immediately unfurl the umbrella and jam it into the fluffy sand, rocking it back and forth to drive it deeper.

"Hey, whoa! Easy!" Will steps behind me and puts his hands over mine, slowing my rhythm. "It helps to twist it down a bunch first, *then* you rock."

Do I like having Will boxing me in, his body bumping against mine? I consider it, and decide I might. That maybe it could even enhance the distraction effect. "That's what she said," I murmur, adding a little innuendo to a flirtation we've both been keeping very PG thus far.

He laughs, and I duck out from between his arms and grab one of the shovels. "Should I do you or do you want to do me?"

"That's what she said," he replies, grinning.

I lie on the sand, tucking my arms by my side and stretching my legs. "I meant who wants to be first getting covered by sand. But you were too slow, so it's me!"

My eyes glitter with challenge now, and not an easygoing, flirty one.

"Um, *okayyyy*." Will's normal confidence is wavering as he tries to track my swinging moods. I half expect him to call bullshit on my behavior and hop the T home—the Blue Line has a station just a few blocks down. But he doesn't. He drops to his knees and begins pushing mounds of sand into the hollows of my hips. My body is humming with a restless energy that makes it difficult to hold still, so when he switches to scooping handfuls and drizzling them over my jeans, I'm grateful for the weight of it, grounding me.

Will pushes sand into me, dumps it onto me . . . but he doesn't pat it down to hold it in place. For the most part, he's keeping his hands from directly touching me; I can sense he's still puzzling out what's going on with me and whether he should ask about it. He shouldn't. Rivulets of sand escape from each side of my kneecaps.

After a few minutes he breaches the silence. "I can't remember, were you there the time my parents took us to the sand sculpting competition here, or was it just Alex who came?"

"The what?"

"I guess that answers my question." He moves to the end of my body and covers my feet, cementing them into place. "They hold the International Sand Sculpting Festival here every July, or at least they used to, I'm not sure if they still do. These sand artists from all over the world create unbelievable sculptures throughout the course of a couple days. Then there's judging the last day and they shut down part of the road and set up a street fair. It's fun."

I raise my eyebrows. "Sand artists? That's a real thing?"

"You mock, but I'm telling you, they are *seriously* talented. You should see pictures."

I take a deep breath, fighting to rein in the instability pulsing in my veins, urging myself to relax into the here and now, to find my banter, to let Will provide the escape from reality I'm craving. Exhaling, I try. "If only something existed that could show us anything, anywhere, at any time and was small enough to fit in your pocket and connected to, I don't know, some kind of web of information—"

Will cuts me off. "Shut it, smartass. Point taken."

He rocks back on his heels, brushes his hands on his pant legs, and pulls out his phone. After typing for a few seconds, he holds the screen a couple feet above my face and slowly scrolls through a photo gallery.

I was picturing sandcastles, but these are so much more; they're huge and detailed sculptures of all types. Pirate boats that are practically life-sized, enormous sea monsters rising from under the sand, and two people embracing. Some are abstract and others are incredibly intricate. They all command my attention. I can't wrap my brain around how they could be made out of regular beach sand.

"Wow! They sculpt these in a couple of days?" I ask.

"Yup."

"But what about high tide?"

"They do them up there, away from the water line." He gestures toward an area behind me, closer to the sidewalk and the open-air pavilions lining it.

"Don't they need the sand to be wet to make it stick together?" The castles of my own happy beach days were all constructed in the low tide flats.

"They use hoses. It's big-time."

Will tucks his phone back into his jacket and shrugs. He moves above me and begins filling in the scoop of my shoulders, leaving my neck and head free. Now that we're in the rhythm of a conversation and the sand covering my chest is as heavy and comforting as the weighted vest my dentist uses when she takes X-rays, the adrenaline buzz I've been riding since running out of my house earlier begins to recede. I still can't stomach thinking about my fight with Sibby or the words my parents spoke when they thought I wasn't listening, but at least I can hold focus without my attention jerking here, there, and everywhere.

"And then what, they just knock them over at the end?" I ask.

"I assume so? Or maybe they leave them to fall down on their own? I'm not sure—we never stuck around for that part."

"New subject. That's depressing."

Will coughs in surprise.

I try to turn my head to see him, but my movement causes my shoulders to break free of their sandy constraints.

"Hey!" he protests.

"Sorry. Why'd you react like that?"

He shrugs and resumes his task. "I wouldn't have expected to hear a girl who erases her own chalkboards every week say that knocking down sandcastles is depressing."

"Oh. Well, that's different. I acknowledge there is *some* level of craftsmanship to what I do, but you just showed me a museum-worthy, twenty-foot Grecian god. I color chalkboards that give you the price of cupcakes."

Will laughs. "There's a distinct value to that."

"Yeah, a literal one: three ninety-five each, a half-dozen for twenty."

Will shifts to my right side, his hands methodical as he scoops and releases piles of sand grains. "I meant to your artistic contribution."

"Maybe. But no one is crying tears when I erase a menu, least of all me."

"So are you saying that you *would* feel sad about erasing your work if your designs were more intricate? Or twenty feet tall? What's the qualifying factor? Won't your mural be both those things?"

"But my mural won't be erased—it's paint, not chalk."

Will glances at me, and he seems to be guarding his words when he says, "So that gives it more value, in your eyes? The idea that it's permanent?"

My knee-jerk response is to answer, "No!" but then I make myself consider his question. "Maybe? I guess there's some value in how many weeks it will take to create. Compared to an hour or two on one of my chalkboards. You know? Which is not to suggest it wouldn't be heartbreaking to see two days of work on a sand sculpture knocked over in thirty seconds, though."

"You would *really* cry over sand mandalas then."

He huffs an annoyed breath when I move my neck again, to try to see him. "Stay still!"

"What are those?" I ask.

"Something Tibetan monks make. They start with an insanely detailed geometrical design, and then take days, or weeks in some cases, using small fragile tubes and funnels to fill in every tiny shape with colored sand. I'm talking ridiculously detailed and delicate designs."

He retrieves his phone once more and types for a minute. "Here, screen time!"

Will tucks his head next to mine and extends his arm straight over us so we can watch a sped-up time-lapse video showing a group of orange-robed monks bent over a table, completing a pattern that looks like a hundred stained glass window designs, each fitting inside of one another. I'm intrigued and not at all expecting what happens at the end when . . . they brush the whole thing away. All those endless hours of tedious, painstaking work just—poof! Gone. A tabletop of swirled sand is all that remains when the music stops.

"What just happened? Why did they do that?" I'm incensed.

"To honor the Buddhist belief that all material things are transitory."

Danger! Danger! This is edging far too close to subjects I'm not considering tonight—not ever, but *especially* not tonight.

Will rolls to his side and rises into kneeling position again. He pushes sand into my left side this time and I'm nearly encased. I try wiggling my fingertips and toes underneath the sand to see how trapped I am, and my big toe on my left foot pops through.

Will swats at it. "I said to hold still!"

"Sorry."

He ignores my apology and resumes his task. "I don't know. The mandalas and the sand sculptures—I think part of what makes them so magical and awe-inspiring *is* the fact that they won't last. If they were made of marble and in a permanent museum exhibit, I don't think they'd capture people's attention the same way. You're kind of breathless that they exist and also sad at the same time because the beauty is fleeting and you can't keep it." He shrugs. "It makes you appreciate them more while they're here."

He moves back to my feet and the sand now fills in my clavicle enough to prevent me from lifting my neck to watch his progress, so I'm stuck with my head turned toward the ocean in the distance.

The reckless abandon I felt earlier is gone now, my mood overtaken by his words, the steady slap of waves, and the drowsy weight of the sand. I'm quiet, but far from peaceful. I won't find peace tonight, not after everything that happened earlier or Will's contemplative words now. I'd happily settle for the blissful oblivion of escape he's always offered in the past, but that's not coming either.

The harder I stare into an endless black sea that bleeds into an even more endless black sky, the more I get swallowed up by the atmosphere. The water is emptiness. The sky is emptiness. The shadows are emptiness. And I am small and inconsequential and lost. A hollowness twinges in my belly and I fight to center myself in the sensation of the sand blanketing me or the car horn sounding far behind me, because if that hollowness goes spinning off, I'm scared I might go with it.

And then it does. There are fingers encasing my brain, starting to squeeze, but instead of feeling it in my head, it's in my stomach, where acid bubbles over, and in my chest, where hysteria climbs.

My limbs are slogging through a swamp I am certainly no feral goddess of, as I thrash my head and try in desperation to free myself from the prison of a hundred thousand tiny grains holding me captive. Will appears in my field of vision, his movements also frantic as he shovels sand off me. "It's okay! It's okay—calm down, Decks!"

I finally twist free and scramble up, jumping away from him. "You BURIED ME!" I accuse him.

"You *asked* me to! I didn't know you were claustrophobic!"

"I'm *not* claustrophobic!! I'm— I might be—" But I can't say the word *dying*. I can't ever say the word *dying*, because then it will be out there, in the realm of possibility. "And you—you—BURIED ME!" My finger is an accusation, jabbing through the air at him as I back away. I angrily scrub the sand from my sweater with my other hand.

"Oh shit, I'm—I'm so—" He takes a breath and tries again. "I'm sorry. I was only trying to follow your lead with your big plan for a nighttime 'day' at the beach."

The mania is back, heating my blood, stealing my logic. Because, yes, of course I was the one who ordered him to do it and it's not like my brain went to "bury" at first either. But I don't care. I don't care. My skin is crawling and I'm desperate again.

This isn't working. None of this is working.

Will, frozen in place, is watching me warily, his palms turned up in defeat.

Over his shoulder, a wave crashes ashore and moonlight forms a path to the water, beckoning me, and a new escape plan forms.

"Let's go swimming." I issue the words as a dare, but inside I haven't quite decided if I hope he'll agree or if he'll try to stop me.

Will tries to play them off as a joke, snapping his fingers. "Darn. Too bad there's not another polar bear plunge scheduled until next January."

His deflection firms my resolve. I know what I want now. "I'm not kidding! Our night *needs* this," I insist.

To prove how serious I am, I yank my sweater over my head, then my T-shirt, standing in front of him in my bra. His eyes widen and his Adam's apple bobs as he swallows. I hold his stare as I peel off one leg of my jeans, then the other. I'm hit with a rush of power and I like it. It has a dark edge to it, but it's far from the awful nothingness of a few minutes ago, and that's something.

My hands go to my hips and my head tilts. "Are you afraid of a little cold water, Will?" I coo. "Don't be afraid. Let's not be afraid tonight, okay? Pact?"

I hold my hand out for him to shake, but he ignores it. His face is now full of concern, which I pretend not to notice. I don't want to imagine what this twisty-turny night must look like from his perspective. What *I* must look like.

"I don't think this is responsible, Decker," he says, calm and reasonable.

But I am neither calm nor reasonable. I don't know if he's referring to me stripping down to my underwear or my suggesting a frolic in frigid water, but I don't need clarification because my answer would be the same either way.

"Fuck responsible."

"Decks—" He takes a step toward me, hand outstretched, but I dip to the side and step away from his grasp, cackling. I turn and race across the sand, letting the salty air invade my lungs. My ankles sink deep with each step and I've only gone about thirty feet before I begin to experience hints of the same fatigue from the derby track, happening so much sooner than it did there. I slow slightly, darting a look behind me to see if Will is following—he isn't—but I don't let anything stop me. I hit the flat sand and my legs move more easily now, my breath deepening. And then I'm at the water's edge. I halt and take a single breath before plunging in.

The water is an icicle to my heart, sharp and harsh and unfor-giving.

Yes.

More.

I dip lower, nearly immersed now.

Alive, alive, alive! my brain screams.

A wave takes my feet out from under me, tossing me through a roll, but I scramble for purchase and reemerge in the shallows as the remains of it pull back to sea. I stand, throw my arms wide and toss my neck back, spinning in the surf as I soak up the moon on my face.

I'm shot through with starlight.

Alive, alive, alive!

"Amelia!!" Will calls. He's panicked—I can hear it in his voice and see it in his posture as he jogs to a stop a few feet away, just out of reach of the creeping surf. He holds my belongings in his hands. Dropping my clothes, he opens the blanket in outstretched arms and pleads, "Come out! Please!"

But I only grin at him, feet planted wide, as water swirls around my ankles and droplets of it cluster in salt-clumped chunks of my hair, releasing in streams down my bare shoulders and collecting in the cups of my bra.

A strand of seaweed cuffs my calf as the ocean attempts to lay claim to me. But no one and nothing can own me in this moment. I shake it free and finally move, striding toward Will, strong and sure along the carpet unfurled by a single strip of moonlight.

I am a selkie, trailing luminescence.

Alive, alive, alive!

I walk straight into the blanket and Will closes it around me and steps to my outside, patting me dry with movements as impersonal as any guard at an airline security checkpoint.

No. Not okay with me.

We're alive—*I'm* alive—and there is nothing impersonal about that, and he needs to feel the enormity of it too. I press my ass into his hands, spinning to face him and weaving my fingers into his hair.

I am a siren, gold-throated bargains. Alive.

My intent must be telegraphed on my face because his eyes widen. "Decker, I—"

I rise on tiptoes and press my lips against his. They are heat personified, his breath steamy as I nudge his mouth open with my tongue. For one faltering instant, I wonder if he's going to push me away; I even acknowledge that I'd deserve it for taking, instead of asking.

But then his fingers press into my hips and he drags me closer, a groan escaping his throat.

I am a sea witch, tidal tendrils and tremors.

I smile into his mouth, and curl my fingers deeper into his hair. *Alive, alive, alive.*

His breath winds through me like smoke wisps, the kiss tangling my brain so intently it takes several seconds to register a noise that's out of place among the crashing waves and the swirling wind. The moment I isolate the sound I rip my mouth from Will's, dropping to the sand and tossing my sweater and jeans over my shoulder to reach my coat underneath, then digging through its pockets to locate the ringing.

If it's Telemarket Suzy, so help me I will smash this phone to pieces.

"Hello?" I answer on an exhale, keeping my gaze on Will. His expression is guarded, revealing nothing about his reaction to our interrupted kiss.

"Amelia Linehan?"

The voice isn't familiar and it isn't robotic. It steals my focus instantly. "Yes? This is she. I mean, me."

"Hi. My name is Kendall Spinks, and I'm a transplant coordinator at Mass General." It's so quiet on the beach that her words spill out across the sand and Will's mouth forms an O. Then my attention snaps away from him again, to the woman speaking in my ear.

"I don't want you to get your hopes up too high, because we're calling you in as a backup to a primary recipient who's already been identified, but . . . is there any chance you could get here tonight? Now, I mean?"

She pauses, then speaks pure magic. "We might have a liver for you."

21

EVERYTHING SLIPS. THE SEA WITCH FROM MY SKIN, THE PHONE from my hand.

I am a jellyfish, spineless and limbless.

My cell lands on my crumpled jeans, where I stare at it, willing myself to react, but I can't. Will takes over, swooping it up and introducing himself to the transplant coordinator as a family friend.

"Would it be possible for you to filter things through me temporarily? I think the shock is hitting her," I hear him say, from the other end of a tunnel.

I sink to the ground, sand glomming to my underwear and against the fresh sweat on the backs of my knees.

I am plankton, infinitesimal, assailable.

Will uses his free hand to drape the blanket around me, then tucks the mouthpiece against his shirt. "She wants me to walk you through the risk factors. If the primary recipient can't make it to the hospital in time, or if there are any complications precluding them from accepting the liver, you'll need to have determined whether you want to accept it or not."

I blink myself back into my body. "What?"

"I don't know! She said it's protocol."

This breaks the spell and I snatch the phone from him. "I accept it!"

"I understand," the woman says. "But it's important that we provide some background information on the donor's health history, so you can make an informed decision. Would you prefer to go over this with the surgeon in person, once you get to the hospital and have had a chance to process things a bit more?"

"I—yes. Yes, please."

I hand my phone back to Will and he puts it to his ear, using his own cell to take notes as she goes through a list of instructions with him. In the empty night air, I can hear her speaking clearly as I wrestle my sweater over my neck and tug damp legs into my jeans, but the words are all a series of consonants and vowels without actual meaning. I slog through the sand, following Will to our umbrella, where we pause to scoop up our things, then start for the street. My brain is scrambled. I know the woman said "backup," but . . .

The only thing repeating in my head is, *Could this nightmare possibly be over?*

Will is steadfast and solid and does everything you would want someone to do in the midst of a stressful situation.

He holds the car door and smoothly deposits me inside.

He cranks the heat and aims the vents at me.

He climbs behind the wheel and steers us toward the hospital.

He calls my parents.

Me, I squeeze the sea from my hair. The kiss we shared dissolves alongside the water droplets in my palm. A product of the moment.

That moment is gone.

"Breathe," Will instructs, as he skillfully maneuvers the car through traffic until we're streaking straight up to the emergency entrance of Mass General. When I spot Mom and Dad waiting on the sidewalk, everything about the last time I saw them—everything I overheard—vanishes and I step from the car straight into my mother's arms.

My wet underwear has soaked through the butt of my jeans and left a spot on my car's seat, ringed with sand. I know it's no big deal and that it will dry soon, that the sand can be vacuumed away, but I can't stop staring at it as we linger beside the open door while Will briefs my parents on the coordinator's instructions.

"She said Amelia shouldn't eat anything, so her stomach is empty for the anesthesia," Will says. "She wasn't sure if they'd have a room for you guys or if they'd want to keep Amelia in the waiting area until they knew more about the primary recipient and whether he'd be a viable candidate."

My mother tightens her grip on my back, bundling me against her. "We talked to our doctor on the drive here—they're admitting her so they can get her prepped and ready, just in case."

Just in case.

The words wash over me, bathing me in promise.

A room sounds nice. Warm. Dry. Am I having surgery tonight? Will this whole thing be over by tomorrow? Wait, am I having surgery tonight?

I'm not supposed to be having surgery tonight. *Should we be calling anyone else? Sibby! Sib and I are in a fight. I don't care—she'd want to be here.* I *want her here. No, she's on a train to New York by now. Alex. Did anyone tell Alex?*

Somehow this forms on my lips as "T-rex?" and Mom squeezes me tighter. "He's on standby for the first flight tomorrow. We called Babi too; we told her to wait to hear back before booking hers, but she'll come if . . . when . . . I mean, once we know whether—"

"Okay," I murmur, interrupting her before she's forced to speak the words aloud.

Will holds up the car keys. "Um, do you want me to park while you take her in, Mr. Linehan? I'm happy to bring these up to you after or leave them at the nurses' station. I can even drive the car back to Cambridge for you if that would be better?"

My dad snaps to attention. "Sorry, Will! I wasn't even thinking about the car. No, no, don't be silly. Wait—do *you* need a way home?"

Will shakes his head emphatically. "Don't worry about me; campus is a straight shot on the Orange Line."

Dad's shoulders relax. "Okay then. We're incredibly grateful to you for getting her here so fast."

"Yes, truly," my mom adds.

He shrugs and tucks his hands into his jeans. "No problem."

Poor Will. He thought he was doing a simple favor for his best friend, and look at all the drama he got dragged into. Not just my behavior earlier tonight, but being stuck in the midst of all this too. He looks so uncharacteristically helpless and out of his element that my heart squeezes with sympathy.

When he glances up, I meet his eyes. "Thanks," I whisper.

He stares back and swallows, a rueful smile on his lips.

I want to reassure him that I'm good, that *we're* good. That the kiss on the beach was good, even if it wasn't actually about *him*, not really. Except we don't have a language between us beyond flirty, insubstantial banter and my parents are watching, so I have to leave all that unsaid.

"I know I can text Alex for updates after he gets here tomorrow," he says, his eyes on me. "But if you hear anything in the meantime and you're able to . . ."

He trails off when I nod. I still can hardly allow myself to believe there might be something worth sharing.

"We'll keep you in the loop," Dad promises, accepting the car keys and shaking Will's hand before sliding into the driver's seat. "I'll meet you two inside," he tells Mom and me, and eases the car from the curb.

Mom releases me to give Will a quick hug, and I step close to do the same once she finishes hers.

"Thanks again," I murmur into his neck.

He squeezes back—too tightly—and whispers, "Be okay."

I let Mom steer me toward the double set of automatic doors, and when I turn to wave bye to Will, he's still standing in the same spot, staring off into the distance, lost in thought.

Why does a disease only one person is afflicted by get to affect so many people?

Mass General's campus is enormous, but my regular doctor's appointments are here, in the Pancreas and Biliary Center, and the corridor Mom and I walk to the Blake Building is that same path we always take. The only deviation comes when Mom pushes the elevator button for Blake 6, instead on Blake 4. The label beside it reads "Transplant Center" and seeing the words makes me shiver.

This might really happen.

We're greeted at the nurses' station and ushered to a room. There's a second bed in it, but it's made up tight and there are no signs of anyone's belongings, so I guess for now we have privacy. I sink onto the edge of "my" bed while Mom pokes around at the controls, trying to adjust it to a less reclined position.

Dad slips in just as the nurse is telling me, "I'm going to send someone in to start an IV and draw some blood so we have baseline labs. But that might take just a bit because we're short staffed, so settle on in and get comfy in the meantime, okay?"

"Sure. Thanks."

When she leaves, my mother heads directly to the full-length cabinet, carrying the beat-up duffel bag I use when I crash at Sibby's. She unzips it and begins unpacking my belongings.

"Should we wait until we know if—" Dad begins, but Mom levels him with a look. "Or we could do it now!" he chirps, turning away from her so she can't see the face he makes at me. The laugh I bite back is the first sign of normalcy to creep in since my cell rang.

"When Will said on the phone that you'd been swimming at the beach, I thought he was kidding," Mom calls over her shoulder. I open my mouth to deliver some type of explanation, but she stops me before I can speak. "Never mind, I can't decide if I even want to know. But your hair is soaked and your clothes are damp, and you can't catch a cold right when we need your immune system as strong as possible. Do you feel up to a hot shower?"

"Okay." I'm still shell-shocked and I can't seem to get more than a word or two at a time out.

"I'll take this opportunity to make a coffee run so you can have some privacy," Dad says, but Mom seems reluctant to offer me the same, to even let me out of her sight. She trails me into the bathroom, turns on the water, arranges the folded hospital gown on a narrow shelf above the toilet, and sets out tiny bottles of shampoo and conditioner. She stops just short of helping me out of my clothes.

When I glance up to nod my thanks, it's to find her biting her lip. "I can't believe we got the call," she says, almost reverently.

"I know."

Eventually, she backs out of the bathroom and I finish undressing, inadvertently dumping a small hill of sand that had collected in my clothes.

The longer I stand under the pulsing showerhead, the more the fog clears from my brain. *I might be getting a liver!*

Though with that thought comes a barrage of others I've been keeping firmly at bay. This is major surgery and I have no clue what to expect. I mean, yes, I've thoroughly read the patient education guide Mass General offers everyone expecting a transplant, because my denial has its limits. But the only real image I have of an operating room is what I've seen on TV; I have no idea what to expect in any real kind of way. What if it hurts? I mean, of course it will hurt, but . . . *how much*? What if I can't handle it?

I know my first thought should be gratitude because this is the scenario we all wanted—and that feeling is there too—but I'm suddenly apprehensive about what could come tonight. Or what might not. Because there's a good chance I won't get this liver, and I'll have to find a way to be okay with that too. *Can I?*

I turn the shower off, dry myself, and dress in the hospital gown. Fortunately, it wraps all the way around, kimono-style, as opposed to the ones that flap open in the back.

I'm vigorously towel-drying my hair when Mom calls, "Lia? The surgeon is here, honey. Can you come out?"

We were supposed to be going to an information session with all the transplant doctors next week, so we'd have a chance to meet them ahead of time, put faces to names, and ask any questions we might have. Instead, I open the door to a stranger.

"Hi, Amelia. I'm Dr. Somnath."

Her hand is cool and baby soft, which I guess is something you want in a surgeon, but her eyes are warm and that sets me at ease a little.

"Nice to meet you," she says. "Probably a little surprised to be here tonight, huh?"

Even though the gown itself is discreet, I still wrap my arms around me to draw it tighter as I lean against the bathroom's door frame. "Um, yeah, a little."

Her smile is soothing. "Well, the first thing I want to be clear about is that there *is* a primary recipient designated for this liver." She expands her gaze to include my mother and we both nod.

"I don't mean to sound indelicate," Mom says, "but what is . . . are you allowed to say what that person's situation is? Uh, does it seem likely he will be able to— I'm not sure how to ask this without it seeming like—"

Dr. Somnath cuts her off. "I understand what you're asking. I spoke to his doctor briefly on my way in. The patient has something called hepatocellular carcinoma and—"

"I'm here! I was in line when I got the text that you'd arrived!" Dad says, entering the room out of breath. "The elevator stopped on every single floor between the cafeteria and this one."

Dr. Somnath waves off his apology. "Not a problem. You didn't miss much. I was just starting to tell your wife and daughter about the primary recipient."

My dad crosses the room and shakes the surgeon's hand before moving next to my mom. Both of them lean against the long window-sill that forms a bench of sorts. I slide past Dr. Somnath and perch on the far edge of my bed, tugging my gown around myself as best I can.

"As I was saying," the surgeon resumes, "the primary candidate has a condition called hepatocellular carcinoma."

I know this term. It's essentially a fancy way of saying liver cancer. I'm tested for it sometimes because people with biliary atresia have a greater chance of developing it.

"The concern is that, when they open him up, they'll find metastatic disease."

"Does that mean his body would be likely to reject the liver?" I ask.

"It would mean the cancer spread elsewhere," my mother murmurs.

Dr. Somnath nods. "We may determine it wouldn't be the best use of a recovered liver, in that instance."

The mood in the room is somber, and I'm guessing all of us are reflecting on the poor man on the operating table. I squeeze my eyes in a silent wish that he'll be okay, but there's a small voice that whispers, "If he is, then *you're* not."

I feel evil even forming the words in my head, and it makes me remember what Dad said about the siren passing the hardware store. I swat away the ugliness. I want this liver so badly my stomach aches. It doesn't seem fair that that guy would have to get bad news in order for me to get good.

Not that any of this is fair.

Tears prickle behind my eyelids, but when Dad clears his throat the sound brings me back to the room. I glance over to find his eyes on me, and he mouths, "Are you okay?"

I nod, swallowing thickly, then force my attention back to the doctor.

"There's an equal chance they'll open him up and it won't have metastasized. I don't want to give you any false hope."

"No such thing," my dad whispers. I'm struck by how quietly he speaks. I know it's not an occasion for goofy jokes or anything, but I rarely see my father this subdued, earlier tonight being a definite exception.

"Sorry?" Dr. Somnath asks.

"Oh. It's, uh, just a line from the show *West Wing*." He's clearly embarrassed she heard him, but he nods at me and continues, "This one here has a thing for presidents, so we binged it a couple years back, right, Sunshine?"

"Right."

"Well, now you have me curious," Dr. Somnath says.

Dad concedes. "In one of the later seasons, the presidential hopeful announces his candidacy with a speech that talks about how we might be living in cynical times, but hope is one thing that's not up for debate. He says something along the lines of: there's false science and false promises and false starts, but there is no such thing as false hope. There is only *hope*. Lines from TV shows don't usually stick with me, but that one always has."

"With good reason. It's a keeper." Dr. Somnath touches my knee. "As are you, Amelia. So settle in and we'll see how tonight goes, okay? I'll check in periodically to deliver any updates I get from the OR. Sound good?"

"Sounds good." I muster a smile.

My mother chimes in from her spot by the window. "Is there anything special we should be doing?"

"Nope," the doctor says. "Things will pick up pretty dramatically if it does look likely we'll be operating tonight. A nurse will be in shortly to place an IV and draw blood. Meantime, no food or drink for our patient here—we'll need her stomach empty. And otherwise, just . . . wait. I'll be back once I have any news."

Once the doctor leaves, Mom busies herself retrieving my things from the bathroom and returns holding my damp jeans. "Okay, I think I want to know now—what earthly reason would you have to go swimming in the ocean in *April*?"

Fortunately for me, a nurse comes in just then and saves me from answering (as if I could ever find a rational explanation). He suggests distracting myself with TV while he inserts the IV and seems perfectly content to hang out making small talk with us afterward. Once he does leave, I turn up the volume on a rerun of *Friends* and pray my mother doesn't resume her line of questioning. Fortunately, she merely scoots my feet aside to claim space at the bottom of my bed, while Dad takes the chair on my other side.

We watch and we wait. One episode. Two.

Alex keeps calling in for updates until we finally just put him on speakerphone so he can listen to the TV with us.

Dr. Somnath pops in after about an hour and a half to say the liver safely arrived on-site and that it looks "beautiful." I've seen enough pictures of organs in Anatomy to know that's not an adjective I would ever attach to one, but honestly, I don't care if it *looks* beautiful, so long as it *works* beautifully. Inside me.

We wait more.

There is literally nothing more passive than waiting, and yet somehow, it's utterly *exhausting*.

Around one in the morning, near the middle of our fifth episode, Dr. Somnath returns and the air rushes out of the room.

"I have some news," she says.

22

I KNOW BEFORE THE SURGEON SAYS ONE WORD WHAT SHE'S going to tell us: I'm not getting a liver tonight. Her face is blank, but the slump in her shoulders clues me in and her exhale when she reaches my bedside seals the deal.

"I'm afraid it's not the news you've been waiting for and I hate to be the bearer of it, but it looks like it's not going to happen tonight. I'm going to have to send you home without this liver. I'm so sorry."

If I'd been frustrated before tonight about all the different things I've been trying lately, pinning my hopes on each as a way to possibly make me feel better only to have them dashed one by one, this is the ultimate deflation.

I try to cover, shaking my head more aggressively than I mean to. "No—I—it's good. I'm glad that man's cancer hadn't spread. That's—great. Really great."

My mother turns and takes my hand, squeezing hard. "My brave girl," she whispers, and I have to tamp down my scoff.

I may have challenged Sibby on her definition of bravery, but even I know there is nothing brave about doing, well, nothing. All I did was sit here and wait. Which is what I'll have to do much more of for the foreseeable future. A sigh slips out and I'm instantly guilty. A man got a new liver tonight because of someone else's generosity. That's a beautiful thing, even if it's not happening to me, right?

Right?

"But this should mean you're at the very top of the list for the next one, Li," Alex offers, his voice echoing through the phone speakers.

I turn to Dr. Somnath. "That's my brother, Alex."

My eyes ask, *Are you going to tell him or should I?*

"Hi, Alex," she says, her gaze on me, acknowledging. "It's possible, of course, but it's not *probable*. If I can explain the distinction: the matching system UNOS—the United Network for Organ Sharing—uses is a bit more fluid than that. Priority is given to patients with the most urgent need, which means that, honestly, it's a little unusual Amelia was called tonight, given how asymptomatic she still is and what her MELD scores are."

I refrain from telling her about my fatigue during derby practice and crossing the sand tonight, because I know that's nothing compared to the severity of symptoms she probably means.

"How *did* she, then?" my mother asks. Her posture is slumped and I swear there are dark circles under her eyes that weren't visible an hour ago. I flash back on the wonder in her voice earlier, before my shower, when she said, "I can't believe we got the call." Her voice is flat now, devoid of inflection.

"Well, here's where Amelia's blood type of ABO B works in her favor. It's the most unique," Dr. Somnath says.

That's a kinder way of saying "rarest." She makes it sounds as if I'm some special unicorn, when really everything would be so much easier if I was AB D, the universal recipient type. Then my body could accept literally *any* liver.

"Okay, not to be crass," Alex says. He sounds so close but feels so far away. "But wouldn't having fewer recipients on 'the list' who are ABO B essentially mean she's got less competition for the ones matching that type that become available?"

"It can, in that respect." She glances at my parents, and softens her voice when she says, "The downside is that there are fewer ABO B donors overall. Sometimes we'll get a bunch in quick succession and other times it can be . . . somewhat longer between them."

Longer than I have?

The question burns in my throat, but I shove it away and focus instead on my father's hand, clammy in mine.

"The point is, there's no real way to know when the call will come," the surgeon says.

Which is exactly what Dr. Wah told us too.

"Essentially, all this means is that we're back to waiting and hoping." She pauses, then adds, "But not falsely," offering a small smile to my father, which is grimly returned.

"For now, we'll work to get you out of here so you can catch some rest tonight," Dr. Somnath says. "However, it'll be just a bit longer while we get all the paperwork done for your discharge. Someone will be in to remove your IV shortly and I hope the next time I see you the circumstances are much happier, Amelia. I'm sorry again."

We all thank her and she departs. Even though we were told we wouldn't be leaving imminently, no one makes a move to unmute the TV.

"I guess I should try to get a couple hours' sleep before I have to leave for the airport," Alex finally says.

"No!" I surprise everyone—myself included—with the force of my protest. I take a breath. "There's no reason to fly here now."

If Alex comes home, he'll only try to tease me out into the light, and now that the events of tonight are starting to sink in, I am being dragged under the darkness again. I'm so tired of fighting it. I want to be left alone to let it swallow me up.

"You should save your frequent flyer miles for a visit later, when everyone's had some time to recover," I say. "Right, Dad?"

My father hesitates, silently conferencing with my mother, so I go directly to the source again. "Please, Alex? What if you came next weekend instead, or the one after that? I'm not sure I want to be around people right now."

"People?" Alex asks, clearly hurt that I'd lump him in with the masses.

Dammit. I hadn't intended it like that. I am not fit for humaning right now, that much is obvious, and it's exactly why I don't want him here, in my face. "You know what I mean."

He sighs and Dad says, "Up to you, Alex."

"It sounds more like it's up to Amelia, but if that's what you want, Lia . . ."

"Thanks, T," I whisper.

Dad takes the phone into the hallway to continue talking to my brother and to call Babi. Mom slumps lower in her chair but jumps up five seconds later. She charges to the armoire, where she begins yanking my clothes out. At first, she folds them neatly, but soon her movements become haphazard as she abandons that and stuffs them into my duffel instead. Her back is to me, but the way she jerks her wrist across her cheeks several times during the process is telling.

My father returns just as the zipper snags when she tries to close it and she lets a loud curse fly. I exchange looks with him as he crosses the room to wrap his arms around her from behind. He tucks his chin into her neck and whispers something, his back sagging, while I cast about for the right thing to say or do.

Me. I caused this. Everyone is hurting and it's all because of me. The guilt stabs my heart.

I can tell my mom is fighting to contain her tears, probably for my benefit, and I don't know how much I can take of this. Yes, I watched her cry plenty the other night in the back seat of her car, but that wasn't over anything personal. This is entirely different. These muffled sobs sound ripped from her gut, the same place where I currently have an empty yawning pit.

23 ~

IT'S ALMOST FOUR IN THE MORNING WHEN I SHUFFLE INTO MY
room and fall face-first on my bed. I use my heels to nudge off my
ballet flats. It takes Herculean effort to push up again long enough to
move my covers aside and crawl underneath them. Pressing my face
into my pillow, I pray for the nothingness of sleep.

It doesn't work.

The second my eyes close, the panic returns. I try to shove it
away, but now my every fiber is shouting.

You wanted that liver.

Don't be selfish. It wasn't yours to have.

But you wanted that liver.

I don't think I even realized *how* badly I did, until Dr. Somnath said "It's not going to happen tonight."

But what if "not tonight" is "not any night"?

I scream inside my head to try to drown out the doubts: *FEAR IS NOT THE BOSS OF ME!*

But the what-if is a splinter, ripping through every protective layer I have and burrowing, hard and sharp, into the base of my spine.

I try to soak the splinter in guilt, to loosen it. *You should be happy for the person who had his dreams answered tonight. He deserves to live every bit as much as you do. Maybe more. Maybe he feeds the homeless or volunteers for a suicide prevention hotline. Maybe he doesn't do either of those things. Maybe he's no one special but is simply a really decent person. Or not. He still has every right to it.*

My pep talk isn't working. The fear creeps along my vertebrae, spreading its poison. It's in my bloodstream now.

"Mom! Dad!" I shout, before I'm even fully aware of the words in my throat.

My mother charges in seconds later. She flips the light on and darts wild eyes around my room. "What? Amelia, what happened?"

I press my lips together tight and shake my head, because I won't be able to answer her without crying. Her response is to exhale and sink onto my bed.

"Oh, baby." There's raw emotion in her voice. "I wanted it too."

My dad appears in the doorway and Mom waves him off. "We're okay. Switch the light off, though, please?"

She stands again and pulls back my covers before nudging my

leg to signal I should make room for her. Then she climbs in beside me. Our knees fit against one another's and we lie face-to-face on my pillow.

The sharp tang of fear retreats to the base of my spine and curls up in a ball, not altogether gone, but no longer taunting me either. I close my eyes as her hand rubs gentle circles on my hip. I feel about five years old . . . and it's enough for now.

For a long time neither of us says anything, at least not with our voices.

Then my mother breaks the silence. "I'm so sorry I couldn't keep it together better for you tonight."

I suck in a breath and keep my eyes screwed tightly closed, so I don't have to see what's in hers. "Mom, I'm not one of your clients."

Her fingers gently untangle strands of my hair. "Which makes it even more important. You're my child and I'm the grown-up; I'm supposed to have the answers and I'm supposed to be strong for you. I believe it's item number one in the job description of a parent."

Her voice wavers on the last bit and I burrow into her shoulder and let her arms curl around me.

We stay like that for several minutes and then I whisper, "I think maybe *this* is item number one."

She doesn't respond, but her arms tighten. We cling to each other, the steady *click* of my flip clock keeping us company, and eventually my eyelids grow heavy. The sun will be up soon and tonight has been endless. Having her hold me is keeping the panic at bay enough that sleep seems possible. Not just possible, but inevitable.

Mom kisses my temple. "Go to sleep, sweetness," she says, before setting her head back on the pillow next to mine. We're both quiet as our breathing slows and evens out.

I'm on the very edge of sleep when I whisper, "Someone died tonight. Whoever's liver that was to begin with."

I open my eyes to peek at her as she brushes my hair from my face with her fingertips. Even after my shower, I can still smell traces of salt water on the strands, mingling with her vanilla lotion.

"Yeah, baby. Someone did," she murmurs. Her fingers capture a small chunk to add to the wisps in her hand and she tugs gently. Our private "I love you." "And someone else was saved."

"Bittersweet," I whisper, my eyelids fluttering closed again.

"Bittersweet," she agrees, the last thing I hear before drifting off.

Words With Friends notification:

You have not signed into your account for four days.

24

TO DESCRIBE THE LAST FEW DAYS AS CRAPPY WOULD BE LIKE saying the *Titanic* hit a minor snag on its maiden voyage.

Easter's never been a huge holiday in our house—we're not all that religious—but this year I slept through it entirely. While thousands of marathon runners were #BostonStrong on Monday's Patriots' Day, pounding the pavement just across the river from me, I stayed under my covers, waking here and there when Dad delivered food on trays, like he used to when I had the flu as a little kid.

I mostly leave my phone across the room. Sibby's in New York, probably still pissed off about our fight and definitely clueless about what happened back here, and I don't need to see any Instagram pictures of my classmates living it up on their own vacations. After the other night, Will definitely can't provide an escape for me anymore, though he did text me to say he was thinking about me and hoped I'd reach out whenever I felt up to it. Alex can get his updates from my parents.

But what is there to update? That my bloodwork at the hospital led to my being assigned a new MELD score of twenty-seven? (Twenty-*seven*. Three away from "needs a liver within weeks" and possible moves to faraway states.) That when I went to the bathroom yesterday I could have sworn the whites of my eyes had a tinge of yellow to them? That I've taken to peeing in the dark ever since and pretending to be asleep when my parents enter my room so they won't notice?

That I don't want to talk to anyone or do anything.

My disappointment over the missed liver is a cobra in a basket and at random intervals the lid gets knocked off and the snake uncoils and strikes.

All the negative thoughts I've tried to keep at bay since that day at the derby arena join forces and overpower the floodgate in my brain.

I'm Dorothy trapped inside the tornado as my world spins around me, only I don't know if the place I'll land at the end of all this will be anything like Oz. It could be better. Or worse. It could be blank nothingness.

I'm terrified.

It's Tuesday afternoon when my phone rings, probably the only thing besides bathroom trips that could get me out of bed. I'm not harboring much hope of hearing from the hospital again so quickly, but my heart trips when the caller ID displays a number I don't recognize.

It takes me three swipes to get the screen to respond because my thumb is instantly damp with sweat.

Calm down—it's probably another robocall.

"Hello?"

"Amelia?"

"I— Yes?"

Okay, she sounds like an actual person, but that doesn't mean—

"Hi! This is Claire Layzell, from the Cambridge Arts Commission. I sit on the committee that awarded you the grant for the mural?"

My breath whooshes out and then catches again as I simultaneously process that this isn't a "We have a liver for you!" call, but in fact is probably about to be a call*out.* I haven't touched the mural in six days now. I'd made good progress in the early part of last week, but once Thursday hit, that was that.

I scrub my T-shirt across a day and a half's worth of fuzz on my tongue. "Oh! Yes, hi. How are you?" I'm trying to sound professional, or at least halfway normal, but my voice is froggy from underuse.

"We-*ll*," she says, giving the word two syllables in a way that reinforces something is wrong. Usually this would cause my stomach to sink, but my reaction instead is surprisingly *meh.*

"I'm calling because I wanted to check in with you on your progress. I'm standing in front of your mural as we speak," she says.

The contract I signed with the arts commission stipulated that all work had to be done prior to May fourth since the restaurant is slated to have its soft opening the following week. It's now the middle of April, but I hadn't been feeling particularly stressed about the deadline, especially because I knew I'd have this whole week off from school to work long hours on it. Except the thought of dragging myself out of bed and into the real world now . . .

The place in the core of my belly that usually bubbles up with eagerness whenever I contemplate getting my hands on that wall gurgles once, and disappears in a black hole of apathy. Who cares about a ridiculous mural? What's the point? Besides, Sibby was right—it's just a generic design anyone could do; it doesn't have to be me.

Just like that, biliary atresia claims another part of me and I know I'm possibly being melodramatic, but I don't care. I don't care about *anything*. I don't even recognize myself.

I've been quiet on my end of the phone and Claire clears her throat. "So, maybe you could fill me in on where things stand? I ride by it every day on my route to work and was really excited about what I saw taking shape. When progress halted, it gave me pause. If you're struggling with some aspect and I can be of any help, well, that's the reason for my check-in."

Her tone is coddling, like I'm some temperamental artist wrapped up in my creative genius and needing a dose of reality. Ha! I never *used* to be temperamental—I was exactly what Coach wrote in my college recommendation letters: hard-charging and enthusiastic. In the good ways. But that Amelia isn't here right now. That Amelia has all the doses of reality she can handle and then some. That Amelia would never have even *contemplated* uttering the words that form instantly on my tongue.

The ones I now speak. "I'm sorry, but I have to quit."

I don't know which one of us is more surprised. There's a small gasp on the other end and then . . . silence. I wait, scanning my emotions for the relief I thought would come from unburdening myself of this added pressure, which I really don't need to be dealing with at the moment. Instead, I'm wooden.

Claire recovers before I do. "Can you please tell me why that is?"

"Um, I'm just having a really hard time making it work with my schedule," I tell her. I keep my tone breezy; I don't need any pity on top of her reproach. "I'm sorry," I add once more.

"No, *I'm* the one who's sorry." Claire's upbeat manner is gone, replaced by something much snippier. "I didn't share this when I called to award you the grant, but the committee was very hesitant to give this project to someone so young. They were concerned that you'd ditch it when you got caught up in the other hoopla that comes with graduating high school. But I went to bat for you! I thought your application essay spoke to your maturity and I called them on their bias. You're putting me in a difficult spot here."

"I really am sorry." Even a week ago, her words would have fired me up. Right now, though, the most my brain musters is a small internal outcry over the indignity of leaving her to believe that all teenagers *are* flakes.

I'm *not* a flake! I'm dying!

The echo of those two words bounces against my brain, stopping my breath.

I'm dying.

I'm *dying*.

Two months ago, that sentence would have sounded as far-fetched as believing that my mother would start a diet or that a guy I hadn't seen in years would ring my doorbell out of the blue or that I'd go night swimming in the ocean in April. But all those things happened.

And so might this.

Oh my god, so might this. The knowledge settles in my spine. I could die.

My score is twenty-seven and if it reaches thirty, the need for a transplant becomes urgent. Meaning I could die *soon*.

Like, actually . . . die.

Dead.

Gone.

Forever.

It's such a bizarre and abstract thing to try to get my head around and yet I can't deny it anymore. It could happen.

The room spins and I sit hard on the end of my bed. I exhale, aware that Claire is still on the other end of the phone line, possibly waiting to see if I'll add any further explanation. Well, maybe I will. If I've already gone entirely against character by quitting the mural, I might as well go the distance and concede defeat. What do I have to lose at this point?

"You don't have to be embarrassed when you talk to them." My voice is hollow. "Just tell them I'm not wrapped up in any graduation hoopla, and that it's not a prom dress I'm in the market for—it's a liver."

"I'm sorry, I don't? I'm not following."

I screw my eyes shut and speak the words, as much for me as for her, letting myself taste them on my still-fuzzy tongue for the first time. "I have a serious liver condition and things aren't looking great for me at the moment. I need a transplant soon or else . . . I could die."

Her inhale is sharp. A beat passes before she speaks. "I—oh. Um, wow, I—had no idea. I don't even know what to say here. You—"

I cut her off. "I didn't know my circumstances myself until after I'd already accepted the commission. I should have updated you on my diagnosis."

"Oh, Amelia, my heart is breaking. I'm so sorry. Please don't give one more second's thought to the mural. We'll contact the runner-up and see if he—well, it doesn't even matter where we go from here, that isn't anything you need to worry about. I—is there anything I can do to help you?" She's a totally different person than she was five minutes ago.

My mood is so black I'm tempted to snap, "Not unless you happen to have a type ABO B liver you're not in need of," but of course I don't. It's not this woman's fault she happened to be stuck on the phone with me the first time I allowed myself to truly acknowledge what my fate might be.

Instead I thank her for her understanding and stumble over yet another apology, before disconnecting the call. I stare at the phone in my hand for a long time, in disbelief that I did the thing I swore I wouldn't do: I used my disease as an excuse, for sympathy.

I just surrendered to being Dying Girl.

It's not just my liver that's being overtaken by scar tissue; it's all of me.

25

MY CURTAINS SNAP OPEN AND I SQUINT MY EYES AGAINST THE harsh glare.

"Sweetie, it's *Thursday afternoon*," my mother says, wielding a can of Febreze. "You have to get up at some point."

I roll to my other side, bringing my iPad with me and readjusting my pillow. "I'm tired."

"You probably have a vitamin D deficiency at this point! This isn't healthy, Amelia." She sighs and perches on the end of my bed. "What if you just spent a couple hours on the patio? Bring your laptop and finish whatever you're watching out there. That's not asking a lot, is it? To get me off your case?"

It might be, but the worry is etched deep in her face, so I change into a fresh T-shirt and shorts and drag myself into a patch of sunlight in our backyard. The patio is covered in ants, so I settle in the grass and prop my iPad against one of the many sundials that my grandfather collected, which litter the yard.

I only have a few scattered memories of Gramps, but I do distinctly remember wandering around out here by his side when I was little and him teaching me about gnomons and styles and why his sundials with straight hour marks told time differently than his ones with curved ones (it has to do with the fact that the sundial's face is a perfect circle but the Earth's orbit changes throughout the year from circular to elliptical).

Back then, I was more interested in Disney princesses than scientific principles, but I did love the funny little sayings etched into the stone or metal of the dials. For example, the sundial next to the back door reads *Let others tell of storms and showers, I tell of sunny morning hours*. That one's in English, but most of the others are written in Latin and I've long since forgotten Gramps's translations.

Sundial mottos usually reference time in some way. The one holding my iPad at the moment reads: *ultima latet ut observentur omnes.*

Omnes like *omni*, probably. Something about *all*, or maybe *always*? I open a translator app on my phone and type in the phrase. As soon as I see the words in English, I wish I hadn't.

Our last hour is hidden from us, so that we watch them all.

I can't appreciate any "seize the day" sentiments when my last hour doesn't feel so hidden at all. More like it's dancing right in front of me taunting: *Nanny nanny boo boo, I'm gonna get you.*

Crap. Coming out here was supposed to let me dip a toe back

into the world. Vacation week is nearly over and I have my regular appointment with Dr. Wah tomorrow, where I'm sure she'll tell me how much worse my MELD score is, even if the yellow I thought I saw in my pupils the other day was either a trick of the light or has gotten better since. I know I'll have to be back in school on Monday, given how alarmed my parents are growing about my total withdrawal from everything and everyone. Yet I can't imagine mustering the strength to wander past our property line.

And *this* is exactly why. There are hidden minefields everywhere. I thought the backyard would be safe, and still the shadow of death found me within five seconds.

"Excuse me, do you have the time?"

It's a joke Dad makes at least once every time we're out here, surrounded by Gramps's collection, but I hadn't heard or seen him approach so I jump sky-high. My elbow sends my iPad toppling into the grass.

"*Dad!* You shouldn't sneak up on people—you scared me to death!"

He winces at my word choice, and there's the shadow, peeking out again. If anyone ever wanted to be hyperalert to just how many of our offhand sayings are morbid, they should try getting diagnosed with a terminal condition. *I'm dying to know. Stop, you're killing me. I'll just die if I can't get tickets. How can you drive this death trap? I'm so hungry, I could murder this pizza. I wouldn't be caught dead wearing that. I'm going in for the kill. It's your funeral. Over my dead body. Knock 'em dead!*

"Sorry, Sunshine. I didn't realize you were lost in thought."

I focus my attention on untangling my headphone wires and avoid his eyes. "I'm not. Mom's on my case about getting fresh air, so I'm continuing my binge out here."

"Netflix and chill? Can I join you?"

I choke. "Um, Dad, that definitely does not mean what you think it means."

"It doesn't mean 'hang out and watch consecutive episodes of a show'?"

"Er, no."

"Oh. See, what would I do without you keeping me on fleck?"

"On *fleek*, Dad, but a. never say that again, and b. you don't need me; you need urbandictionary.com."

"I need *you*, Sunshine," he says quietly.

Peekaboo, taunts the shadow.

I swallow and try to compose a response, but before I can formulate anything he's plopped down next to me and crossed his legs. "So . . . what are we watching?"

"*Project Runway*, but—"

"Sounds good." He reaches past me and unplugs my headphones, then hits Play.

He's not out here to watch a show with me, I'm sure of it. My guard goes up, but when five minutes go by and he doesn't attempt to initiate any conversations, I relax a little and settle onto my stomach.

We finish the last few minutes of my current episode and begin another.

Aside from the fall of tenth grade when we watched every season of *West Wing* together, my father adheres mainly to a TV diet of sports, CNN, and home renovation shows, so I'm having a hard time believing he could be into catwalks and catfights. But, to his credit, he does seem to be paying close attention and I have to confess it's kind of nice to *just be* with someone after my forced isolation this week.

When the credits roll, I ask, "How much would someone have to pay you to wear an avant-garde jacket made from the contents of a Jersey City storage unit out in public?"

I slide a quick look at him and note the smile poking at the corners of his mouth. "I don't know," he says, "although I kind of dig the cape the nonbinary contestant created. The way they repurposed that carpeted toilet seat cover was pretty genius. But the tattoo artist? C'mon. She's clearly only getting through these rounds because the producers need someone in the sewing room to stir up the drama."

"Totally. The judges aren't even being subtle about it."

The countdown to the next episode begins and I settle back into place, but he pushes the pause button. Warning bells clang again. I *knew* he had an ulterior motive for being out here.

"So . . . ," he says, with a breathiness that holds his nerves in it. The fact that my *dad* is nervous is hard to reconcile with the version of him I carry around in my heart—this all-powerful superhero who would kiss my boo-boos and make them better, and toss me over his head in the community pool, masterfully swat any creepy crawling thing that made their way into my bedroom at night, and use his bike to chase down cars so he could offer a salty-worded lecture to whoever just drove around the flashing lights of my stopped school bus.

"Mom and I have been trying to give you space, but we're worried."

I knew this already. They've both tiptoed around me this week. Neither has tried to "wake" me when they've checked in, though I'm sure they could tell I wasn't really asleep. There's been no mention of my previous—reluctant—agreement that April vacation would be our deadline for contacting Amherst's admissions department to ask about options for the fall. They haven't forced me to join them for any meals.

But Mom's pleas for me to get fresh air today held more than a whiff of desperation and I was half expecting this "big talk," just not the person delivering it.

"So you drew the short straw?"

"Hey!" Dad says. "I may be a little . . . emotionally challenged, but I can handle a chat with my daughter without being forced into it. We didn't draw straws—and I resent the accusation!"

I don't point out that he just sat through an hour plus of sewing challenges to avoid starting this "chat."

"So rock, paper, scissors then?" I ask.

He sighs. "She *always* plays scissors! Why would she pick *today* to play paper?"

In spite of my own nerves, I laugh, sitting up and tucking a leg under me. "I hate to break it to you, Dad, but you're not emotionally challenged. You're actually super-embarrassing about your, um, I think the right word could only be *effusive* shows of affection. Remember when I had exactly one line in *Once Upon a Mattress* in fifth grade and you stopped the whole play after I delivered it with your very embarrassing standing ovation?"

We both smile at the memory, then I force myself to be serious because it's suddenly really important to me that he really, truly believes I don't see him as some emotionless robot just because we don't indulge in daily heart-to-hearts. "Dad, I always know you do, okay? Love me, I mean."

He smiles and bumps my knee with his. "Thanks, Sunshine. That means a lot to me. Except that's not what I'm referring to. I think our family is pretty decent about showing our love, in our own goofy ways, but we don't really *talk* about stuff so well. Especially the, well, the darker stuff. And I didn't want you to interpret my avoiding that as some kind of indication that I'm not here for you during all of this."

"I don't," I whisper around a lump in my throat that appears.

"Good," he says. Then, more quietly, "So, how *are* you? Honestly."

My pulse races because it feels dangerous to continue this conversation, not because I don't expect him to be supportive, but more because it feels like there's no going back from here. Like somehow, having an open discussion about this stuff, the way two grown-ups would, is this line in the sand that would mark the exact moment I stop being his little girl. I don't know if I'm ready for that. I know how to be his Sunshine. I don't know how to navigate "two mature people having an adult conversation" with him yet.

But I'm eighteen years old; I'm *not* a little girl, no matter how much of a baby I feel like these days. And I can't be alone with all these thoughts anymore—I just can't. I'll break. So I bury the edgy jitters and confess to him: "I'm upside down."

My dad grimaces. "Yeah, I can see that. I might need more to go on, though, sweets."

I sigh. "It just seems like everything I believed in was wrong and backward. I thought I'd figured all this important stuff out about myself and what I cared about and what I wanted to use my time and energy fighting for and I was feeling really confident about who I was as a person before all this. But now . . ." I sigh. "But now this happened and it—it pulled the rug out from under me. Not only because of all the medical stuff and the uncertainty about . . . you know."

He nods. "Yeah."

"But also about who I am as a person, ya know?"

"That's easy, though. You're my Sunshine, best daughter a guy could ask for."

I smirk and award him a small smile. He doesn't disappoint, my father. "Thanks, Daddy, but that's not what I meant."

"Gimme an example, then."

I sigh, then tell him about Sibby's accusation that I am full of bravado but not bravery.

I've missed Sibby something fierce this week; as out of it as I've been, a small part of me has been keeping tabs on how many days until she comes back from New York (two more, at the moment). I'm still upset about our fight, but so much has happened since then and I don't even know which parts of my anger about the way things went down with us is directed at Sibby versus at me versus at this fucking disease that's ruining my life—literally. It's all a jumble. What I do know is that we won't be angry at the other forever, especially since I might not *have* forever.

But Sibby challenged me on the one thing I most needed right now: my identity.

As frustrating and impossible as it's been to try to get everyone else to see me as anything but Dying Girl, at least *I* was able to see myself as fierce and confident and kickass.

And now I'm doubting all of that.

Which hurts.

I try to hold my tears in, but a couple slide down the crease of my nose. I swipe them away when they reach my lip, and my dad shakes his head, moves my iPad to the side, and pulls me in for a hug. He's wearing one of his many T-shirts advertising the hardware store, and this one's been washed so many times that nestling against it is like nosing into a burrow of bunnies. He smells like Bounce fabric softener and *Dad*.

There was a time a hug from my father could make the whole world safe and friendly again. I'm too old now to accept intellectually that he has this power, but a part of me still believes, and as he holds me close my few remaining tears air dry on my cheeks.

"Does Sibby need me to drop-kick her all the way back Down Under?" my father mutters into my hair.

I muster a smile and turn my head so I'm not speaking into his shoulder. "Nah. She's so tiny, I'm pretty sure I could handle it myself if I wanted to." I pause. "But I don't. I just want to know whether she was right."

My father releases me from his embrace and considers me for a few beats. "You want me to answer that?"

I nod, bracing for the truth. Dad likes to joke around, but he'll always be brutally honest with you if you ask for it.

What I'm *not* expecting is for him to begin with, "Did you ever wonder—"

I cut him off with a groan. "Hey, I'm kind of having an existential crisis here, so I'm not sure I care what hair color they put on the drivers' licenses of bald men."

"Ha! That's one of my favorites." He flicks my arm. "But if you'd let me *finish*, I was going to ask if you'd ever wondered why I like 'Did you ever wonder' questions so much."

"I figured it was because you love being cheesy and making us roll our eyes at you."

"Well, yeah," he agrees, "that's a definite plus. Your mom's world-weary sighs are seriously cute. But the real reason I like them is because they point out how little sense we humans make. And how contradictory we can be."

He takes a breath and adds, "Mostly, I love that they force people to answer with the greatest three words in the English language."

I squint at him. "I love you?"

He scoffs. "Meh. Those are *okay*, I guess. But I prefer mine." He ticks them off on his fingers: "I. Don't. Know."

"Seriously? What is remotely great about being clueless?"

He smiles. "Nothing. But if you're the curious type, the not knowing is going to make you want to find answers. And if you have curiosity, you have everything: 1. It's nearly impossible for you to be bored. 2. You'll be a lifelong learner. 3. You'll probably be a traveler. 4. You'll definitely be an empathetic person, because you'll want to learn people's stories and what makes them tick. So bravery/bravado?

To me it doesn't matter. I don't care *what* other qualities someone has, because curiosity's the critical one."

Oh.

Do I *have it? I'd say I do, but maybe there's some nuance or distinction that I don't grasp and need someone else to point out. Like, I might think I'm curious but really I'm . . . I don't know,* thoughtful *or—or something close but no cigar.*

Dad hears my unspoken question and smiles. "The thing that makes me most proud of you—and the reason I've never, ever worried about who you would turn out to be as a person—is that you have curiosity in spades, Sunshine. You jump into every new interest with two feet—literally, in the case of derby. But you did the same with your art. And, though my ears have only just stopped bleeding, the ukulele. Heck, it's because of you I retain the unsettling mental image of Calvin Coolidge's morning ritual of having his head rubbed with Vaseline *and* of John Quincy Adams's daily skinny-dips in the Potomac. I want you to see the incredible person I do when I look at you. If you did, you wouldn't doubt your identity, I promise you that."

Something warm and peaceful settles in my abdomen, like an unexpected hug or reggae music. Like a gulp of oatmeal spreading across my rib cage, sticky and sweet.

"Thanks, Daddy," I whisper.

I like the girl he described better than any other version of me I've tried on. I think I could get very comfortable inhabiting Curious Amelia; she feels like the best aspects of all the others combined. She feels like *me*.

But then my eyes fall on Gramps's sundial and my confidence whooshes away. Because the one thing I've been fighting off any curiosity about, any consideration of at all, is death. Specifically, *my* possible death.

Even if I did let the possibility of it settle around me as I spoke to the arts commission woman earlier this week, I still haven't let myself explore what that *means* for me. What I think about it or feel about it. I mean, other than that it sucks, which is a given. I've refused to let myself wonder what might happen afterward or what it would feel like to have to say goodbye to everyone I love or how much it might hurt physically to have my liver fail and how fast things will spiral after that.

Am I ready to stare any of that in the face now?

I don't know.

I don't know.

Dad's favorite words.

The one thing I have to admit is that nothing else I've tried has worked. If the last few weeks haven't shown me that, I don't know what could. But it still feels too dangerous; there's too *much* unknown. The questions are too *big* and potentially unanswerable, and then what am I left with?

Dad has begun aimlessly pulling weeds within his reach, clearly picking up on the fact that I'm working through some big stuff in my head. But now he says, "I gotta tell you, I certainly never expected to be having a conversation like *this* with my kid. God, when you're young and innocent and caught up in baby fever and considering trying for one, you don't know what you don't know. *If* you even bother to think about those babies one day turning into teenagers, you *might* imagine having the sex talk or the 'don't do drugs' talk, but this stuff? Never ever."

"Yeah, but if you *had* imagined it, would Alex and I still be here?" I keep my tone light, when what I really want to know is, *If you'd known you might lose your daughter at eighteen, would you still have had me?*

"From this vantage point, knowing you and your brother as two amazing people who've made my life about a million times richer? No brainer. As that nervous twenty-five-year-old who wasn't sure he could hack a diaper change and was more interested in biking the Minuteman Trail on the weekends than pushing a stroller? Am I a terrible person if I say . . . maybe?"

I smile. "Yes."

He's trying to turn the conversation light and part of me appreciates that, but another part hates that he didn't *really* answer my question.

Maybe because you didn't really *ask it, Lia.*

"Don't worry, I have zero regrets about you and Alex or any other decision I've made," Dad continues, laughing, oblivious to my inner turmoil this time.

"Really?" This surprises me—he's forty-three, so I don't see how that could be possible.

"Nope. Not a thing I would have done differently."

The question lingers in the air in front of me. I know I need to grasp it; need to ask.

"But what if—" I drop my eyes and whisper, "If things go bad from here . . . would you—would you regret it then?"

Would you regret me?

His sigh is shuddering and harsh, and he shakes his head so hard it could almost be described as violently. "Never. *Never.* Not for a second."

He pulls me against him roughly and my throat closes up so tight with emotion I can barely breathe.

"Don't you ever think that, even for one tiny instant!" he orders.

I burrow into his shirt, struggling to keep it together.

"There's only one thing I'd regret then, because there's only one thing I want for you."

"A liver. I know," I murmur.

His laugh is biting. "I'm pathetic. Yes, that, of *course.* But that wasn't what I was thinking of. Two things, then."

I hold my breath, almost afraid for his next words. What does my father want for me?

"You know earlier, when you asked me if I remembered when I clapped so loud and long at your school play?" he whispers, stroking my hair.

I nod into his shoulder and he continues. "That's what I want for you, Sunshine. More 'remember-whens.' I want you to have a whole lifetime of remember-whens."

I'm too choked up to answer, and I'm grateful when he simply holds me quietly. After a minute or two he says, "I love you like fireworks, Sunshine."

He's been saying this to Alex and me since we were little. It stretches back to the first time my parents took us to the Fourth of July fireworks on the Esplanade. I was only a toddler, so I don't remember it, but as Dad tells it he had me up on his shoulders as the fireworks burst and I put my arms out wide and yelled, "It's just like how love feels!"

Even though I've heard the expression from Dad a million times, it's never hit me with the force it does now. I lean my forehead into his chest. "I know, Daddy. Same."

He collects his breath in his lungs and it's shaky when he exhales.

We sit like this for a few more minutes before he says, "I guess I should go start dinner before Mom sends a search party out." He releases me and stands, brushing grass from his legs. "Think you might feel up to joining us and experiencing a meal at an actual table today?"

I inhale deeply and try to compose myself too. "I could probably hack that."

Dad stretches his neck. "Good. Then we await the pleasure of your company." He leans down and picks up my iPad, passing it to me. "In the meantime, I'll be sorry to miss out on that tattoo artist's sewing room mayhem. Maybe you can give me the SparkNotes version over burgers."

"Count on it," I tell him.

We stare at each other for a second, something indefinable passing between us, then Dad nods and heads toward the patio.

Before he reaches it, I call out, "Wait! I have a question about your theory." I struggle to remember one of Dad's recent "I wonders,"

then say, "Even the most curious person isn't going to be able to figure out an answer for, say, 'What is the exception to the rule that
every rule has an exception?' So what *then*?"

He winks. "That just means some of life's mysteries aren't meant
to be solved."

He ducks around the flip-flop I throw in his direction.

26

THE UNEXPECTED KNOCK ON MY BEDROOM DOOR THE NEXT afternoon sends my pulse jumping. My parents dropped me off at home after my doctor's appointment—no MELD score change!—and left again to run errands. The only other people who have keys to our house are Sibby, who's not due back until tomorrow afternoon, and our next-door neighbor, Mrs. Taholi, who needs one of those motorized lifts to get up a set of stairs these days.

I wish interior doors had peepholes.

"Who is it?" I venture, creeping closer.

"Special delivery" comes the reply, in a deep, familiar voice.

"Alex!" I yank open the door, my jaw dropping. *Of course* there's someone else with a key to our house: its other occupant.

My brother stands in front of me with a Scrabble board held in both hands like an offering. "You were ghosting me on Words With Friends, so . . ."

"Mom said you were coming up the weekend *after* this one."

"I am." He shrugs. "Also."

I grin at him. I said I didn't want him here because I knew he'd try to tease me out of any wallowing I wanted to do, but I am ridiculously and unexpectedly happy he ignored me. And it turns out he doesn't even need to resort to teasing, because my mood takes an instant lift just seeing him in my doorway. Despite the fact that we're not all that physical with each other and it doesn't feel completely natural to do it, I throw my arms around him and squeeze tight.

He hugs back hard. After a few seconds, he peeks over my shoulder, wrinkling his nose. "It smells like ass in here. Or maybe it's you. Slap on some deodorant and meet me in the kitchen."

I narrow my eyes, but I'm secretly grateful he's being the same Alex as ever.

"You're going down so hard," I tell him. "There aren't any cheats to save your butt in analog."

"Cheats? Why would you think I—" He gasps, pretends to be scandalized. "Wait, do you use *cheats* when you play me?" His eyebrows are in his hairline.

"Oh, please. As if you don't!" I laugh and close my door in his face.

He clomps down the back stairs as I search for my phone, open Words With Friends for the first time since last week, and play "owned." Then I open the chat box within our game and type: *That's what you're about to be.*

A few seconds later his bark of laughter travels up the heating vents.

27 ~✽

ALEX DROPS ME OFF AT SIBBY'S APARTMENT ON SATURDAY afternoon with a pep talk. "If she gives you a hard time, we'll ditch her and buy you a cuddly koala from Australia instead."

I steal his baseball cap and fling it onto the sidewalk, ignoring his yelp as I slide from the car.

"You'd better not make me get out for that," Alex calls from the driver's seat.

I don't answer, but I do dip down and retrieve his hat, dangling it through the open window.

He snatches it from me. "Anything you want me to tell Will when I see him?"

Alex hasn't pushed back on my vague answers about Will, but he does know from Mom that his BFF was the one to bring me to the hospital last week, meaning he knows we were continuing to hang out together after that first time. I have no idea what Will may or may not have said to him about it.

I smile and shrug. "I texted him yesterday—we're good."

I did, too. I thanked him for being there when I needed him, and he responded to say he was so sorry about my not getting the liver and that he understood if I wasn't in the right headspace to hang out, but he'd be a text away if I ever was. We're cool.

Although I'd never admit this to my brother, Will was the exact right guy for the job and I'm grateful he was around. But hanging out with Will was all about keeping it light and breezy, and I realize now that my much bigger priority is setting things straight with someone who pushed me to keep it real.

My *person*.

It's been a week since our fight—nine days, technically—and Sibby and I haven't spoken a word to one another. Not a text, not an Insta tag, not anything. That's never happened before and I have no idea how she's going to react to my apology today. I haven't been in the position of having to utter one to her before.

I mean, over minor stuff, sure. *I'm sorry I forgot to grab you a Gatorade when I stopped at 7-Eleven on my way to practice. I'm sorry I didn't notice your "Save me" eyes when you got stuck talking to Carmen Moreno about League of Legends for twenty minutes. I'm sorry I accidentally barged in on you making out with Justin Bolt.*

Never *I'm sorry we've been giving each other the silent treatment for nearly the entirety of our last-ever school vacation week.* Or even just *at all.*

But as much as Alex's showing up and my parents' nudging has helped pull me back from the brink this week, things will never *really* be okay if I don't have my best friend. I need to fix us.

I wave bye to my brother and enter Sibby's apartment building, climbing the stairs to stand in front of her door. I'm not completely sure what time their train was scheduled back and whether they'll even be home yet, but Sibby answers on my first knock, her eyes wide when she sees it's me.

"I'm sorry," I whisper.

Someone in one of the nearby apartments is cooking something that smells like extra-pungent fish and it assaults my nose, but I force my expression to hold on one that I hope conveys true repentance.

She shifts her stance to lean against the doorway casing. "Me too."

When I exhale, her chin juts out a bit and she adds, "But I can't take back what I said the other day, even if I wasn't expecting you to react the way you did."

"I don't want you to. Turns out you were right anyway."

Her eyebrows flicker. "Which part?"

I purse my lips and sigh. "Probably most of it. Maybe the part about me not being brave."

Sibby's posture relaxes at this, and her eyes soften. "Lia! You *know* I wasn't try to drag you. I think you're *totally* capable of being brave, I just don't think you've been letting yourself go there lately and I thought maybe if I pointed it out, it might, you know, shake you up a little. But in a good way." She pushes off the door casing. "I was trying to help."

I nod. "I know. At least, I know that *now*. Turns out losing your shot at a liver and locking yourself in your room most of the week to mourn makes you realize some stuff."

"*What are you talking about?*"

"Can I come in?"

She rolls her eyes, another sign that we're gonna get past this. "What are you, a vampire? You need an invitation?"

I follow her down the hall toward her room and we assume our regular positions—Sibby on her stomach across her bed and me sprawled out on one of her floor cushions.

"So I got *the* call," I say.

She sits straight up, her eyes wide. "*Holy shit*," she whispers. "What—how—"

I fill her in on the stuff at the hospital, scooting closer to brush away her tears when they fall.

"I'm the worst friend in the world," she says. "I was watching *Hamilton* and you were prepping for major surgery, and then having to deal with not having it, without me by your side cheering you up."

"Yeah, well, the Worst Friend Award is all mine for making everything about me lately and for being so all over the place."

"Will this award be hand lettered? Because if so, *I* want it."

I make a face. "Might as well use my talents there, since I won't have the chance to anywhere else."

I tell her about quitting the mural.

"Was that a heat of the moment thing, or is it still what you want?" she asks.

Leave it to Sibby to know instantly that I've been regretting my decision for days now.

Shrugging, I say, "Now that I'm feeling a tiny bit better again, I wish I hadn't done it, but it's too late now. The arts commission lady was already super worried that I wasn't going to be able to finish by May fourth—"

Sibby interrupts me to say, "May the fourth be with you." She turns her palms up in apology. "Sorry, it's *physically impossible* for me to hear that date and not finish the saying. You *know* how I feel about all things Carrie Fisher."

"Yeah, yeah, Jedi Master. Anyway, I'm sure she was on the phone lining up a replacement the minute we hung up."

Sibby pulls at a thread on her quilt. "Oh, babe, that sucks. I'm sorry. And I really *am* sorry about the other night too. I think maybe . . . I think maybe I *was* trying to start a blue that day, just to get that stuff out of my head and into the open."

"Does blue mean fight, you Aussie freak?"

She nods. "But it wasn't because I was angry at you specifically, I'm just pissed off about all of it. Although, I'm *kind of* pissed at you because I don't feel like I can talk to my best friend about how I'm feeling, since you don't want to delve into anything related to all of this. I get that it's happening to you and this is your way of dealing with things, but . . ." She pauses and lifts her eyes to mine. "It's also kind of happening to me too, and *my* way of dealing with anything confusing is usually to talk it to death with my best friend—argh, sorry. Terrible word choice."

I shake my head and gesture for her to continue.

"Except if I complain about how I'm feeling, I come across as a twit because it's so much worse to be in your shoes and I feel like the biggest wanker ever, whining about how much this is all tearing me apart." Her voice cracks and a tear slips down her cheek when she adds, "But it is."

She raises her eyes to mine and sees that I'm about to cry too, and then we both burst into teary laughter. Because what else is there to do?

"I messed everything up," I say. "With me, with you, with—just with everything. I *want* you to be able to whine to me. I want to be able to talk about it with you too, and to find a way to stare down some of the stuff I've been avoiding, I'm just not sure how to do that yet."

"I'll help!" Sibby says, without hesitation. She tumbles off her bed and crawls over to me, wrapping her arms around my neck. I grab back and hang on for dear life.

I speak into her hair. "I'm so sorry. I know I keep saying that, but—"

"No, *I'm* so sorry!"

"Well, I'm *more* sorry."

"Fuck right off, *I'm* more sorry, you gronk," she insists.

"Don't call me a gronk when I don't know what that means, you shitfrisbee."

She pulls back enough to look at my face. "You just made that up!"

I half sniffle, half giggle. "I totally just made that up."

"I love you," she says.

"I love you more." We cling to each other even harder.

Then Sibby lifts her head from my shoulder slightly and says, "Ugh, this crying is making my nose run. Do you care if I wipe it on your sweater?"

"I really, really do."

There's a pause. "Oh. Then, um, whoops."

28

WHEN I RETURN TO SIBBY'S ROOM AFTER WASHING MY FACE (AND shoulder), she's perched on the edge of her bed tying her shoe.

"Going somewhere?" I ask, raising an eyebrow.

"Yes, *we* are."

"Okay. Do I get to know where?"

"I thought we might celebrate renewing our vows of everlasting friendship with a little Sibby + Lia Back in Action reunion mission."

I stare, waiting.

"We're getting you that mural back," she states, plucking my bag from the floor and sliding it over my shoulder.

I shake my head. "Even if I thought that was a remote possibility, it's the weekend. No one's going to be at the arts commission office."

Sibby peeks up at me from under her bangs. "Um, don't be annoyed but when you were in the bathroom, I kind of got that woman's cell number off your phone. Sorry, not sorry."

"How? I didn't have her saved in contacts!"

"Yeah, but seeing that you only had one phone number in your recents from mid-week . . ."

I don't know whether to hit her or hug her. Actually, yes I do.

When I release her, she says, "She's going to meet us there in an hour. I figure, on our way we can wander by the mural and get the scoop on what's happened with it since you quit."

"You're kind of amazing, you know that, right?"

"Of course. I am the keeper of light and the bringer of dawn," she replies.

"Ooh, that one's got staying power. I kind of want to steal that for our next rally."

She waves her hand. "All yours. I like it better for you anyway."

What would I do without my Sib?

Ten minutes later, we're staring at a very plain, very *white* brick wall.

Sibby tilts her head to the left. "Well. The bad news is Maya Angelou's brilliant words are no longer. The good news is that who-ever's working on this now isn't very far down their own path. Uh, how would your design look on a white background?"

"Not *terrible*, I guess. Although it only took a day and a half to paint the green, and with you as my servant—er, I mean *helper* . . ." I grin and she gives me a thumbs-up.

But the more I look at the literal blank canvas in front of us, the more "meh" I feel about repainting my design. "I don't know, Sib. Maybe this isn't the best idea after all."

"You're changing your mind again?"

I try to sort through my emotions. When I think about being up on the ladder, creating, there's a hint of that secret jolt of excitement I always get when I'm planning or doing anything artistic. But when I picture my *design* up there? Solid *blah.*

Sibby's waiting patiently for me to respond so I try. "Maybe it's the quote? I mean, all bow to Maya, and I buy into every word of it, but maybe it's not . . ." I pause to consider what the right word is, but the answer already waits on my tongue. "*Me* enough?"

My design is pretty, the sentiment is inspiring, the whole thing is Instagram-worthy—which I know because I've seen a hundred variations of the same thing on there.

Sibby is right.

I've been a little bit chickenshit about a lot of things, and my art is one of them.

I plop down on the asphalt and stare up at the wall, twisting a lock of hair around and around my fingers as I examine the vast expanse.

"Whoa," Sibby says, joining me. "What's happening now?"

"What's happening now is that I'm acknowledging my art is generic."

She shrugs. "I think *generic* is a big exaggeration, but let's go with that for a sec. So? Ditch that design and come up with something more *you.*"

I scoff. "Oh, sure, under a huge time crunch I just—*presto!*—come up with something amazing and personal and then slap it up on a ginormous wall so it can be permanently displayed for all my friends and neighbors to see for years to come. Easy-peasy."

She grins. "I mean, when you put it like that."

But after a pause, she says, "Okay, so the issues are: too big, too fast, too long."

I raise my eyebrows at her, smirking.

"Ew! Gross! Get your mind out of the gutter and work with me here. Can we change any of those obstacles?"

My neck is starting to hurt from staring up, so I lean back on my elbows and stretch my legs in front of me. "I guess I don't have to use the *entire* wall, but either way it would still have to be large enough to detract attention from this nasty parking lot, so ginormous versus plain old huge? Same same."

Sibby matches my position on the cracked pavement. I realize too late that we're probably going to be covered in asphalt dust when we meet with the arts commission woman.

"Can we change the timeline?" Sibby asks. "What if it wasn't ready for the soft opening, but for the hard opening? Is that a thing? Argh! Why does everything coming out of my mouth right now sound like sexual innuendo?"

I laugh, but then ponder her first question. "Maybe? If I could buy a couple more weeks to work on a design . . . The painting part itself goes pretty fast—and it's not like I have anything else going on, so if I can stay healthy—" I break off when I see her face fall. "Sorry."

She nods and whispers, "I know."

We are literally saved by the bell when the alarm on Sibby's phone goes off, telling us we need to start walking to the arts commission offices. We stand and brush each other clean as best we can, then set off up Brattle Street.

Claire is waiting outside when we arrive. I'd been expecting someone working in this capacity to express herself a little more like Sibby and me—funky, individual, artistic. But her appearance is a perfect match for her phone voice, bland and professional. Unless she changed outfits after receiving Sibby's call, she kicks it on Saturdays in a sweater set and pencil skirt.

"Which of you is Amelia?" she asks, stretching out a hand.

"That would be me," I answer, shaking it.

Her eyes flicker over me in surprise; she was obviously expecting someone who fit that Dying Girl stereotype a little better, maybe dragging around an oxygen tank behind me or something.

But she recovers quickly. "I'm glad to put a face with a name. Come inside, girls."

She uses her key to unlock the door and ushers us into a small but comfy lobby, where she points us to chairs.

When we're all seated, she leans forward. "So, Sibilla, is it? You're very persistent and I applaud that, but as I told you over the phone and I'm happy to repeat to both of you now, I don't think I'm going to be able to help here. I've already contacted the restaurant group that owns Zuzu's Petals and informed them of your decision not to proceed." She glances at me as she says this and I seize on her attention to interrupt her.

"Has someone else been assigned to replace me yet?"

Sibby chimes in. "We were just there and noticed the wall had been painted white."

Claire leans back in her chair. "We had one of our interns do that last week, rather than leave a half-finished design up while we waited to hear back from the few different artists we've approached."

Sibby shoots me a triumphant look. "So, you *don't* have anyone specific lined up then."

Claire sighs. "No. Not yet. And, I'll be honest with you, it would solve a lot of my problems to simply hand it back over to you, but as I said, I've already told the restaurant group about your situation and—"

"And you're not sure they'll want to take a chance on me being alive to finish it," I blurt, studying my hands.

She and Sibby both gasp.

"I would never put it that way!" Claire says. "Amelia, I am so, *so* sorry for everything you're dealing with right now. I would like nothing more than to see you better, truly."

Sibby slaps her hands on her knees. "Perfect. Because getting back to work on this mural is going to help Amelia's mental state quite a bit. So then. Let's sit here and brainstorm our way through this obstacle."

I appreciate Sibby's initiative, but I'm two steps ahead of both of them. "What if we could line up a replacement to wait in the wings—someone ready to see the project through to completion if I'm not able to?"

Claire's foot jiggles as she thinks. "I mean, we'd have to vet the artist, make sure his or her work is of a certain skill level."

"I'm just spitballing here," I say. "But how about if I approached the set designers at the American Repertory Theater. Would they pass muster?"

Sibby catches on now and straightens in her chair.

Claire laughs derisively. "Obviously! They have a great track record for supporting worthy causes too, but good luck getting a meeting with them. I've been trying to schedule something with their director of partnership for months now to pitch them on working with us and the Cambridge Youth Initiative to create a back-to-school program for underserved kids, and I'm afraid September is going to have come and gone before her calendar has an opening."

I drop my chin. "Oh. Hmm. You're probably right."

With my head still ducked, I wink at Sibby from the corner of my eye, and she stifles her grin and whips out her cell phone.

Holding up a finger to Claire, she says, "'Scuse me for one quick sec." Then, into the phone, "Hi, Mum? Hey, so Lia needs a favor." She laughs. "You haven't even heard what it is yet! I know . . . I *know* . . . she needs you to take a meeting with the Cambridge Arts Commission tomorrow before work." She listens for a sec, then puts her hand over the mouthpiece and asks Claire, "Is seven thirty too early for you?"

Claire uncrosses her legs and closes her mouth. "Uh, no. No! Tell her I'll bring the coffee."

Sibby nods, relays Claire's message, and listens for another few seconds before saying, "Ta, Mum! I'll tell her."

She presses End on the call and turns to me. "Mum got you a Statue of Liberty piggy bank she said reminded her of you, and she wants you to come home with me after so she can give it to you in person."

I smile, then we both turn back to Claire.

"Your mother is Kyra Watson. I should have put it together from the last name combined with the accent," she says, sounding begrudgingly amused.

"Like mother, like daughter," Sibby says, shrugging. "And if you couldn't tell, Lia here might not sound like either of us, but she's family all the same. My mum would do anything for her. *Anything.*"

Sibby isn't the least bit subtle, and Claire holds up her hand. "Okay, girls, point made. I think you've given me a lot to work with here, but let me have a few days to try to sort it out with everyone involved, okay?"

I cringe, but force myself to ask, "Um, this might not be the best time to push our luck, but if they go for it, do you think there's any chance they might agree to a short extension on the completion date? I know that means it might not line up with their soft opening, but with the lost time this week and however much longer it might take to get their decision, plus I was thinking about making some changes to the design, which of course I'd send to you for approval, but—"

She holds up a hand again. "Let me stop you right there. We learned on Friday that the opening is already going to be delayed a couple weeks over a slight snafu with the liquor license. The next meeting of the state's Alcoholic Beverages Control Commission is May fourteenth. Would that give you enough extra time?"

"Wow, that's—that's like a gift from the universe!" Sibby says.

Claire examines a fingernail. "Mmm. I'd term it more of a gift from a well-placed woman who doesn't take kindly to a restaurant manager calling her daughter-in-law *babycakes* during the building inspection, but you girls are free to look at it however you want. That guy was immediately fired, by the way, and the team's response was enough to assure me the rest of them are decent people. We wouldn't associate ourselves with them—or ask you to do so—otherwise."

I jump up and hold out my hand. "I trust you. Whether it was the universe responsible for the delay or this mother-in-law, or both, I'll take it! Thank you for agreeing to go to bat for me—again. I swear you won't regret it."

I'll make sure of it.

29

LIQUOR LICENSE DELAY OR NOT, IF I'M GOING TO HAVE TIME TO design and paint a whole new mural in a matter of weeks—even without allowing for the possibility of health-related distractions—I can't afford to wait for the official greenlight before getting started on concepts.

Except I slam straight into a hard reality: it can be, er, *challenging* to design a piece of art that tells the world, "Hello, this is me!" when you've recently determined you might not have the most decent handle on which parts of you *are* authentically *you*.

My art teacher Miss Leekley's wispy voice is in my ear. "Isn't that what the process of making the art is for, to reveal to yourself who you truly are? Let the blank page whisper to you."

Yeah, Miss Leekley can suck it.

"If I could just find a starting place," I moan to Alex and Sibby on Sunday afternoon, as we polish off slices of pizza bigger than our heads. As soon as Sibby learned a side trip to Santarpio's was included, she wasted no time volunteering to come along while I dropped off Alex at the airport.

Well, pizza *and* the fact that we have a lot of lost time to make up for after a whole week apart.

"Whatever direction you decide to go in, it should have a llama in it," Sibby says.

"*What?*"

Alex crams his crust into his left cheek and speaks out of the right side of his mouth. "She's got a point. Llamas are super trendy right now. People will eat it up."

"*You* should eat it up." I point at his chipmunk cheek and the crumbs escaping it. "I'm not sure I'm going for super trendy, but I'll keep it in mind."

Sibby grins conspiratorially at my brother. "There are always owls."

"So last year," he says.

I appraise them, then steal the last slice of pepperoni without the slightest twinge of guilt. "Quite the comedy duo you two make."

Sibby wipes her mouth with a napkin before balling it up and stuffing it into her empty cup. "Does it need to be some huge statement piece? I mean, it's your first attempt at going rogue—can't that be achievement enough?"

Alex nods. "She has a point. This doesn't have to be your

masterpiece. You wouldn't even *want* it to be, because who wants to peak at eighteen?"

People who might not see nineteen? I nearly say aloud.

But why *am I not saying that out loud?* my brain chides. *You told yourself you wanted to be more open about facing this reality, so why are you still shoving the thoughts aside, refusing to give them air?*

I draw in a deep breath, then fling the sentence into the world.

"Don't say things like that!" Sibby points at me, eyes wide. "I refuse to let that happen."

Alex merely drops his eyes to the table and stares hard at his empty plate.

I rub my neck. "Obviously, I don't want it to either, but it's part of my reality right now. And I think . . . I think it has to be in the design, if it's going to be personal. That would be the expectation."

Alex stands and gathers our trash. "Screw that, Li. You don't owe anyone anything," he says, before leaving to throw it out.

Sibby stands too. "For what it's worth, I agree with him. I'll be right back—I gotta change my tampon."

I remain at the table and consider what Alex said. He might be right: I don't owe anyone. I owe *me*, though. I can't see any way to put my own voice on this piece right now, at this moment in my life, and have the design be all bunny rabbits and sparkly rainbows. Or llamas. (I'll keep that last bit from Sibby, though.)

But that doesn't mean I have the first clue how to start, or that I have faith I'll figure it out before the mural's deadline.

What do *I* have to offer on the topic of death?

The thing is, when somebody lives to be a hundred, people say things like, "Oh, she was blessed with a long life," or "She achieved so much in her time on Earth." Even *making it* to that age is considered an accomplishment.

But when someone's really sick at eighteen, no one says that. They say, "Well, if anything tragic happens to her, it must have been for a reason; she must have been sent here to teach us some lesson."

The alternative is that life is cruel and random and pointless and who the hell wants to accept that?

But I don't have *anything* to teach anyone; I'm just as confused as everyone else.

Maybe more so.

I am one giant fucking I Don't Know. My dad would be so proud.

Alex is back. "We need to head out. The line for security's always a nightmare on Sunday nights. I don't want to cut it too close."

"Fat chance of that. We're, like, what? *Three minutes* from the airport?" Sibby says, reappearing as well.

Alex snickers. "That reminds me—you ready for Jeff Linehan's latest?"

Sibby and I start for the exit, Alex on our heels, as he says, "Did you ever wonder why slim chance and fat chance mean the same thing?"

Sibby halts mid-step. She brings her fist to her forehead and explodes it.

Alex laughs and ducks out the door I'm holding for us. "Each one is worse than the last. What was last night's, Lia? Something about invisible ink."

"Oh, I've heard him ask that one before," Sibby answers, before I can. "Did you ever wonder how you'd know if your invisible ink pen ran out of ink?"

They both groan, but my pulse starts racing as I remember something I read about last month.

"Can I borrow your phone, T-rex? Mine's at five percent."

"Does that mean I'm driving?" he asks.

I trade him the keys for his cell and open his browser as I slide into the back seat and stretch out, completely distracted by my search.

"Uh, I guess I'll take shotgun then," Sibby says, amused.

Her words barely register, because I've found the article I wanted and am reading through it closely while ideas tumble over each other in my mind. They're both staring at me when I look up a minute later. Alex hasn't even started the car.

"What just happened here?" Sibby asks, waving her hand to indicate my entire head.

"A stroke of genius," I answer, half my brain still on my idea. "It would take a freaking miracle to pull off, though."

"I believe in miracles!" Sibby proclaims. She elbows Alex when he doesn't agree fast enough for her liking.

"What she said!" he offers, rubbing his side. "Do all Australians have such pointy elbows?"

Sibby buckles her seat belt. "I don't know. Should we call Hugh Jackman and ask about his?"

"Well, he's Wolverine so his sharp parts are on his—"

"You guys, seriously," I interrupt. "Would you want to help me?"

Sibby and Alex exchange looks.

"What does she think we've been trying to do all this time?"

Sibby asks him, one hand over her mouth and speaking in a stage whisper.

Alex's shrug is exaggerated for effect. "Hiding right here in plain sight."

Hiding in plain sight. The universe winks at me again, another sign I'm on exactly the right track with this idea.

30 ❧

LATER THAT NIGHT, I STAND WITH MY HAND HOVERING IN THE
air outside the tiny alcove off our dining room that my mom turned
into her (very cramped) home office when I was little.

Partly the hovering is habit. Mom's rule for Alex and me was
always, "Pause here and consider whether whatever you need is worth
interrupting me for. If there aren't bodily fluids involved, I expect
your conclusion to be no."

And partly it's sheer apprehension.

Knock, knock.

"Come in!"

I turn the knob and enter, my pulse racing. Which is ridiculous, it's just *my mom*. It's not the person who has me nervous, though. It's what I'm about to ask her.

"Is that popcorn?" she asks, her eyes widening.

"Air popped with spray butter. Zero Weight Watchers points." I use my free hand to slide my iPad out from under my armpit and set the bowl on her coffee table. Mom clears aside a slew of file folders to make room for me next to her on the leather love seat.

"I must have been really into my project—I didn't even hear that popping," she says.

"Whatcha working on?"

She gestures at the piles of paperwork. "Trying to get things in order to pass on some of my caseload to a coworker."

Hearing her talk about giving up her cases makes my throat ache a little, but far less than it did last week. Selfishly, I want my mom around right now, and I guess I'm finally ready to admit it. Although if she's going to suggest moving to Tennessee next, I *will* have something to say on the matter.

But she merely glances at my iPad. "Did you want to show me something?"

"Kind of." I bite my lip, buying time.

Bravery, not bravado. Be vulnerable—it's your mom. *There is no safer person to test the waters with; she's obligated to love you no matter what.*

I straighten my back against the cushion. "Actually, I wanted to see if you might have time to watch a *few* things with me."

"These aren't soldiers sneaking into their kids' school assemblies in mascot costumes, are they? Because I am fresh out of tissues in here."

I shake my head. "It's not that, but we still might need to track some Kleenex down at some point."

She tucks a leg under her and scoots closer. "Well, I don't know whether to be intrigued or scared. Let's see it."

I don't turn on my screen just yet, though. Instead, I force myself to get out the words I'd rehearsed in the kitchen while I waited for the kernels to pop.

"So you know how you said that thing the other night—morning, I guess—after the hospital, about not being able to be stronger for me? How you wish you had all the answers?"

She's taken aback. She shifts now, tugging down her skirt and glancing to the side before settling her gaze back on me. "Yeah?"

I inhale, then force out my breath. "The thing is, I don't have any answers either. Which will surprise exactly no one, I know." My laugh is weak and Mom's eyes soften on mine, waiting for me to go on. So I do, following a shaky exhale. "But the bigger part is, I, um, I also haven't been letting myself ask the questions. And, uh, I think I have to start doing some of that now."

I need to look away to get these words out, so I busy myself unlocking my iPad screen and opening up the YouTube app. "I, um, I bookmarked a bunch of TED Talks by people who've had near-death experiences or been diagnosed with terminal diseases and, uh, a couple by people explaining different religions' takes on what happens when, uh, when someone dies, because . . . because I think I need to let myself go there and, um, I was hoping—" I'm too choked up to continue and when I pause to collect myself, Mom's hand settles over mine.

It's exactly the encouragement I need to get the last bit out. "I was hoping maybe we could learn how to let it be personal together."

Mom's eyes are already filled with tears threatening to spill as she nods over and over.

Words With Friends notification:

QuitWithTheT-rex has just played: ENROUTE for 22 points

31

IT PAINS ME TO ADMIT THIS, BUT IT TURNS OUT I HAVE NOT given Dying Girl enough credit.

She's a lot of things I'm not (doe-eyed, ethereal, wise beyond my years) and one big thing I refuse to ever become (sweetly and resignedly accepting of her death sentence), no matter how things progress with my BA from here. But she does have one superpower I underestimated: she can command some serious help when she needs it.

"He's not even late yet. You're being annoying, you know that, right?" Sibby asks.

"Yup. Ask me how many shits I give?" I pace the parking lot abutting my mural, impatient for my brother to show up so we can get this project underway.

"Zed-E-R-O?" she replies, staring up at the brick wall that is about to be turned yet another color. Bye-bye, plain white. Hello, chalkboard paint.

Bitterly, some of the help Dying Girl gets is given with pity.

I may not be wise, but I *am* smart—enough to realize the concessions the arts commission and the restaurant group behind Zuzu's Petals made for me are ones they probably would never, ever have considered under "ordinary circumstances."

Such as letting me convince them I need to do my design in chalk, even if that means a new, permanent design will have to be painted in its place later this summer (*if* we can even get the chalk one to last that long).

Such as bumping up the budget by $200 to fund a swimming pool cover on a roller.

Such as allowing me permission to temporarily mount that on the roof of the building, so I'll be able to unfurl it to protect the chalk from the elements as I work and, after the reveal, any time there's rain in the forecast.

But sweetly, some of it is given with pure heart.

Such as Alex coming back again this weekend to assist. Such as Sibby declaring that nothing dramatic will go down on her watch without her participation.

"There he is!" Finally, *finally*, I catch sight of Mom's hatchback with my brother behind the wheel. He pulls into the lot and he's scarcely parked before I yank open his door.

"What, did you detour to walk the Freedom Trail? That text saying your flight landed is over an hour old!"

He holds up his hands as he slides out. "Relax! I'm here now. Mom needed us to swing by her office on the way back from the airport so she could pick up some paperwork she needed. Apparently she's doing a deep dive into case stuff she's trying to wrap up; said we're on our own for dinner." He lifts his chin at Sibby. "Hey. I see you're dealing with some cuckoo here."

Sibby smiles at me. "She's cute when she acts all Picasso-y."

I roll my eyes at both of them. "Tease all you want, just do it while you lend a hand. It's supposed to rain tomorrow *and* the next day and there aren't extra hours to spare as it is, so the roller has to be completely installed *and* both coats of chalkboard paint have to go on TODAY."

Alex's gaze sweeps over the wall. "Wow. That's quite a lot to paint."

"Twice," Sibby adds.

"*And* we have to assemble the roller," I remind them. "It shipped in pieces and the instructions are all in Chinese."

Alex faces me. "Is that hyperbole or are you being serious?"

"Oh, I *wish* it was hyperbole."

"You know who speaks Chinese, don't you?" he asks.

I stare back at him, at a loss. "*Noooooo*. Should I?"

"Will."

My jaw drops. "Damn, Alex. Will's *Thai*, you asshole. It's not the same thing."

Alex rolls his eyes at me. "Thanks, I hadn't realized. It's not like he's *my* best friend or something. Which is how I know he took Mandarin as his language elective all through high school. Now who's the asshole?"

Sibby snorts a laugh and I have to duck my head and murmur, "Okay, sorry."

"So? It's okay to call him to help out?" Alex asks.

He and Sibby both watch me as I consider. It's a little awkward that I kissed the boy the last time we hung out (oh, and also dragged him to the beach at night, accused him of burying me, stripped to my underwear in front of him, and had him drive me to the hospital for a possible liver transplant), but if we can put all *that* aside, I wouldn't complain about having Will around today. Not one bit.

In fact, when I texted him a week and a half ago, in the midst of my epic mope, I believe his exact response to my thanking him for being there when I needed someone was: Happy to do the same any time you do again. I'm a text away. So he *did* offer already . . .

"Yeah, see if he's around," I say, hiding a small smile.

Sibby jumps up and down and claps. "I finally get to meet Fuckskillet!"

Alex looks up from typing on his phone and mouths, "What?"

I shake my head. "Nothing. Never mind. Sibby's just being Sibby."

She sticks her tongue out at me. "You love me."

"He's in," Alex says, a few seconds later. "I told him we could pick him up before swinging by the store for the paint supplies."

I raise a skeptical eyebrow as I gesture to Mom's car. "No way all four of us are fitting in there *plus* the roller plus everything else I ordered through Dad."

Alex sighs. "Fine. I'll go get the stuff and Will. Just means you're stuck waiting on me again."

Sibby flutters her eyelashes. "Oh, Alex. You're worth the wait!"

He rolls his eyes at her and I pretend to puke.

I wait for Mom's car to turn onto the street before I turn on Sibby. "You're not suddenly into my brother, are you?"

"Yeah, nah, luv—the brother's best friend trope is all yours."

I nudge her. "It's not like that."

She nudges me right back. "Why not? Maybe? You said the kiss was hot, right?"

"I mean, it *was*, but I wasn't exactly myself that night and I'm mostly hoping he kissed me back for the same reason I initiated it to begin with—because it felt right for *that* moment."

"I'd be happy to ask him for his take on it," Sibby offers.

"Don't you *dare*! I'm counting on you to be casual."

She examines her fingernails. "Good thing casual's my middle name."

I have to laugh at that. "About the farthest thing from. Hey, while we wait, want me to help proofread the Prom with a Purpose website once more before you take it live?"

"Obviously."

We're still bent over Sibby's phone a half hour later, when my brother pulls back into the empty lot. It's loaded with supplies, including a long cardboard box hanging out the open hatchback. And Will.

He crosses the lot and smiles at me before sticking out his hand to Sibby.

"Hey, I'm Will."

"Oh yes, I'm well aware. Sibby."

"Your accent . . . are you . . . British?"

Sibby chafes at this. "Hardly! Proud Aussie, through and through."

"Aussie, Aussie, Aussie!" Will responds.

"Oi, oi, oi!" she answers, shaking her fist in the air.

He grins at her. "I was just kidding with the British thing. Amelia's told me all about you."

"Thank fuck," she says. "I was just about to clobber her."

I step closer. "*Amelia*, huh?"

He fixes his familiar smile on me again. "Hi, *Decks*. Amelia's only for when I'm talking about you to someone else."

Sibby and Alex begin unloading supplies from the car, but Will pulls me to the side and asks, "Hey, so . . . are we good?"

"I'm good if you're good," I tell him.

"Totally," he says. "I'm glad you guys reached out; I wasn't sure when I'd get the chance to ask if you knew that President Ford was a former fashion model who was once on the cover of *Cosmo* before he changed careers and went into law!"

My bark of laughter holds relief inside it—today's gonna be okay. "Somebody's been doing their homework!"

"What can I say, I'm the curious type."

Turns out, so am I, Will Srisari, so am I.

"Okay, are we getting down to business here or what? I was promised power tools would be involved, so gimme!" Sibby declares, rubbing her hands together.

"Plenty of those in the back seat," I tell her. "I'm thinking two of us should take the box with the pool cover roller up to the roof, while the other two get the first coat of chalkboard paint onto the bricks? Anyone have a preference? I kind of want to be up on the roof, personally, since I've already painted that entire wall once and I'll be spending a whole lot more time on that ladder after today."

"Will has to do the roller too because he's the only one of us who can read the directions," Alex reminds us.

"Boo. No power tools for me," Sibby says, pouting.

"I'm the one forcing you to be here today, so I can totally paint if you'd rather—" I begin, but she puts a hand on her hips and points to the building.

"Go!" She punctuates her word with a smile, so I know she's really okay.

Alex volunteers to help Will cart the box up, which I'm grateful for because even without carrying anything heavier than a cordless drill, it takes me twice as long as it would have a month ago to climb the stairs. But for once I'm not trying to cover my symptoms, even from myself.

After Alex heads back down to paint alongside Sibby, Will and I spread all the pieces out and begin trying to make heads or tails of the assembly. At first we work in relative quiet, only speaking to give the other instructions, but finally we reach a point where we've sorted out what we need to do pretty well, and Will says, "I hope there's a moratorium on the whole Scout's honor thing at this point, because I really want to tell you that I have tons of respect for what you're doing here. Alex told me you were planning to explore some of what's been going on with you through this mural and I think that's gonna really resonate with people when they see it."

I pretend to be very absorbed in fitting two pieces together while I school my expression to something neutral, but my stomach churns because Will just confirmed exactly what I've been so worried about—everyone is going to look at this mural expecting some brilliant statement from me about how it feels to be dying or what it all means.

I'll never be able to escape being Dying Girl.

And short of painting "It freaking sucks and it's senseless and messy and complicated so thanks for coming, but I got nothing for you!" up there, there's nothing I have to offer them.

"Uh." I literally have no idea how to respond.

"Sorry—if you're still not wanting to talk about this stuff—"

"It's fine." I give him a friendly smile to let him know he hasn't overstepped, though I'm snorting hard at myself on the inside. *It's fine,* says the girl who, prior to the last week and a half, has been actively and acutely avoiding the topic at all possible costs. I'm such a phony.

Although I really am trying more now; Mom and I have been logging serious video time this week.

"I get it. Most people consider it a pretty taboo subject," Will says. "Which never used to be the case—during Victorian times, little girls were given death kits for their dolls that had mourning clothes and play coffins, so they could play 'funeral.'"

"I'm sorry, *why* do you know that?"

"You're not the only one carting around useless factoids, Decks," he says, grinning at me.

I hit his arm. "Mine aren't that morbid, though."

Will shrugs, and adjusts the position of the roller so it's snug up against the edge of the roof. Then he leans over the edge and calls down, "Hey, we could use some extra sets of hands for this next part," before turning back to me and asking, "Sure, but at the same time, it's healthy to have the topic out in the open, right?"

I mean, can I really argue? Watching TED Talks and listening to podcasts *has* actually been helping me some. Only a little. It's not that the idea of *my* dying doesn't scare me anymore—god, it terrifies me beyond belief—but being able to put language to some of the mysteries surrounding the concept of death is helping.

Being curious is helping.

Which is why I point to his head and respond, "What other creepy factoids you got in there?"

Will peeks up at me while *whrring* a screw into place. "I'm not sure if creepy is the right word for it, but one of my roommates is *convinced* we're all just avatars in a giant simulation being run from the future and any time someone dies they simply re-spawn and play on."

"What's going on up here?" Alex and Sibby burst onto the roof, carrying bottles of water.

I accept one from Alex and answer, "Nothing much. Just building a kickass tarp roller while we chat about Victorian funeral dolls and re-spawning. As one does."

Sibby's gaze slides immediately to me, her eyebrows asking the question, *You okay with this?*

I purse my lips and nod. Would it be my first choice of topics? Maybe not. But am I hyperventilating with fight-or-flight symptoms? No. Weirdly, no.

And besides, this fits my curiosity mission. "I'm almost afraid to ask, but tell me more about this 'we're all in a simulation model' concept."

"Oh man, not that crap," Alex says. "Sibby, can you pass me that drill?"

"Nope, but I can *use* the drill wherever you point me," she replies. "What crap? What's a simulation model?"

"According to my roommate Arun? Widely respected scientific theory," Will replies.

"But what *is* it?" I ask again, squatting gently on the roller to hold it in place for Alex and Sibby.

Will lines up beside me and lends his weight too. "Okay, so, many scientists think it's very possible that we are all living in a simulation right now, kind of like the Sims game, but created by an advanced civilization."

"Um, what now?" Sibby asks.

Alex scoffs. "I've read about this—it's ridiculous."

Will laughs. "I'm not saying I don't agree, but way smarter people than us believe it could be a genuine possibility. Elon Musk. A ton of physics professors at MIT. They've had entire conferences about it."

"So you're saying we're living in the Matrix? What would be the point? We're some alien's entertainment?" Sibby asks.

"More likely it's an evolved version of the human race. And maybe not for entertainment. They could be running different versions of our history, altering essential details here and there to find the best possible outcome for our race. Like, they could run one where someone else won the 2016 election to see if—"

"I want to be in that model!" Sibby interrupts.

I can't help but smile at her, despite the fact that this entire conversation is weirding me out a little. Still, I'm proud of myself for being here, for listening.

"This is the dumbest BS I've ever heard," Alex says, shifting out of the way to accommodate Sibby's drilling.

"Although you have to admit, it does explain déjà vu perfectly," I say.

Will laughs. "I have a hard time believing someone would make me—their avatar—do so much ridiculous minutia, like flossing my teeth or sitting in traffic or standing in the soup aisle for twenty minutes trying to figure out what I want for dinner. I'd like to think our lives mean more than that!"

Me too. If only I knew what that was, though.

"Shit, it just shifted and I can't line up the last screw," Alex says. "I need all three of you to lean our weight into it and push."

We're too consumed by the task at hand to continue the conversation from there, and once we finish securing the roller, we all head back to street level to examine the progress Sibby and Alex have made with the chalkboard paint. They've painted a whole quadrant in the time Will and I were up there—it's *amazing* to have so much help. If only they could do my whole design for me, this mural would be done in no time flat.

"I'll take a turn on the ladder," Will offers, reaching for a paintbrush. "What do you think the odds are of cranking down the windows on your mom's car and putting the Sox game on the radio?"

"I'm all over it!" Alex says, darting to the hatchback.

Sibby and I watch Will climb the ladder and she whispers, "I'm feeling really guilty about calling him a fuckskillet because he's way too nice for his own good."

"You *should* feel guilty, you coldhearted bitch." I pause. "I'm feeling really guilty about sticking my tongue down his throat."

Sibby throws me a look. "Yeah, I'm wondering if he might not have minded that so much."

I laugh. "Could be. Maybe somewhere out there, there's a simulation version where my phone never interrupted us that night."

"Or a version where it did, but you got the liver and then both rode off into the sunset together," she adds, somewhat wistfully.

"Or a version where he noticed me back when I was crushing on him in middle school and we had all kinds of time together before . . ."

"Or a version where you were never born with BA in the first place," Sibby says, which makes us both stop and sigh.

We're quiet for a few seconds. Alex finds the game right as the opposing team scores on a double and Will's spare paintbrush falls off the rung below him when he kicks the ladder in annoyance.

Sibby's smile returns at that, and she says, "Maybe in *this* version of reality, at some future date to be determined, you guys might . . ."

Will looks down after his brush, then over at us, his eyes widening when he finds us staring up at him. But then the corners of them crinkle into his familiar smile and my lips follow unbidden.

"Mmm," I answer Sibby. "Maybe someday."

I bend over and pick up my own paintbrush and a bucket of paint. "First things first, though," I tell her, nodding at the wall.

As I paint, I replay the conversation I just had with Sibby and the one I had with Will on the roof. I still can't quite believe I was able to talk to them about stuff related to death. So yeah, the research I'm doing *is* helping, though it's not like I'm expecting any of this to suddenly get easy. I'm nowhere near cured. And I don't mean my BA—I mean my fear of everything that comes with it. I'm very much in the messy middle.

But that still counts for something, right?

No more novocaine.

I tune back in when the guys cheer over a Sox hit, just in time to hear Sibby say, "If you guys are into this baseball stuff, I should introduce you to cricket. Pretty much baseball, except the games last for something like three days. You'd adore it."

"Introduce *me* to?" Will scoffs. "I don't think so! My grandfather spent some time in India as a kid and he played in a club there. You're being conservative, he told me about one game that lasted *nine* days."

Sibby is nonplussed. "Will, if you're gonna hang around with us, there's something you need to learn real fast."

"What's that?"

Oh, this should be good.

My best friend uses her brush to add a swooping tail on the giant unicorn she has painted on her section of wall, instead of brushing back and forth to cover the bricks in straight lines like the rest of us have been doing. "I am never—*never*—conservative."

I bite the inside of my cheek to keep from laughing and then I figure *screw that* and let loose with a chortle that earns me a flick of paint from Will's paintbrush, which only makes me laugh again.

This right here?

This is a pretty decent remember-when.

~ 32

I FEEL ABOUT FIVE YEARS OLD AGAIN. MY MOTHER IS TUCKING me into bed and I should be embarrassed about it, but . . .

"Hey. Just try to get some decent rest tonight, okay? We're headed back to Dr. Wah's first thing in the morning so she can reassess this cold of yours."

"It's probably just allergies, Mom. The guy on the news tonight said the pollen count is"— my case isn't helped when my protests get interrupted by a coughing fit that burns my lungs, and my mother's eyes sharpen as she watches my chest cave in on my inhales—"off the charts," I finish weakly.

"Nothing's 'just' when you have a compromised immune system, sweetness." She sighs and tucks the blanket around my chin. "Do you need anything? More water? Want me to run a white noise app on your phone to help you fall asleep?"

I shake my head. Falling asleep is not going to be a problem. I can barely keep my eyes open as it is. As far as colds or allergies or whatever go, this one has me knocked on my ass. I've missed the past two days of school, including our first graduation rehearsal, which sucks. Not just because that actually sounded fun, but because the gossip mill is starting to go into overdrive. Sibby stopped by earlier with the news that the "Save Amelia" chant went up twice as the seniors practiced their line formation for filing in and out of the Fieldhouse.

I can't even.

"I'm fine," I insist.

"How about we let Dr. Wah decide what is and isn't anything to worry about, huh?" Mom says.

She perches on the edge of my bed and rubs my arm through the blanket before leaning over to kiss my forehead.

Like I said, five years old.

Except I can't lie; it's not the worst.

I jerk awake.

"Shhh. It's okay, Sunshine," Dad whispers. "I'm just trying to prop you up a little more to help some of the coughing."

Coughing. As soon as he says the word, my chest rattles and I have another fit of it. I feel like utter crap.

"What time is it?" I ask when I can speak again.

Dad tucks a second pillow under my head and helps me adjust. "Middle of the night—go back to sleep." He leans closer, his breath tickling my cheek. "Love you like fireworks, baby."

I'm halfway asleep already. "Love you, Daddy."

"Sunshine?" Dad's voice is tunneling through a thick fog. I try to roll away from it, but even that slight movement makes my spleen ache with raw tenderness and my blanket is a straitjacket.

Not my blanket. My chest.

Breathe, I order myself.

Can't. Hurts.

The words drift closer, edged in haze. "I wish I could let you keep sleeping—I know you were up half the night, but Mom got you an appointment first thing with Dr. Wah."

Shapes. Haze. Snap of shade. Wince of light.

Breathe.

Can't. Hurts.

"Hey. Am I gonna have to tug you out from—"

Cool fingers. Clammy cheek.

"NATALIE!!"

AFTER

33

USUALLY THERE'S A HEADS-UP WHEN YOU'RE APPROACHING moments that will mark a permanent Before and an After in your life, like a "Welcome Guide for Incoming Freshmen," or a printout of an ultrasound picture, or a save-the-date postcard for a wedding.

But sometimes they slam into you with no notice at all.

It was a cold. My best friend got a simple fucking spring cold.

The kind where you feel a bit knackered, sniffle for a couple days, then resume your life.

The kind that can sometimes turn into pneumonia, if you happen to be living with a compromised immune system, say due to organ failure.

Lia's liver was the wanker, but it was her spleen that caused the bigger problem. The larger it grew to help compensate for her liver's failures, the less it was able to do its own job of filtering out the damaged blood cells and producing white blood cells to fight off bacterial infections—or so I learned that nightmare of a morning.

They took her straight to the ICU.

When your best friend tells you she's got a disease that could end her life, you put on a brave face and you fight like hell because anything less would make it seem as if you're giving up on her, and you are literally her blocker; your job is to clear all obstacles from her way.

You don't say goodbye. Goodbyes would be admitting defeat and you would never do that, not until she reached her dying breath.

But then she goes into septic shock and she *does* reach her dying breath and you *still* don't get to say goodbye, because your cell phone gets terrible reception at school, because even when you finally get the voice mail and "borrow" a moped from the student parking lot and run every red light, you aren't even allowed into the ICU despite some *very* aggressive protesting. Because you could never have imagined that morning would be your last chance to—

Because even though you knew your best friend had this serious disease, you still never let yourself imagine she might actually—*Fuck. I can't say the words.*

Goddammit, if she'd just gotten that liver the first time. If there was a surplus of them instead of a shortage, she never would have—

For her sake, I'm glad it was sudden like that. I hope like bloody hell she didn't have time to be scared.

But *I* have time to be scared. I have all the goddamn time in the world to be *terrified*.

I'm afraid of the space between blinks and of the hollow in my belly . . . because now I know.

Now I know that you can soak your skin in starlight and scrub your lungs with noonday winds and trail your fingers through ombré sunrises and call yourself the granddaughter of the witches they couldn't burn, and none of that breath or beauty or blaze is ward or amulet.

Because the harshest truth, the truth that's been there all the while, is that the worst thing you can ever imagine happening . . . ?

Some days it actually does.

34 ~

I'VE BEEN STARING AT LIA'S MURAL FOR FOUR MONTHS NOW. There's a lot I get and a few things I really, *really* wish I could ask her about.

It's unfinished. Like her.

Though she'd made heaps of progress on it in just the few short weeks she'd had to work, it takes up most of the wall, a series of circles inside one another. The outermost one is a clock face, more specifically it's a sundial face, with bright, happy rays extending from its edges. Roman numerals marking the hours form a semicircle around the top three-quarters, and tick marks between each designate the quarter hours. A swirling wave fills the bottom quadrant, and inside it is a compass rose marking north, south, east, and west. Around the outer edge of all of it is a Latin phrase in Lia's perfect calligraphy script.

It reads: *Time is too slow for those who wait, too swift for those who fear, too long for those who grieve, too short for those who rejoice. But for those who love, time is not.*

The piece is titled "Only Questions." It's subtitled "This Is Not My Masterpiece."

I am obsessed with it.

Most of the people who've walked by this over the past few months—at least on sunny days when the tarp wasn't protecting it—never thought to step closer, would never have known to look for the tiny images Lia hid among the mandala pattern of the innermost circles. They wouldn't have noticed the saluting soldier wearing the bottom half of a furry costume or the phrase "false hope" with a line through it or the game controller. Or the word *oxyphenbutazone*, which I googled and learned was the highest scoring word ever played in Words With Friends.

They never saw the sea witch or the washing machine, both of which make me wonder if I really knew her.

Or the llama that tells me I did.

"Ready?" I whisper to Alex.

"No. But yes." Alex's eyes are glued to the mural.

Despite us being vigilant about keeping the tarp in place whenever rain is in the forecast (even if it's meant trekking back from my dorm at Tufts these last couple weeks) and despite our retracing some of the lines that have flecked away over the weeks, the chalk won't hold up forever.

It's time.

Lia's death was rushed and messy and inelegant. This send-off won't be, even without her parents here. I wish we'd been able to talk them into it, but they're not really doing all that well these days. Who could blame them?

At this hour on a Sunday morning the sidewalks are nearly empty, though it's not so early that the line cooks at Zuzu's Petals haven't already clocked in to begin prepping for brunch. They helped us hook up our hose to one of their sinks and propped the back door open enough for us to snake it out to the parking lot.

"Should we say something first?" Alex asks.

"I don't know. How about just . . . I love you, Lia."

"Love you, Li," Alex whispers, closing his eyes briefly.

We catch glances and nod to signal our readiness, then squeeze the trigger together.

A spray of water arcs onto the lower third of the wall and streaks of colored chalk bleed and run in rainbow rivulets down the wall. I thought I could watch, but I can't. I know it's just a chalkboard, but it's my best friend's heart and soul up there and my tears are salty in my throat. I spin so that my back is to the melting mural, swapping hands to keep one in place next to Alex's on the trigger.

A second later, Alex's arm drops, bringing the nozzle and my hand with it. "Sib," he whispers, wonderstruck.

I pivot to take in what he's seeing.

The lower half of the mural is gone, the bright colors of the sundial/mandala washed clean. But instead of just a plain black chalkboard beneath, pale letters shimmer where the sun meets water droplets.

Sweet fuck all!

It's another design entirely.

She hid a complete other design underneath her chalk rendering.

"Lia, you dazzler," I murmur, allowing my grin to crack my face in two. It's like she's reached out from . . . wherever she is . . . and laughed at me. I can hear her too: *Sib, you Aussie freak, did you really think you'd get rid of me so easily?*

"Oh my god, I've heard about this stuff!" Alex says. "There's this spray you can get that has a chemical in it that repels water. A group in Boston uses it to paint sidewalk poetry that only shows up on rainy days. The stenciled words 'appear' because the rest of the concrete darkens when it gets wet, and the part that's been treated with this stuff stays dry. She must have coated the chalk layer we painted, after we left. Before she started the actual mural design." He pauses, then adds, "Wow."

"How long will it last?" I ask.

I thought I was prepared for today, to say this final proper good-bye to Lia, and get back to my private grieving. But now I know I'm not; I need to hear her laughing at me more.

Alex is already punching away at his phone. "Got it! It's called Rainworks."

My limbs jiggle with adrenaline as I wait for him to click around the website.

"This'll fade as soon as the wall dries," he tells me. "But it says the chemical itself can last for months, maybe even up to a year, which means until then it'll reappear every time it gets wet."

The air catches in my lungs and I savor the exhale that follows.

A year. A piece of Lia for a whole year.

I jump into action, scrambling to retrieve the hose. "We have to get the entire wall wet—I need to see the whole thing!"

Alex ducks out of my way so I can point the nozzle again, this time staring intently—and in awe—as the rest of the colored chalk streams away and the wall saturates with water, revealing an artfully stenciled quote against the wet chalkboard backdrop.

"UNANSWERED QUESTIONS LEAVE MORE ROOM FOR POSSIBILITIES."
—MAYBE/MAYBE NOT DYING GIRL
(WHO GUESSES SHE HAS SOMETHING TO SAY AFTER ALL)

"*Lia*," I breathe.

"I know your parents didn't want to be here, but they'd want to see this, don't you think?" I tell Alex.

He turns his neck so I can see he already has his phone to his ear. "Mom?"

I step closer to the wall to give him some privacy.

Underneath the parentheses is a row of tiny letters I have to squint at to read: *This Isn't My Masterpiece Either.*

I abso-bloody-lutely love this girl. *She* is a masterpiece.

She was a badass and chickenshit and fierce and flawed and perfect and messy.

She was real.

She just wasn't invincible.

Lia's dying changed *everything* for me. I no longer believe in the concept of "fair." I no longer believe being a good person guarantees you a happy ending. I no longer believe any of us are invincible. I no longer believe *I'm* invincible.

A woman in yoga pants and a yellow jacket rounds the corner, juggling a coffee cup in one hand and her dog's leash in the other. She pauses in a patch of early morning sun to squint up at the still-dripping wall and I hesitate for only a second, glancing at Alex to confirm he's still on the phone with his parents. I cross the lot and offer the woman a friendly smile as I wordlessly ask permission to pet her corgi. She nods and I squat down to scratch the pup between his ears before venturing, "Do you reckon I could ask you a question that'll come off as a bit random?"

Her smile is slow to form, but it's there. "Well, now you have me curious, so I guess I have no choice but to say yes." She lifts her chin to gesture to Lia's quote. "Though I'm not sure if I should answer you or leave room for possibilities."

I grin in response. "Cheers. Don't worry—in this case the right answer leaves room for those too. I was just wondering, are you registered as an organ donor?"

Despite all the assurances Lia's death stole from me, it also left behind one shiny new one. Because now I understand that if I'm forced to accept the positively worst things imaginable *can* actually happen . . . it means I have no choice but to also believe the best possible things can.

And I am here for those. We all are.

Author's Note

I know there will be some readers who may feel betrayed by Amelia's death, after spending the majority of the book inside her head. There is even a for-my-eyes-only draft where she does survive, because I promise, it was *really* hard to doom her to this fate. But although being an author means having the ability to play God with the fictional characters we bring to life, I wrote this in honor of one specific girl who wasn't saved and, above all, I wanted to portray *her* story.

The spark for this book was a newspaper account of a girl in the small town where I live, who passed away at the age of twenty after a long struggle with organ failure *on the very day a liver was procured for her*. I didn't know her personally, nor did I reach out to people in my circle who did, because I didn't want the details of her condition (which was different from Amelia's) or her specific circumstances to seep into this story in any way that might intrude upon her family's privacy. But I was captivated by the cruel tragedy of missing out on a lifesaving donation by a matter of hours, after having waited years and years. It was only in researching this book that I learned how often this same scenario plays out across the world, because the shortage of organs means patients are forced to ride an incredibly fine and dangerous line between staying healthy enough to accept a transplant and being sick enough to warrant one.

While there *are* plenty of happy and hopeful endings, there are still too many that are not. All of the facts and figures Sibby uses during the school assembly that opens this story are accurate as of this writing, including the statistic that twenty-two people die every day while awaiting an organ donation.

Telling Amelia's story challenged me to take my own ideas about what this weird thing called *life* is all about and put them under a microscope, but one constant that remained from beginning to end was the conviction that at least some aspect of its meaning lies in helping one another, when we can and where we can. The majority of characters in this novel were named after actual organ donors who did just that through their generosity, some while living and some following their deaths. First and last names have been scrambled to protect privacy, except in cases where permission was granted or the donation received news coverage that stated names publicly.

I was humbled by all the stories of organ donors and recipients I had the honor of hearing and reading, especially that of my close friends John and Cara Ventresca, godparents to one of my children and favorite goofballs of my other two. John, who has polycystic kidney disease, received a kidney donation in 2016 from a complete stranger several states away who simply "wanted to do something nice for someone." When John's wife, Cara, learned she wasn't a blood type match for her husband, she didn't allow that to stop her from donating her own kidney, to a stranger she knew must be feeling the same vulnerability and helplessness her family did as they searched for a match for John. That people like this exist in our world—and in my life—gives me hope for humanity.

There are others who have made organ donation and organ transplant a cause they champion daily and I also borrowed their names for this book. In particular, Sibby's last name, Watson, is in honor of New York volunteer Roxanne Watson, who—at the time of this writing—has single-handedly signed up more than ten thousand donors (and counting).

Personal stories aside, one of the other things I find most compelling about organ donation is that it is a global health crisis that's entirely solvable. Today. Yesterday, even. We don't need to wait on that one brilliant doctor or on a team of dedicated scientists to discover an elusive fix—because, combined, we *all* hold the cure to this problem within our own bodies, whether we're able to offer an organ while alive or gift many after our own deaths.

While there are also hopeful signs for technological and medical advances on several fronts, that elusive "someday" has not arrived yet. There remains an urgent need for organs here and now.

If you are interested in registering as an organ donor, learning more about donation, or volunteering to lead a donor registry drive in your area, please visit www.donatelife.net. You can also register to become a donor through your state's Department of Motor Vehicles, which you can link to via www.dmv.org. It is further recommended that you take a moment to discuss your wishes with those closest to you, who are now or who might become responsible for making medical decisions on your behalf. Sibby would offer a hearty "Good on ya!" and I'd have to second her.

And if a fictional character's death can lead to saving a real life, I'm very certain Amelia would be just fine with the way things turned out for her within these pages. I hope you agree!

Acknowledgments

Foremost acknowledgment goes to my editor, Alyssa Miele: If only there existed a version of Rainworks for stories, so her many contributions to this book could come shining through . . . but I hope she know that the marks she left are indelible to me. (Ha! A set of ellipses she can't put a red line through—I couldn't resist, Alyssa!)

Special thanks to my agent, Holly Root, for being both trusted blocker and badass jammer with respect to my publishing career.

I would not have been able to plot or execute this story without the patient (no pun intended; well, maybe just a little, in honor of Amelia's dad) guidance of Dr. Douglas Mogul. You might think someone who holds the impressive title of medical director of pediatric liver transplant at a hospital as esteemed as Johns Hopkins would not be as gracious about answering so many of my truly ignorant questions. But Dr. Mogul was that and more as he helped me find inventive solutions to my dilemma of "How can I have a terminally ill patient who spends very little time in a hospital and is asymptomatic enough to do all these other things I want her to be able to do?" I am truly thankful for his guidance, and take full responsibility for any errors I may have made in interpreting the information he shared. I would also like to make mention here of an app that Dr. Mogul has created as part of a Johns Hopkins study to help parents of newborns identify signs of gastrointestinal illness or problems with their baby's liver. It's free and is called PoopMD+. Spread the word!

I also leaned heavily on other experts in their medical fields to provide information and fact-checking as I wrote. These include Lisa Bos in Endoscopy at Rhode Island Hospital; Chris Pierce, nurse practitioner at University Emergency Medicine Foundation and ED nurse at RI Hospital; Claire Watson, development and coordinations coordinator at New England Donor Services; and her clinical staff.

Further gratitude to those in the biliary atresia Facebook group who welcomed my intrusion, offered requested information or steered me to valuable resources that could and, in the exceptional cases of Jen Alpard and Amy Montgomery, allowed me to interview them about their personal relationships with the disease.

I am so appreciative of all the time given by one and all and, once again, any errors in text are mine alone.

An extra special dose of love and thanks to Pintip Dunne for helping me conceive of Will during a late-night conference sleepover and for checking me every step of the way to ensure I was accurately portraying him as a proud Thai American. I treasure all the care and time she took in allowing me to form a greater understanding of and appreciation for her experiences and her culture.

Gratitude to Dygo Tosa for taking time away from teaching Latin to high school students (including my own) to help me with the sundial mottos.

A hearty "Cheers!" to my Down Under mate (and talented author) Sharon Johnson for checking Sibby's Aussie-speak for accuracy.

Speaking of talented authors, I have many more to thank for lending their writerly muscles and hearts to aiding me in creating, shaping, and polishing this story, including: Dana Levy, Darcy Woods, Pintip Dunne (yes, again), Jen Brooks, Kate Brauning, Lori Goldstein, and Gail Nall. You are treasures and I am so lucky to count each of you as friends.

To the entire team at Harper, so many of whom work tirelessly and anonymously behind the scenes to get books into readers' hands and who do so with passion and integrity, a humble thank-you. Special shout-outs to editorial director Rosemary Brosnan, copy editor Jessica White, and publicist Aubrey Churchward. An extra-special thanks to Sophia Drevenstam and Molly Jacques and designer Jessie Gang for a cover I positively drool over and one so perfectly befitting a story about a chalk artist/hand letterer.

And lastly, to you readers: it's all nothing without you! Thank you for seeking out stories to help you figure out the world—it lets us authors write them to do the same and this author, in particular, is very grateful to have that opportunity.